I0564198

Beggar's Pardon (A Lady Marmalade Mystery)

by

Jason Blacker

PUBLISHED BY:
Lemon Tree Publishing

Visit www.JasonBlacker.com on the web to stay up to date

Editing: Andrea Anesi

ISBN: 9781927623404

For Angela and Kraigh as always

Table of Contents

One

Eric was sitting at the dining table with the Sunday Times open wide in front of him, his eyes and nose just peeking up above it. Frances came downstairs to join him for breakfast. It was the 2nd of April, 1939. The month before, Lord and Lady Marmalade had celebrated their thirty- sixth wedding anniversary. Thirty-six very happy years, she had said, toasting him with her champagne flute.

And as she entered the dining room and he looked up at her with a twinkle in his bright blue eyes and a rakish smile on his face, she was certain that another blissful thirty-six years awaited them.

"Good morning, luv," he said.

He got up as she came round and he kissed her on the lips. He folded the paper and put it down off to one side. He was still handsome for his sixty-one years, though his once jet black hair was no longer as black as it had been, but it still had the same natural wave in it as when she had first met him at the start of the new century.

Frances sat down and looked at him as Ginny entered in her clean white uniform.

"Would you like a fresh pot of tea, m'lady?" she asked.

Frances nodded.

"That would be lovely," she said.

"Anything else, sir?" she asked, looking at Eric.

"No thank you, Ginny, I think that'll be fine."

Ginny left and headed out into the kitchen.

"Unless you wanted warmer toast," he said.

Frances picked a piece out of the toast holder and put it on her plate.

"It's still warm enough. Should be just fine. Anything interesting in the news today?"

Eric looked over at the paper that lay beside him. He picked up the last half piece of toast that was on his plate, slathered it with marmalade, and took a bite.

"The usual, you know, the world's going to hell in a hand basket and the political leaders don't seem to have a clue."

Frances looked up at him as she spread butter and then marmalade onto her toast.

"Just yesterday the Spanish Civil War came to an end. And I'll tell you, it's a bad situation. Those fascists have gotten into power and it'll lead us all into war eventually."

Frances put down her knife and took a bite of toast.

"I thought they were called the Nationalists."

"Yes, they are, but underneath their thin facade of nationalism they're fascist through and through. Mark my words, this Franco chap is going to end up being a dictator."

"I thought we quietly supported the Nationalists."

"Well, the inept leaders of this country, including that milquetoast Neville, are more scared of the reds than they are of Hitler, so yes, they're quietly celebrating this victory. But the reds are of far lesser concern than fascism."

"Do you think then, that the Republicans would have been any better?"

Frances was finishing up her first half of the piece of toast when Ginny came back in carrying a silver tray with teapot, milk jug and sugar bowl. Tea cups were already on the table. Frances smiled at her as Ginny poured the tea. One sugar and a splash of cream.

"Thank you, Ginny."

Ginny smiled as she poured tea for Eric. Black with a wedge of lemon which he squeezed into it after Ginny had finished.

"Thank you. That'll be all," said Eric.

Ginny curtsied herself away.

"I do think the Republicans would have been far better. They're far less brutish and in any event, I think this big monster of Communism has a bigger bark than he does have bite."

Frances nodded her head.

"Well, time will show us the error of our ways, won't it?"

Eric shoved the last bit of toast into his mouth and chased it down with a sip of tea.

"Yes, I suppose it will. Though war is very seldom good for business. Any decent business I should add."

Frances started on her second half of toast, pausing to sip her tea. Sweet and milky. It reminded her of so many things. Everything was made better with tea.

"Anyway, enough about politics on the Lord's day, what are you up to this coming week?" he asked.

"I'm going up to see Florence Hudnall, she's been begging me for our marmalade recipe."

What most people didn't know was that marmalade was named after Eric's great grandfather, the first Lord Marmalade. He was known for enjoying marmalade and for making his own recipes with it. Before that, the English had simply borrowed the French term, marmelade.

"Oh yes, she's one of your old school friends, right?"

Frances nodded.

"Yes, she's up in Puddle's End now. Never been married, which I find strange, she was such a pretty girl in her youth."

"Weren't we all," said Eric sipping tea.

"Not likely. I can't imagine you being a very pretty girl however young you might have been."

Eric laughed.

"Don't, you almost made me spill my tea. You know what I mean."

"I do."

"Maybe she didn't find the right sort of fellow."

Frances shrugged.

"Could be, though I sometimes wonder if it wasn't rather a choice. And you darling, what are you doing tomorrow?"

"I'm heading up to Aberdeen for the week. We've started a new project out there, hotel and golf course. One of our biggest projects yet and it's hit a bit of a snag with the local council, so I'm going to see if I can't go and smooth some ruffled feathers."

"I'm sure you will, you're very good at that."

Outside the sun was shining and the lawn was green thanks to all the spring rain they'd received in London so far. The flowers against the far garden wall were starting to bud and soon the wall would be painted with the colors of the rainbow. Frances took another piece of toast and enjoyed it with more butter and more marmalade.

The two of them sat quietly in each other's company, conversation bubbling up and then quieting down. After many years of marriage, the company was more important than the conversation. Though they still had many things to share and talk about. Although there was one area Frances wanted to speak with her husband about, and that concerned their first born, Declan. It was a difficult topic that they had wrestled with before, Frances wanted to try and help Eric come to terms with it, but now wasn't the time.

Two

The morning train had been quiet and serene. Lady Marmalade had spent most of the time in the dining carriage watching the English countryside drift by. It was lush and green. A heavy mist had enveloped much of England and the train cut through the thick of it as it carried its passengers towards Blackpool. Puddle's End was the last stop before it ended its journey at Blackpool.

It was Monday, late morning, when Lady Marmalade had left London. Those who were heading up to Blackpool for work had left much earlier. Her 9:30 a.m. train was filled with young women and children as well as retirees. It was a three and a half hour train ride, straight through the heart of England's green countryside.

In a moment of weakness, Lady Marmalade thought of traveling on straight through to Avalon at Ambleside, her home in the Lake District, but her friend was expecting her and she was looking forward to seeing her. It had been a long time since they had gotten together.

The steam engine pulled into Puddle's End Station with a huff and slow squeal of its wheels, the conductor informing everyone of the same. It would be a five minute stop before it groaned out of Puddle's End towards Blackpool.

Lady Marmalade got off the train, her paisley scarf across her head, wearing a khaki dress suit and brown oxfords. She looked around and saw her friend coming towards her, waving her hand as she did so. Florence was almost a foot taller than Frances and carried it well. Her awkward teenage days were well behind her. She had a kind face that was otherwise nondescript. Not someone you'd remember from a crowd. Her smile was warm and her teeth straight. Her eyes were the same brown that matched her hair which was short and kept in a pageboy. She wore no makeup. There were very few people on the platform and Lady Marmalade's bags were easy to find.

"Hello dear," said Florence as she came up to Frances and they hugged each other.

"Flo, so lovely to see you again. It's been too long."

"Hasn't it? Where are your bags, Fran?" asked Florence looking around.

"I just have this small one and that other larger case over there," said Frances pointing to the wall where three bags stood still as soldiers.

"Then let's get one of these strapping lads to help us with it and be off."

Florence walked up to one of the porters at the train station and asked for his help with Frances' luggage. He was happy to oblige and hauled it all the way to Florence's Alvis Speed 25 Tourer. Florence tipped the young man and he tipped his cap back in return before heading back to the train station.

"Lovely car, Florence. It must be new since we last got together?"

"It is, I got it just last autumn. It's wonderfully fast and stable," said Florence, laughing. "Sometimes I think it might be too fast. You drive don't you?"

Frances nodded her head.

"Would you like to drive us home?"

"No, that's quite all right," said Frances. "I'll leave the driving in your capable hands."

They got in and drove away from the station. Puddle's End is a small community of only a few thousand. As small town or even a hamlet really. Not far from Blackpool, many of those who own the larger estate homes around here work in Blackpool. But that is the exception to the rule. Most of the population both works and lives in and around Puddle's End.

"So how have you been since you moved up here?" asked Frances, as they drove along slim winding roads.

Florence looked at her as she changed gears and drove with determination towards her home.

"Absolutely wonderful. The English countryside has done wonders for my asthma and the costs are very reasonable."

"Why did you leave London?"

"Well, when my father died a few years ago, he left me some money. All he had, which turned out to be a small fortune really. Well, not like yours, but an amount I could easily live off for the rest of my days quite comfortably. And London wasn't for me. I'm not a big city girl, I prefer open spaces and countryside and gardens. Besides, my job for the financial firm I was working with was made redundant, so I've come out here to live life."

"Wonderful, Flo. I'm so happy for you."

"Listen," said Florence, turning to look at Frances. "I have two thoughts for lunch. First, you must be famished. Secondly, would you prefer to head to the Wet Whistle, which is a wonderful quaint and cozy pub just up the road or would you rather have something simple at home? I can make some tea and sandwiches."

"I think I'd rather just head to your home Flo and relax for a bit. Then we can get started later this afternoon making some of Lady Marmalade's famous marmalade."

"Super, though why don't we just relax this afternoon. A friend of mine out here, Ginnie Forsyth, has invited us for dinner this evening at six. She seems wonderful, not sure about her husband, but I said I'd ask if you were up to it. She really is quite excited to meet you."

"Sounds lovely."

Florence pulled up to her driveway and got out of the car to open the gate. She drove them through, then got back out and closed the gate behind them. Her home was a small but elegant cottage. The front of it green with growing ivy and the grounds were lush and verdant. Her flowerbeds were already well manicured and ready for the bursting colors that would be arriving soon.

Florence carried Frances' large suitcase into the house and showed her to the spare bedroom. Its decor was warm and simple. Florence put Lady Marmalade's bag on the bed and Frances put her smaller case on top of it.

"This is wonderful, Flo. I'm so happy to be here and to spend time with my dear friend."

"I know," she said, "and no boys to bother us...though I don't mind Eric."

"Neither do I," said Frances smiling.

"Come, let's retire into the living room and I'll get started with tea and sandwiches."

"Nonsense, I won't just sit around and watch you work. Let's do it together."

"If you insist."

"I do."

They made their way into the kitchen where Florence took out a loaf of bread from the bread bin, butter that was covered in a butter dish, and a glass jar of marmite.

"Do you like marmite Fran?"

"I love marmite."

"You're just like me. I thought we could have marmite and cucumber sandwiches with some nice Earl Grey tea."

"Perfect."

Florence reached into her icebox and pulled out a single cucumber.

"Do you have one of those new refrigerators, Fran? I've been thinking of getting one."

Fran nodded.

"Eric got us one just a few years ago. Works like a charm. I don't know how we ever got by without it."

"I'm thinking of getting one too."

"I would definitely support that. We got one of those monitor-top ones. It's very spacious and keeps the temperatures more consistent than our old icebox used to."

Florence took her bread knife and cut four slices of the whole meal bread.

"How many sandwiches can you eat, Fran?"

"Just one. Where is your Earl Grey? I'll get us started on the tea."

"Just up there in the left cupboard. The teapot and teacups are up in the right cupboard."

Frances made the two of them a pot of tea and Florence made the sandwiches. They took them out to the living room and sat across from each other. Frances poured them tea and put in her own cream and sugar. Florence handed her the sandwich cut into four triangles. A table lamp on the side table where Florence sat gave the atmosphere in that room a warm glow. Outside it was cool and misty still.

"Lovely sandwiches. I haven't tried cucumber and marmite together, but this really works well."

"Thanks, Fran, I haven't tried it either, but I thought I'd give it a try. So glad you like it. It is good, I must say."

They sat in silence for a while enjoying each other's company and eating their sandwiches. When she was done, Frances put the plate on the coffee table in front of her and leaned back into the armchair. Her left hand cradled the saucer while she took a sip of her tea with her right hand. It was a fine bone China teacup with rose flowers on it.

"Tell me about your friend Ginnie," said Frances.

Florence finished up her sandwich and leaned over the coffee table and put her empty plate on top of Frances'.

"Well, acquaintance really, but she seems very nice. They live in the estate across the road and up a ways. I've seen her in town a few times and said hi. She's had me over for tea once or twice. Nice woman, but shy."

"How old is she?"

"She's a little younger than we are. Early fifties at most I think. She's married, her husband's name is Jack. Not sure exactly what he does, but they must be well off to afford the estate they have. Almost as big as yours at Ambleside."

"Did she say what she had in mind for dinner?"

"No. But I get the impression it'll be good. I think she likes to impress her guests."

Frances took a last sip of her tea and put it down on the table. She picked up the teapot and poured herself a fresh cup.

"Can I top you up, Flo."

"Please."

Florence put her cup out for Frances and she got a refill.

"Nothing like a pot of hot tea to set the mood on such a misty day."

Lady Marmalade was looking out into Florence's back yard, as the mist hung thick and gray like an old man's beard.

"Yes, we get a lot of rain up in these parts, especially at this time of year, but it is so good for the garden that I don't mind much at all."

Frances nodded her head and sipped tea.

"I noticed your garden as we came in, and this one in the back is just as wonderful. Do you do it all yourself?"

"I do. It's not much, and I like to potter around in the garden and see the flowers and shrubs blossom and bloom. Do you not garden?"

"Oh yes, but only in London. The garden is small enough that I can handle it. And like you, I enjoy it. Up at Avalon though, we have a groundskeeper. I'd spend my whole day in the garden otherwise. Not that I'd mind, but there is so much else to do. Liam does such a wonderful job up at Avalon that frankly, I don't think I could compete with his talents in any event. I see your crocuses and daffodils are blooming out in the back. But nothing out front yet?"

"No, I try to plan my gardens for the seasons. The back garden is my spring and summer garden. The front is summer and fall. I'm out and about a lot more in the summer and fall so I like to drive back home to the welcoming arms of my blooming front garden."

"That's such a clever idea. I think I might do something like that myself. We don't have a front garden in London, but I could divide up the back garden into two halves."

"What I'd do, Fran, if I was you, is I'd intersperse the flowers for the different seasons rather than carving up the garden into two halves. I think it'll be more picturesque, so anywhere you look at any time of the year, you'll see colorful blossoms."

Frances nodded her head and looked out at the purple crocuses and the yellow daffodils.

"You do have such a green thumb, Flo. I'm green with envy."

They laughed together.

"Tell me again how you ever got into sleuthing," said Florence.

Frances took a sip of tea and lay the teacup onto its saucer.

"I sort of fell into it," Frances said. "Almost literally. Shortly after Eric and I were married— in fact it was 1905— I went to the neighbor's to borrow some sugar. I was baking tarts and had run out of sugar. Our neighbor, a dear old woman by the name of Betsy Hummingham. I knocked on her door and the door opened all by itself. So I called out for her but received no reply so I entered into her home and kept calling her name. I got no answer."

"How dreadful."

"Well, it wasn't dreadful at that point, just a little eerie. But as I entered into her office, I almost tripped over her. She was lying, dead, across the floor with her head towards the door. She must have been in her eighties."

"Terrible shame, poor old dear."

"Yes it was. And I could tell that she hadn't died naturally."

"How do you manage that?"

"Well, she was lying with her head off to the right and I could see red marks around her neck, suggesting she had been strangled by something or someone."

"What did you do?"

"I called Scotland Yard and then went and waited outside. They suggested I not wait in the house in case the murderer was still there."

"That's terrible. Weren't you scared?"

Frances picked up her teacup again and took a sip. She shook her head.

"No, I wasn't really scared, I was more...horrified. This was the first time that I had ever seen a murdered person and I felt a little sick to my stomach. Actually, I felt that way the first few times. It wasn't so much the death, I had been with my grandmother and mother when they both passed on. I think it was the senselessness of it all. The utter uselessness of murder and the callousness of the act that horrified me."

Florence nodded.

"You know, I can't imagine ever being that upset or insulted or angry to kill someone. And yet you'd be horrified by the small petty reasons that some will kill over. It's pointless. I mean you can't take it back. It's the final act of deceit and betrayal. An awful loss of control and selfishness."

"So why do you still do it?"

Frances looked at Florence and her brown eyes were hot and determined.

"Because I can't stomach the thought that somebody might ever get away with such a despicable crime. You see, Flo, what happened is that Scotland Yard sent this very young inspector to the house. His name was Devlin Pearce. He wasn't an inspector then, I think he was just a Sergeant at that point. Anyway, he was very serious and police-like."

"What does that mean, 'police-like'?" asked Florence.

"When you get to know them you'll understand. They're sort of distanced, like they put a boundary between themselves and others. Anyway, he's not like that anymore, he's actually quite funny and charming now that I've got know him, but at the time he was very aloof. That's the word, aloof."

"I understand."

"Yes, aloof and all police professionalism. He didn't care to have me, a young woman at the time, interfering with the murder investigation. So we butted heads. I wanted to help but he wouldn't let me. In any event, as it turned out, I complained to Eric who at that time was quite friendly with the Commissioner."

Florence laughed.

"I can only imagine what happened then," she said.

"Well, yes, I got my way and much to the chagrin of Devlin he had to let me tag along. Now, without trying to sound pretentious or arrogant, but honestly, Flo, Devlin and his men were heading right in the wrong direction, and I believe, and I'm sure that Devlin will back this up, now that we're on good terms, that I helped steer them towards the true killer."

"And who was that?"

"The milkman."

"Really?"

"Yes, it's quite the fascinating story that I'll have to tell you at some point."

"I'd love to hear it."

Three

Florence waited for Frances in the living room. She was sitting in her armchair, her purse on her lap and a thick gray sweater over her dress. The nights were cool and they were walking to the Forsyth's to have dinner. Not a long walk. No more than five minutes, but still, it was enough to get a chill if you didn't have a sweater or jacket.

Frances came out of her room. She had put more effort into making herself presentable than she had in some time. Eric and she had tried to limit the number of social engagements that overpopulated their already busy calendar. Though truth be told, Lady Marmalade was looking forward to meeting a few new people this evening and enjoying a warm meal.

She had a red scarf over her head and underneath her hair was an organized mess of tight curls. She was naturally wavy, and naturally brunette, but the color of her hair and the tightness of her curls had been helped this evening by science. Even still, as she edged towards sixty, Lady Marmalade cut a dashing figure and a pretty face.

Her lips were red, matching the color of her scarf as well as that of her sweater. It was a cardigan and the buttons in front were large and burgundy. Underneath was a long heavy navy dress that fell past her knees. Tonight, Lady Marmalade wore black oxfords.

"You look like an absolute vision," said Florence, getting up from her chair.

"Thank you, my dear, and you look dashing yourself."

They smiled at each other and Frances exited Florence's home behind her. Frances paused for a moment expecting Florence to lock up after them.

"You don't lock down the hatches?"

"Good heavens no," said Florence, "this is Puddle's End. Nothing of note has happened here since I got here a few years ago."

"So you're not worried that someone might come and rifle through your things."

Florence took Frances' crook of her arm in hers and they started walking off down the lane.

"This isn't big bad London, Fran. And besides, if they have a fancy for anything I have, they're welcome to it. In any event, I don't think I have much worth stealing."

"We still lock up at Ambleside," said Frances.

"I can imagine, but you're up there at the Lakes and you've got valuables that some might want. You also entertain a lot and have all sorts coming and going in and out of the castle."

Florence grinned at Frances then.

"Hardly a castle," said Frances, bumping into Florence gently. "We're not royalty."

"Pardon me then, your ladyship, I'll call it your humble estate then."

"You're being silly."

"I am, but I'm happy for you, Fran. Who would have thought, over forty years ago now, that you'd be a Lady. Did you ever dream of it?"

"No, I was hardly dreaming of boys back then."

"I suppose though, we did go to a good all-girls school, so in some ways we were heading in the right direction just because of circumstances. Do you ever wonder what might have come of us if we had been born to poorer parents."

The sun was a heavy ball of spilled milk, sighing at its inability to burn off the mist as it settled in for the night in the western sky. It was quite bright out still, and the two women walked down the lane towards one of the larger homes in Puddle's End, alone, nobody else within sight.

"I do sometimes think about it, Flo. We are the lucky ones. Though I do believe that those poorer than us can get lucky too, but having the cards on your side certainly helps. One thing I'll say though, is that the crimes I seem to investigate have a deviousness all to themselves. Much more so than those crimes I read about committed by the working classes."

Florence nodded her head.

"How so?"

"Well, what with unemployment still so terribly high, most of the working poor or perhaps even more so, the jobless, steal and commit crimes out of desperation rather than for more nefarious reasons. As such, the crimes and the minds behind those that commit them are more straightforward. With us though, or those who lead more leisurely lives, the mind seems to become more imaginative and the crimes mirror that."

"Fascinating. That's something else for the history books, who would have thought you'd ever become a detective."

Frances smiled at Florence and nodded her head.

"I know. I was squeamish about blood, wasn't I?"

"You certainly were."

"And how about you? You're so courageous and brave. You've never married, you practically balk at current fashions and you never feel the need to mask your natural beauty with makeup."

"Well, you're certainly not bursting at the seams with the most forward fashion. Look at us, neither of us are wearing gloves for instance."

"That's for the young women to enjoy," said Frances.

"Enjoy! I think that's tongue in cheek. I find it terribly uncomfortable to wrap my arms up in gloves like I'm some sort of living mummy."

Frances laughed.

"Oh Flo, it is so good to see you again. I missed this, our conversations and your wit."

"Me too. In any event, I'm really not trying to make a statement or anything like that, I just like to be comfortable. I can tolerate, but I don't like the feeling of paint on my face and as for my clothes, well, I just like to wear what's comfortable, not what's in for the season."

"Well you still look absolutely marvelous."

"Thank you, Fran."

And she did. Even in her plain gray dress and black shoes, there was something about Florence that one could find very appealing. Perhaps it was her natural healthy look, though more likely it was her charm and wit.

"But what about marriage, Flo, I've always been curious about why you never married?"

"Well, it's not because I never had any suitors. I've had a few charming men court me. But honestly, Fran, I never met the right chap, and I don't think I ever would have either. I've never really been interested in having children and I suppose that being an only child I got used to my own company. I never felt I was missing anything."

"But don't you worry that people might think you're, well, um...lesbian."

"Oh Fran, you're awful," said Florence, laughing heartily. "Not at all, I can't help what people might think, and besides, would it be that awful if I were?"

"No, of course not," said Frances. "I'm just curious, it wouldn't matter to me, you know that, what with Declan being gay."

Florence nodded her head.

"How is that, by the way."

"Well it's fine, Declan is doing very well in Eric's business."

"I meant how are he and Eric getting along?"

"Well, I think they tolerate each other. Or rather, I think Eric tolerates it. I keep hoping he'll come around, but it's hard for him you know. His only son being gay and all. I really think he was hoping for a grandson, you know, to continue the Marmalade line."

"Do you think that's all?"

Frances shook her head.

"No, I think he doesn't know how to deal with Declan. Eric's very old school you know..."

A 1938 Alfa Romeo 6C 2300 Spider drove up beside them and stopped. A young man was in the driver's seat. He was good looking, with a square jaw and gray eyes and black wavy hair.

"Good evening, ladies."

"Good evening, Garrett. Lady Marmalade, this is Garrett Forsyth, Ginnie's son," said Florence.

Garrett held out his hand and Frances shook it.

"Lady Marmalade, our guest of honor. I'd offer you a lift but, as you can see, it's a bit cramped in here."

"That's quite alright, we can see the end in sight."

"Well, I look forward to visiting with you this evening."

Garrett nodded his head and continued on. The driveway was about a hundred feet up on the left and he disappeared through the gates and they lost sight of him as he went past the hedge.

"Charming young man," said Frances.

"Spoiled more like it, and petulant too. He's twenty seven, I think Ginnie said, and still lives at home with his parents, living off of them. Doesn't work from what I can gather..."

"Neither do we," said Frances smiling.

"Yes, Fran, but we're both old enough to be his mother and idle hands attached to a young healthy man like that I fear might make devil's work at some point."

"Maybe he's trying to find out what he wants to do with his life?"

"You're too kind, Fran. I think he's had plenty long enough to figure that out."

They walked in silence the rest of the way to the home of Ginnie and Jack Forsyth. It was a large estate, large by Puddle's End's standards. The grounds were lush and green and well kept.

Moss and ivy ran up the front of the stone faced home. Florence used the door knocker to announce their presence. It was a little after six.

In the front of the house was Garrett's Alfa Romeo, as well as three other more sedate-looking sedans. A well-dressed butler answered the door and welcomed them into the home.

"Can I take your sweaters, ladies?" he asked.

Florence and Frances took their sweaters off and handed them to the butler. An average-sized woman came down the hall to greet them. She had long red hair and green eyes. A plain countenance with freckles and severe lips. But when she smiled her face showed great warmth.

"Thank you, James," she said to the butler. "This is our butler, Mr. James Gromson. You must be Lady Marmalade. It is such a pleasure to meet you. I am Ginnie Forsyth."

Ginnie took Lady Marmalade's hand and shook it warmly, smiling all the time.

"Nice to meet you, please call me Frances."

"I'm so glad you decided to join us, Florence has said very kind things about you."

Ginnie stepped aside and gave Florence a hug and a kiss on the cheek.

"Please come on in, everyone is here enjoying some drinks in the living room."

Frances and Florence followed Ginnie into the living room where four men and one woman sat in a couple of couches and a couple of armchairs. The men stood up as soon as the three of them entered.

"Our guest of honor has arrived," said Ginnie, Lady Marmalade flushed momentarily, a little embarrassed at the suggestion. "This is Lady Frances Marmalade, she's up here visiting her dear friend, Florence Hudnall, who, as some of you might know, lives not far from us."

Jack Forsyth smiled and walked up to Lady Marmalade.

"Jack Forsyth," he said, taking Lady Marmalade's hand and kissing the back of it. "Thank you for coming."

Jack was tall and gangly with a receding hairline. His black hair was thin on top and he brushed it backwards. His brown eyes were close together and his nose was hooked. He had a gap between his two front teeth and a pencil thin mustache like a rat's tail lay across his top lip. His hand was cold as it held Lady Marmalade's and his fingers twitched like spider's legs.

"It's my pleasure," said Frances, "please call me Frances."

Jack turned to look at the other guests present.

"This is Dr. Luther Garnet, Ginnie's brother," he said as he looked at the man he was introducing.

Dr. Garnet was several years older than his sister. Possibly pushing sixty. He looked very much like a redheaded cousin of Winston Churchill. Rotund of girth with a ruddy complexion and bulldog jowls. His mouth had the same limp scowl that Churchill wore so well but he was as pale and as freckled as his sister. His hair was wispy gray and combed back. He stepped forward and shook France's hand.

"Nice to meet you, my Lady."

"The pleasure is mine. Please everyone, call me Frances or Fran."

"I understand you've already met my son, Garrett."

Frances nodded as Garrett waved his hand in greeting.

"This is my brother, Gerald, we're in business together."

Gerald stepped forward, you could tell they were brothers. Both had thin lips, though Gerald looked older and his face was clean-shaven. He was practically bald on top, but kept his black hair short on the sides of his head. He was shorter and stouter than Jack. He shook Frances' hand.

"Delighted," he said.

Lady Marmalade smiled at him.

"And lastly is my dear sister-in-law, Meredith Church. She was married to my dearly departed brother Roger, who was the oldest of the three of us."

Meredith came up and shook hands with Lady Marmalade. Her hands, though well manicured, were somewhat masculine.

"Happy to meet you, Frances," she said.

"Likewise. I'm sorry about your husband."

Meredith smiled. It was a brave smile. She wore a bright floral patterned dress. She had long brown hair that dropped in curls just past her shoulder. She wore makeup with red lipstick. Her chin was weak but other than that she was pleasant to look at.

After everyone had been introduced to Lady Marmalade, Jack made the same introductions with Florence to those whom she didn't know, which were Meredith and Dr. Garnet.

"Now what can I get the two of you to drink?" asked Jack.

"A gin and tonic," said Frances.

"Make that two," said Florence.

"I thought you might say that," said Frances.

"Old habits die hard, Fran," said Florence.

The two of them went and sat down together on a two-seater couch that was vacant. Meredith looked over at Frances.

"I've heard that you're a detective," she said.

Jack came back with the two gin and tonics and handed one each to Frances and Florence.

"Not a real detective," said Frances.

"She's too modest," said Florence, "we were just talking about that on our walk up here."

"Oh, do tell," said Meredith, leaning in from her armchair.

"Well, I've earned a bit of a reputation for being quite good at solving crimes, so I'm often asked to help out in some cases."

"So it's the police that ask you to help out?" asked Meredith.

Frances smiled and shook her head after sipping on her gin and tonic.

"Not usually, though sometimes they have. No, usually I'm asked to help out by one of the relatives or I'm called in because they've heard about me and ask for my help."

"Fascinating. And you don't mind all the gore and dead bodies?"

"Funny you should ask, I was just talking with Florence about that on our way here. I sort of fell into sleuthing by accident, and indeed the first few dead bodies I saw were quite upsetting. Not because of all the gore as you say, there wasn't much of that, no, what really upset me was the senselessness of it all. To be honest, that's what upsets me the most about crimes and especially murder, the senselessness of it all."

"So intriguing, Frances, you're a veritable Sherlock Holmes," said Meredith.

Frances waved it off and took a sip of her gin and tonic.

"But enough about me, I want to hear about you. Are you still involved in the family business?"

Meredith sat back into her chair a bit more comfortably.

"Yes, unfortunately I am still involved. Ever since Roger died three years ago I've had to feign interest in it. But I leave it mostly in Jack's hands. I believe he's doing a good job."

"And what sort of business is it that you are all involved with? Florence hasn't mentioned it to me."

"We're a small parts manufacturer for cars mostly. We ship engine parts of a variety of sorts all over Europe to most of the car manufacturers. I bet that Garrett's Alfa Romeo has a part or two in it from Forsyth Motor Manufacturing. That's the name of the company."

Garrett's ears pricked up when he heard his name.

"I dare say it does. We manufacture primarily carburetors, water pumps and ignition systems. My Romeo has a Forsyth carburetor in it. We make one of the best in the business, if I don't mind saying so myself."

"But you aren't really involved in the business are you, Garrett?" said Meredith.

Garrett's eyes burned hot.

"Well, I will be soon enough."

And he turned to join the conversation going on between Ginnie and her brother, Luther.

The butler came back into the living room and announced to Ginnie and Jack that dinner was ready. Ginnie stood up and corralled the guests into the dining room where the eight of them sat down at a large elegant wooden table with white linen napkins and genuine silverware.

James Gromson came around with some white wine. He held out a bottle of Chenin Blanc to Jack, at the head of the table, and poured him a small sip. He swirled it, sniffed it before swallowing it. He nodded at James and James took the wine over to Lady Marmalade and filled her glass. Then he went to Florence and on down, serving the women according to their age. His best guess, which was also accurate. Ginnie, the lady of the house was served last before James served the men in the same order.

James left an almost empty bottle on the table and went back into the kitchen where he came out with the housekeeper, Agnus Van Buren, and served the main course in the same order he had served the wine. Frances watched Agnus put the tray on a dumbwaiter off to the side with hands that were large for a woman and spoke intimately with the voice of hard labor.

In front of Frances on her plate was pan fried flounder with lemon and dill. Accompanying it were parsley-encrusted fingerling potatoes. It smelled heavenly and Frances hadn't realized how hungry she was until the aroma of the food teased her nostrils and made her mouth water.

"Looks absolutely wonderful, Ginnie, thank you so much for this delightful dinner," said Frances.

"Yes, smells delicious," echoed Florence.

James and Agnus reappeared from the kitchen one more time, and served up the remaining guests.

"Please, dig in," said Ginnie. "Let's enjoy the meal."

"You don't have to ask me a second time," said Meredith.

Jack lifted up his glass and looked his wife in the eye across the table from him. Frances was seated to Ginnie's right, across from Garrett. Dr. Garnet was to Frances' right, opposite Meredith and Florence was at the other end, to Jack's left and across from Gerald.

"To the coming war, and may it make us all rich, especially Forsyth Motors," said Jack.

Lady Marmalade raised her glass tentatively as did the others. She tried to pinch a smile but it was awkward.

"Jack, that's inappropriate," said Ginnie.

"Well, war is often good for manufacturers like us."

"Only when you don't know how to run a business during peaceful times," said Dr. Garnet.

Jack looked at him and furrowed his brow.

"Not now, Luther, if you don't mind. I don't wish to speak of business matters during dinner."

"That's your problem," said Dr. Garnet, "never wanting to speak of business matters."

"Gentleman, please," said Ginnie. "May I propose a toast? To freedom, friends and good food."

"I'll drink to that," said Meredith.

"You'll drink to anything," mumbled Ginnie under her breath.

They all clinked glasses with those closest to them and began to eat their dinner. The food was delicious. Exceptionally well cooked, but Frances feared that the company might have been overdone.

"Did you all hear about the Nationalists taking over Spain?" asked Garrett. "How incredible and exciting."

Gerald looked up from his plate, a forkful of flounder hovering above it.

"You mean, Garrett, how incredibly depressing."

"Well, no, I meant how exciting. Now the reds are going to have a hard time stretching their stain across Europe."

"How come everyone seems so scared of the communists and not the real threat, right across the channel in Germany?" asked Gerald.

"Probably because we don't want to believe it is why," offered Jack.

"Eric was saying the exact same thing this morning at breakfast," said Frances. "But I wonder though, if Spain's outcome is really going to have any effect on the looming war one way or another."

"I don't think so," said Meredith, "I think men just like to go to war and beat their chests, so we'll have a war one way or another."

Meredith swallowed the last of her wine and reached for James who came over and refilled her. He looked around, but the others at best were only half finished their first glass.

"I think Frances is probably right, at the end of the day it won't make much of a difference to the impending war. And Neville should have stopped appeasing this Hitler chap, months ago. Anyone with such a perfect and orderly toothbrush mustache is not someone to be trusted."

That last comment got a round of laughs and eased the tensions.

"What concerns me, is another big war when we've barely escaped the clutches of the first one," said Florence.

"I agree," said Ginnie, "I find this whole idea of war quite distasteful."

"Well, it looks like it'll be put upon us by Germany. We'll have Hitler and the Nazis to blame for this one. Just like we did the last one, except for the Nazis, they weren't around then," said Jack.

"I think it's a bit of a reach to blame the Germans for everything," said Dr. Garnet. "I'd argue that it was the Serbs and Austro-Hungarians who really started the last one."

"Well, whoever starts it, it's going to be good for business," said Jack.

"If you'll keep the money in the business, Jack," said Gerald.

Jack looked at Gerald with fiery eyes and took a long drink from his wine.

"I said not now. We can deal with the business later."

"Well, businesses have their ups and downs," said Florence, trying to smooth over the ruffled emotions.

"Yes, but they have more downs when you have incompetent management playing loose and fast with the company's funds," said Ginnie.

"Not you too," said Jack. "You have no idea of the pressures that the business is under."

Meredith put her hand up for James who came by and emptied the bottle of wine into her wine glass. He opened another and went round to refill the others. Lady Marmalade put her hand over hers. She had had enough.

"The dinner was wonderful," said Frances, trying to steer the conversation in another direction.

After James had topped up the wine glasses of those who wanted them topped up, which wasn't very many, he went into the kitchen and came back out with Agnus and they started to clear the plates off the table.

"You should let mother be more involved in the business, I'm sure she could help out with the books," said Garrett.

"Your mother can barely keep the household budget from bleeding red, I doubt very much she could help me with the business."

"I could if you'd stop spending it on everyone but the business," said Ginnie.

"And what the hell is that supposed to mean?" asked Jack.

"You know exactly what it means," said Ginnie, looking over at Meredith and then at Jack.

Meredith took a long drink from her glass and looked at Jack.

"I'm sure Jack will have things sorted out in no time, won't you, darling?" she said.

Garrett looked at his father and then at Meredith, then he looked at his mother.

"Do you mean to say..."

"Not now, we can talk about this later," said Jack.

Garrett was about to protest when his mother put her hand on his forearm and he stopped himself and stared into the middle of the table.

"I think dessert will help us all feel better," said Ginnie.

James needed no further encouragement. He left the dining room again and came out with Agnus, each of them carrying a tray containing four Liverpool tarts on each. They served them around.

The tarts were small, single servings with pastry hearts in the center of each and a dollop of whipped cream on the side. The tangy lemon flavor was cut by the sweet sugar. Not exceedingly sweet, but very pleasant and cleansing on the palate.

"This is wonderful, Ginnie, really it is," said Florence.

"Thank you, I thought something light and citrusy after the fish was probably a good bet."

"More than a good bet, I'd say it perfectly hit the spot."

Everyone ate in silence for a while, the mood somewhat somber after the recent outbursts. Finally, Florence cut the silence.

"Frances and I will be making marmalade tomorrow. Did you know that her husband's great grandfather was the one for whom marmalade was coined? Before that we called it the same as the French marmelade with the e in the middle."

"Fascinating," said Ginnie, trying her best to feign interest.

"The reason being, was because Lord Marmalade loved his marmalade and developed several recipes, one of his best kept secrets being a chunky version we'll be making tomorrow."

"Well, if I can be a bother, I would certainly love a jar if there'll be any to spare," said Meredith.

"Oh, there will be plenty," said Frances, "we can bring a couple of jars over tomorrow afternoon for whoever would like some."

"I'd love one too," said Ginnie.

"Super, we should be finished with it by tea time tomorrow, should we not?" asked Florence.

"I'd hope so, at the very latest," said Frances.

"Would four in the afternoon be convenient then?" asked Florence.

"That would be lovely, then we can have some of France's marmalade with our afternoon tea," said Ginnie. "It will be lovely to enjoy your company again tomorrow."

The rest of the dessert was eaten quietly, very little conversation going on, other than some idle chit chat about the weather and the local sporting news amongst the men. Most of that concerned the upcoming Australian matches against the English teams towards the end of spring and summer.

Frances and Florence delicately excused themselves from the rest of the group shortly after dessert, staying only for a small cup of tea while the rest enjoyed coffee. They had to get a good night's rest, said Florence, for they needed an early start for the marmalade making the next morning. It was just after eight thirty when they left.

Ginnie came to the door to send them on their way.

"Are you sure you don't want Jack to drive you home?" she asked.

"Absolutely not, it's only a few minutes walk and we could used the exercise. The dinner was absolutely super. Thank you ever so much," said Florence kissing Ginnie on the cheek.

"Yes it was marvelous," said France. "So good of you to invite me."

They hugged and kissed cheeks and then the two of them headed out into the night air which was cool and crisp.

"I think I'll have to turn up the heat when we get home," said Florence.

"I wouldn't mind, it is a bit chill this evening isn't it?"

They walked to the end of the driveway in silence, and then Florence turned around and looked back at the estate and then at Frances.

"And that, my dear, is why I never got married. I'm sorry to have put you through that."

"Not at all, it wasn't all that bad. Seems to me though, that they have financial troubles and that will always cause some difficulty."

"They have a lot of problems from what I've heard. I believe that Jack is a bit of a philanderer. Did you hear Meredith calling him 'darling', how ghastly to think his mistress might be the wife of his late brother."

"Quite shocking, I feel for poor Ginnie, that can't be easy to cope with."

"I think she should divorce the bastard and be done with it."

"Not that easy, Flo."

"Couldn't be easier, Fran, since they passed that act last year which made it easier to divorce than ever before."

"Yes, I know, but I didn't mean the actual getting a divorce, I meant the financial aspects of it. It will still be terribly difficult for her to get any money from him. You know the courts aren't as sympathetic to the plight of divorced women as they should be."

"True, I suppose. And there again is another good reason not to get married in the first place."

Frances laughed.

"You're incorrigible," she said. "You just have to find the right man. Look at Eric, he's not like that at all."

"Are you sure?" said Florence, and she laughed heartily.

"Flo!"

"I'm just teasing you, I know Eric is a good man."

And they walked the rest of the way to Florence's home in silence. They turned up her driveway and headed towards the front door.

"Thank heavens for decent men and chaste women," said Flo.

"And for order and responsibility. I do hope they come to terms with their difficulties," said Frances.

"I'm not sure that'll happen. There doesn't seem to be any more love to be lost between those two. They've grown so far apart I fear they can barely see each other from across the chasm."

Four

Lady Marmalade woke to the sun bleeding out of the corners of the curtain in her room. The curtains were yellow, but they were a warmer yellow than they should have been for a misty morning. She got out of her bed and put a dressing gown over her nightgown. The mornings and evenings in Puddle's End were still cool.

She went over to the curtains and opened them up wide in one quick pull. The sun was indeed awake and looking over the earth. Frances had to put her hand up to her face to shade her eyes from the blinding sun. It was a wondrous sight, to have the sun beginning to carve its arc in the sky.

The frost on the grass was melting into wet dripping jewels twinkling like fairies. In the corners and shadows the frost was not thick, but it was white on top of the blanket of green grass.

Frances looked at her bedside table and her travel clock was pointing just after eight. She had slept in and she felt wonderful about it too. Usually an early riser, Frances took an early start to her day, getting up between six and six thirty.

But she was practically on holiday and a little indulgence never hurt anyone. Frances pulled her blue satin dressing gown tighter and tied it off at the waist. It had white dots all over but they were not as closely nestled to call it polka dotted. She put on her blue slippers and exited her room.

Florence was in the kitchen working at the counter buttering toast. The kettle just started whistling when Frances got in and she took it off the stove.

“Good morning Fran. Did you sleep well?”

“Too well it seems, I’m not usually up this late.”

“Well, you’re on holiday, and as my guest I want you as happy and relaxed as you can be. Will you enjoy some toast and jam?”

“I’d love some, I’ll pour us some tea then?”

“Please, I’ve already put the tea in the teapot, just needs the water.”

Frances poured the water into the pot and put the pot onto the silver tray that was on the counter. She took the cream out of the icebox that was still left over from yesterday’s low tea and put that on the tray. She put the bowl of sugar as well as the two teacups and saucers on there too with two small silver spoons. Lastly she placed a sieve that lay over a small bowl onto the tray.

“How many slices of toast would you like?” asked Florence.

“Just one, thanks Flo.”

Florence was dressed in a salmon colored dressing gown with white slippers.

"I'm terribly sorry Fran, but I don't have any marmalade...at least not yet."

She grinned at Frances and Frances smiled back.

"Not yet. Speaking of same, we should get started on that after breakfast if you're up for it."

"I think that sounds like a marvelous idea."

Frances carried the tray into the dining room which held only a small table around which crowded four chairs. She placed it in the middle of the table. Florence put a plate on at one end of the table and another plate on the other end. They sat down and started to eat. The jam was strawberry, wet and glassy looking but delicious.

"How strong do you like your tea?" asked Florence.

"A little stronger than it is right now," said Frances.

"I think we like our tea the same then."

"Yes, I remember you complaining sometimes at St. Mary's that the tea wasn't often strong enough."

When the toast was finished, Florence poured them each a strong cup of tea holding the sieve over the teacup to catch errant leaves. Frances had hers with cream and sugar. She'd been preferring it that way over a squeeze of lemon lately.

"Now this is the way to start your day, don't you think Flo?"

"I shudder to think how it might start any other way."

She grinned at Frances. Frances held up her cup and looked over the brim at Florence.

“Here’s to us and our continuing friendship. Forty odd years isn’t it?”

“Only if you think you’re much younger than you are?”

Florence smiled, a mischievous twinkle in her eye.

“Let’s work it out,” she said. “We were in the same year, and you, my dear, are a few months older than me. We started at St. Mary’s in Year 7 and I believe we were both still eleven at the time.”

Florence chuckled.

“Can you imagine us at eleven, looking back.”

“I’d rather not,” said Frances, “a couple of know-it-alls, I’m sure.”

Florence, looked past France’s right and out into the garden through the French doors. She sighed, looked back down at her tea and then decided to take a sip.

“Forty-five years, Fran. Actually a little more. Can you imagine that. Forty-five years we’ve known each other.”

“You say that with a sigh like you’re carrying a heavy burden,” said Frances.

Florence looked up at Frances and smiled. Her brown eyes were soft and kind and Frances could see where the Sandman had carved his trails across her face. The wrinkles showed of great adventures, and more importantly great and long laughs.

“Sorry, Fran, I don’t mean it like that. I just got to thinking, that our ages as we come up upon the hill of sixty, we have less time left than we've used up. That's all. I don't regret a moment of it. Just sitting here with you, reminiscing and looking back, it seems so fleeting doesn't it? I mean, I can still remember that first day at school when we looked over at each other and recognized the friendship to come."

Frances put her teacup back down on the saucer and looked at her friend of many years.

"It is fleeting. Fleeting and so fragile. Sometimes one dares not think about it for fear it might evaporate in front of one's eyes. Yet the memories are so kind and they often warm the cockles of my heart during choppy seas."

Florence smiled and nodded her head, and then sipped her tea.

"And I suppose Flo, if you can live a life well lived, a life of few if any regrets, then all you've gathered along the path of life are handfuls of blooming flowers. And don't you find the years bring with them gifts of their own?"

Florence nodded.

"They do indeed. Perhaps I'm just selfish in wanting more of it. It has been such fun so far hasn't it?"

"It has. We'll have to do something fun for our fiftieth friendship anniversary. Perhaps go back and visit St. Mary's and have a tour. Though I doubt any of our old teachers will be there still."

"You never know, Ms. Bouvier, our English teacher, seemed young."

Frances nodded.

"I remember her well, she was very sweet and kind. Unlike some of the nuns."

Frances chuckled and Florence laughed with her.

"How about another cup to get us started on the marmalade."

"I'd love it."

Florence poured them each another cup of tea and then they moved back into the kitchen.

"You do have everything, don't you?" asked Frances.

"I bought everything on your list."

"You know, the recipe we'll use only makes six pints, and you're giving away two pints, so that's not going to leave you with much."

"It'll be plenty," said Florence, "and when I run out, it'll be an excuse to call you up and have you come out again."

Frances laughed.

"Yes I suppose so. So you got ten pounds of citrus. Seven pounds of Sevilles, two pounds of grapefruit and a pound of lemons?"

"I did indeed, they're just in the bottom of the cupboard. Why so many oranges?"

"That, my dear, is the Marmalade family's secret. An orangey marmalade is so much more enjoyable and that is why so many oranges. If you start diluting the orange flavor more than that, I find it not quite to my liking. But once you've tried this recipe it's easy to adjust to your personal preferences."

"I wouldn't dare dream of it," said Florence.

Frances shook her head.

"Good, because I think you'll really like it this way. Another thing that makes our marmalade different and tastier, in my humble opinion is the chunkiness of our rinds. We also slow cook them longer than most until the rind almost becomes spreadable."

"You're making me hungry just thinking about it. I can't wait to try it."

"Well, we need twelve cups of sugar and about half a gallon of water."

"I have it all."

"Then let's get started. Ought to be a lot of fun."

Five

It seemed like the walk back to the Forsyth's home was quicker than it had been the night before. But that is what a warm sunny day will do for you. Florence was carrying a cloth bag that had the two jars of marmalade in them.

She was wearing a long summer dress with a flower pattern on it as well as a pale blue cardigan over top. Frances was wearing a long yellow dress with a yellow cardigan over top.

"You didn't lead me down the wrong path, Fran. That marmalade of yours is incredibly tasty. I'm almost having second thoughts of sharing any with Ginnie and Meredith."

"Well, I can always come back up and we can make another batch."

"Might be sooner than you think."

They slowly walked up towards the driveway and as they turned into it, passing the hedge, Frances and Florence saw two Wolseley police cars parked up at the top of the driveway.

"Oh my," said Florence, "I hope everything is alright with the Forsyths."

"I hope so too."

They walked the gravel driveway and past the two police cars. A bobby was standing by the main entrance, as if he were guarding Buckingham Palace.

"I'm afraid you ladies aren't allowed inside," he said, in the brisk and authoritarian manner of a British police constable.

"We're friends of the family, Constable?" said Frances.

"Constable Richards, mum."

"Well, Constable Richards, we're friends of the family and I'm sure we'll be allowed inside."

Frances went to walk into the house, trying to move past him, but the constable was not to be persuaded and he moved to block her. Down the hall, Frances saw the butler, James, walking towards them.

"Constable Richards, it's quite alright, Mr. Forsyth has asked that you let them in."

The constable looked at the butler for a moment, his boyish face trying it's hardest to look as stern as possible. His body was bolt upright and his hands clasped tightly behind his back. He turned back to face Lady Marmalade.

"Very well, then," he said and turned to the side to let Frances and Florence through.

"Thank you, James," said Frances as they entered the hall.

"Not at all, if you'll please follow me, my Lady and madam Hudnall, Mr. Forsyth is in the living room with Inspector Henry Gibbard, though he goes by Hank."

James led them down the hallway and then right into the living room where Jack was sitting on the couch with his hand through his thinning hair. He looked visibly upset. His thin mustache quivering on his lip as if it might be blown away any moment by the slightest breeze. His eyes were wet. He wore a white shirt with cream suspenders holding up cream-colored pants and cream-colored boat shoes.

A stout man of average height turned as they came into the living room after James. He had his hands clasped behind him and he wore a gray suit that needed some tailoring. It was tight across the shoulders and too short at the arms. His hair was at that in between stage not certain whether it was still the chestnut brown of his youth or the dull gray of his later years.

The man's face was round and his blue eyes were small. He looked at you as if he were squinting, only he wasn't. His lips were thin and his complexion ruddy. He had the squat red veined nose of a drinker, and when he opened his mouth the most wondrous baritone voice came deep from his belly like a rumbling train. He held out his hand to Lady Marmalade first.

"I'm Inspector Hank Gibbard."

"Lady Frances Marmalade, though please call me Frances."

"Yes, right. I've heard about you. You're that meddling type Scotland Yard has told me about."

Frances cocked her head slightly at him and maintained her composure, smiling all the while.

"Florence Hudnall."

She shook his hand and he turned back towards Jack. Frances and Florence stepped into the room and Florence sat down next to Jack.

"What's going on?" she asked.

"Ginnie is dead," he said, and he blinked his eyes bravely, trying to stem the tears.

Florence put her hand up to her mouth.

"Good God, no," she said.

"Oh yes," said Inspector Gibbard, "I'm afraid so."

Frances looked at the inspector for a moment.

"Are you from Blackpool?" she asked.

He turned towards her and nodded, his hands still clasped behind his back.

"I thought so, as we haven't met, and you don't seem to be aware of the help that I hope to offer."

"My dear Lady, I am well aware of the help you are inclined to offer, but here in Blackpool and area, we leave the sleuthing to real policemen."

Frances looked at him and smiled thinly.

"I think Inspector Pearce might disagree."

"Yes, well, Inspector Pearce isn't here and I'm the man in charge."

"Yes, I can see that. I'll let you get on with your important duties no doubt. But if I can help in any way, I am at your service."

"Thank you my Lady, but that won't be necessary."

"Then you wouldn't mind if I tagged along, quietly and out of the way?"

Inspector Gibbard looked at her for a while, and as he did the corner of his mouth twitched.

"No, I suppose not, if you stay out of the way."

"Thank you, Inspector."

Gibbard nodded and looked back at Jack Forsyth.

"As I was saying, you said that you didn't find her yourself. Is that correct?"

Jack nodded, his right elbow resting on his right knee, his hand still slowly brushing over his thinning pate. He blinked tightly.

"Yes, yes, Inspector, that's exactly what I said. My groundskeeper Enoch Habbit, found her this afternoon. I think it was around three thirty when he came and told me."

"Are you sure it was at exactly three thirty Mr. Forsyth?"

Jack looked up at him and took his hand from his head. He held his hands together loosely in the middle of his knees.

"No Inspector, I'm bloody well not sure it was at exactly three thirty. My wife has been dead just over a half hour or God knows how long, I've only known about it for the past half hour and you expect a grieving husband to take note of the time when his groundskeeper comes to him with this sort of ghastly news. Next I suppose you'll be asking for my notes since then."

"Did you make any?"

Jack hung his neck and slowly shook his head.

"Let me talk to him, Inspector," said Florence.

Gibbard looked at her and nodded. He then looked at the butler. James came up to him. He looked impeccable, a perfect example of calm amongst this brewing storm. He was in his black suit with white shirt and black bow tie. He wore white gloves without a mark on them.

"Bring me this Enoch Habbit fellow. I presume he's still around?"

"He should be sir," said James.

"Good," and then looking at the constable off to the side of the room. "Warren, go with him in case this Enoch fellow doesn't want to come quietly."

The constable nodded his head and left the living room following closely behind James.

"You must forgive them, Jack, they're only trying to do their job," said Florence.

Jack nodded his head. Outside in the hallway someone was coming down the steps, it sounded like a woman, the high heels clicking on each step carefully. Frances looked towards the living room doors which were open to the hallway. In a moment,

Meredith appeared and walked up to Jack where she sat down next to him and rubbed his shoulders.

"My dear Jack, I'm so sorry," she said.

Meredith was wearing a knee length black dress and white blouse over which was a black jacket. She wore a black flat brimmed hat with white trim that was tilted to one side. She looked up at Florence and Frances.

"Isn't it just terrible what happened to poor Ginnie?" she said.

"Most terrible," agreed Florence.

Meredith crossed her ankles and Frances noticed that her shoes were scuffed just a little on the insides. Not quite as immaculate as the rest of her outfit.

"Did you see her?" asked Frances.

"No, I overhead Jack talking to his groundskeeper. Though Ginnie had told me she was going to the greenhouse to check in on the tomatoes. I don't have much of a green thumb."

Meredith stopped rubbing Jack's shoulders and hooked her arm around his. She was sitting to his right. Florence was on his left.

"Where is the greenhouse Meredith?" asked Francis.

"It's around back, you can get to it through those French doors at the far end of the living room. They shouldn't be unlocked, and if they are, the key's in them."

"Inspector, do you mind if I go and have a look at the greenhouse? Has the coroner been for Ginnie's body yet?" asked Frances.

"No, he hasn't, but he should be here any minute. Now don't go messing with anything, we're not quite finished yet, and if you find any evidence you let me know."

"I certainly will, you have my word."

"Would you like me to come, Fran?" asked Florence.

"Only if you want to."

"Well, I think I shall, I'm very curious to see how your mind works with these sorts of things."

Florence got up from the couch and left the inspector with Jack and Meredith. She followed Frances to the end of the living room and just like Meredith had said, behind the sheer curtains, the doors were unlocked and the key was in the keyhole.

Frances opened the door out onto a patio which was starting to be filled in with shade as the sun was easing its way towards the west. Florence closed it behind them. Off to the right towards the back of the yard was the greenhouse. Across from it, on the far left side was the shed. Frances saw James speaking with a man who was presumably Enoch.

In front of the shed, towards the house were the living quarters for the staff. Frances took a moment and looked down towards the greenhouse. There was a bobby standing guard at its entrance. At the very back of the yard, stretching almost all the way between the shed and the greenhouse was the barren garden already tilled and weeded and turned over, ready for planting.

Frances started to make her way towards the greenhouse.

"This is quite exciting in a sort of macabre way," said Florence. "Do you think you might solve it before the police do?"

"I'm only here to help, though I don't have a large amount of confidence in that Inspector Gibbard. He might mean well, but I think he's too stuck in his ways. I've found that when solving crime, the best way to look at it is with open eyes."

"Then I'll help you keep your eyes open."

The bobby watched them come towards him and he stood his ground until Lady Marmalade was face to face with him.

"This is a crime scene, madam," he said with much the same authority coming from as boyish a face as his twin at the front of the house. Only he had a thin wispy mustache that only added to his boyish looks.

"Yes, thank you, constable, I know that," said Frances, "Inspector Gibbard has given me full authority to evaluate the crime scene if you'll let me in."

The constable looked up towards the house and thought about it for a moment.

"If I have to go back up, I'll be sure to bring the inspector back with me so that you can explain in person why you wouldn't let Lady Marmalade into the greenhouse."

The constable's face flushed for a brief moment.

"I beg your pardon, I didn't realize you were Lady Marmalade," he said, tipping his hat to her, "I've heard about you."

"So I've gathered," said Frances, her voice rusty with just the barest hint of frustration.

"Oh, no, it's not like that," he said. "Some of us have heard of your great deductions. It's the older ones who have a different opinion."

Frances smiled.

"Kind of you to say."

The constable moved aside and let Lady Marmalade and Florence enter into the greenhouse.

"Seems your reputation precedes you," said Florence.

"Hardly ever, actually, but I'll use whatever I can to help bring criminals to justice."

Inside the greenhouse it was quite warm and humid. After a short while both Florence and Frances started to glow from the warmth.

"I think I could live in here," said Florence. "So warm and comforting, like a blanket."

Frances nodded absentmindedly. The greenhouse was large. Roughly twenty-five feet by fifteen feet. As you entered near the front there was a rectangular table across the width. Just past it, were two rows of rectangular tables in parallel heading towards the back of the greenhouse. At the back, there was another rectangular table along the width.

All the tables were full of planters sprouting many different varieties of vegetables and flowers. Some of them were already a couple of feet tall with greenery.

In the middle of the greenhouse, in the open space between the lengths of the tables lay Ginnie's body on the soft dirt. She was lying face down with her hair off to the left as her face faced away from Frances towards the back of the greenhouse.

She had on a pair of floral patterned gardening gloves that seemed surprisingly clean. She wore a green dress that fell just below her knees and she wore flat black shoes. Frances walked up to her and looked at the body. Her feet were slightly apart and on her head, just above the right ear was a congealed damp spot of blood.

Frances stepped over her and leaned down to look at the face. Ginnie looked calm, there wasn't much sign of the struggle on her face. Though around her neck was an abrasion.

"Do you think she was strangled?" asked Florence.

"I do. Though it looks like she might have been hit over the head with something blunt first."

Frances stood back up and surveyed the scene. There were plenty of scuff marks by Ginnie's feet as if she might have struggled for a short while. There were also several assorted shoe prints of various sizes across the length and breadth of the greenhouse.

At the far end were a huddle of several large pots carrying the hearty beginnings of tomato plants. The soil around them was smooth other than for various circle indentations from where the tomato planters had been moved and replaced.

"I wonder why they like to move the tomato plants around so much?" asked Frances, mostly to herself.

"Probably to give them better light, I imagine. I can feel slight temperature differences in here from one end to the other."

Frances bent back down next to Ginnie's body and looked her up and down. She didn't have much dirt on her other than what she had come in contact with from lying on the dirt in the greenhouse. Frances picked up Ginnie's right hand and then her left hand. She felt her ring finger.

"Doesn't look like she's been doing much gardening," said Frances, "her gloves are particularly clean."

"Could've been she got surprised soon after she arrived here to do her gardening."

"Perhaps, we'll ask Jack when Ginnie came out to garden. She's also not wearing her wedding and engagement rings."

"Well, I know I probably wouldn't if I was going to be doing any gardening."

Frances smiled up at Florence and nodded her head.

"Perhaps, but you, at least, are a gardener."

"What is that supposed to mean?" asked Florence.

Frances stood back up and looked around again at the Greenhouse.

"Well, just that Ginnie doesn't strike me as the gardening type. This is a very well kept greenhouse and the garden is already tilled and ready for planting. They likely have a strapping groundskeeper who does most of this work. It just seems odd that she'd show so much interest in something she really doesn't need to be concerned with."

"Maybe she just likes to come out and check on things, see how Enoch is getting on. She might also just like to pretend she's more of a green thumb than she is."

"Yes, you could well be correct."

"Does anything else here look odd to you?" asked Frances.

Florence looked around and walked down to the far end. Then she walked back up to the front end and looked around again.

"No, can't say that it does. A nice large greenhouse with a bountiful amount of gorgeous plants. I'm nothing if not envious."

"How do you suppose she got that bump on her head?" asked Frances.

Florence looked around again but didn't find what she was looking for.

"Maybe in the struggle she stumbled and bumped her head on one of those table corners."

"That is a good theory, but I don't see any blood on any of the table edges near her do you?"

Florence bent down to take a closer look but she too had to admit that she didn't see any blood that might support her theory.

"However, if you take a look here," and Frances pointed to the front of the greenhouse where hooks were arranged holding a variety of gardening tools. "It seems that a couple of hooks are without tools hanging on them."

"Yes, I see what you mean. Do you think she was bumped over the head with some sort of gardening implement?"

"Well, I think I'd certainly like to find out what tools belong to those hooks. Wouldn't you?"

"I'd like to do whatever the sleuth feels is best," said Florence laughing. "You don't seem to miss a thing, do you?"

"Not very often. Once you've done this sort of thing once or twice you get an eye for the details. It's the details that are often very telling."

Six

Lady Marmalade and Florence had reentered the house and were in the living room. Enoch Habbit had been brought in and was standing with his hat in his hands. His hands were big and large like shovels and knobbly as tree trunks. The size of the rest of his body was in proportion to his hands.

His face had been weather beaten, unkindly. The years had more miles on them for him than for others his age. He wasn't likely much older than fifty and yet he seemed to be leaning on the decade of sixty.

His hair was a mix of sandy brown and gray, it was thin and messy though kept short. His clothes were well worn and meant for work. His wore a couple of hues of brown. A vest was open over his shirt which was buttoned up a few buttons below his neck. You could see hair on his thick slab of chest, like black and gray wires sewn into his skin.

His eyes were brown and held up heavy lids under protest. He wore a frown better than he wore his clothes, perhaps it came natural to him with years spent in the outdoors squinting out the sun. His nose was broken, perhaps more than once and he had a scar on his upper lip. The teeth he had remaining in his mouth were yellow and crooked.

There was something about the man that Frances didn't like. And it wasn't because he worked for a living. It was something else. The road map written all over his face spoke of dark journeys. He might have been handsome once if his life had been more genteel.

"So you're telling me, Mr. Habbit, that you didn't see the lady of the house out in the garden at all today?" asked Inspector Gibbard.

"Yes sir, that's what I'm sayin'."

Meredith was still sitting down next to Jack. It appeared that drinks were the order of the afternoon as both Jack and Meredith seemed to have made good work on the drinks that they held in their hands. Frances was certain they were alcoholic in nature. Florence's bag of the marmalade was still where she left it, in the corner of the room by the doors.

"Well, then," said the Inspector, "where were you all day, Mr. Habbit?"

The young bobby shifted uneasily on his feet. Seemed that Frances wasn't the only one who was made uncomfortable by Enoch's presence.

"I was out in the garden, an' I was preparin' it for the planting. At two, Agnus call'd me fa' suppa'. I was eatin' suppa' with the staff until three."

Enoch was squeezing his cap, his knuckles going white, one of the scabs on it cracking open.

"Can you confirm that, Mr. Gromson?" asked Gibbard.

"I can sir. In as much as I saw Mr. Habbit come in for his supper at two as he says, but he left at around two thirty and I only saw him again at three when he brought his plate and mug back to Ms. Van Buren."

Inspector Gibbard turned to look at Mr. Habbit and his eyes turned to slits.

"I put men like you in prison, Mr. Habbit, for the sport of it. Looks to me like that's where you're going. A place you're probably familiar with, aren't you."

"Now just a minute, Inspector," said Jack standing up. "Enoch's been with me for over three years. He's a good, honest, hard worker and I've never had a problem with him. You can't seriously believe that he'd kill my wife."

"I didin' sir, I swear I didin' kill the missus," said Enoch. "Listen, 'spector, I ain't much for company so I took my supper and went an' sat down un'er the tree. Being such a nice day an' all."

The tree was at the far end of the garden behind the shed and out of the way. A quiet spot if you were looking for peace. Though Lady Marmalade didn't think that Enoch was a man that spent much time looking for peace. Quite to the contrary.

The French doors opened up behind Frances and Florence and another bobby they hadn't seen before entered carrying a small shovel. Gibbard looked at him.

"What is it, constable?" he asked.

"Well sir, I was looking around in the shed like you asked me too, after Leavens brought Mr. Habbit in sir, and I found this shovel hiding way in the back out of sight behind a wheelbarrow. I think it's the murder weapon, sir. There's blood on it here."

The bobby brought the shovel up for the inspector to take a closer look. There was indeed a smudge of blood on the convex part of the shovel's blade. In addition there were a couple of long strands of red hair stuck to it.

"Um, Inspector," said Frances. He looked at her. "I don't believe that is the actual murder weapon."

"You don't do you? So how do you suppose Mrs. Forsyth was killed then?"

"Well, I believe she was strangled, the shovel was only used to knock her down."

"Is that so, and you are of course a coroner too, I take it, as well as a detective now?"

Jack and both Meredith had to stifle a small laugh.

"I just think it's important."

"Let the police and coroner determine what's important. Speaking of which, go and see what's taking them so long."

He was speaking to the bobby holding the shovel. Gibbard took the shovel from him and handed it to Leavens, the constable standing slightly behind Mr. Habbit. Mr. Habbit was chewing his lip, not looking any happier with the situation.

"Take him to the station, constable and have him charged. We'll let the barristers sort it out."

For a moment it looked like Mr. Habbit was going to put up a fight as Leavens grabbed him by the elbow. He was bigger than Leavens, but Enoch's eyes met Lady Marmalade's and then Florence's and he thought better of it. Perhaps one of the few wise decisions a man like him had made in his long life.

Frances looked up at the grandfather clock as it struck once indicating half past the hour of four. The coroner was running late. And as if hearing her thoughts, the coroner and two men carrying a stretcher came in and walked up to Gibbard. He pointed them in the direction of the greenhouse and they walked out again through the French doors.

Running into the living room after them was Garrett. His eyes wide and his hair a mess. A white and blue scarf was around his neck and he wore gray slacks and a navy blazer over blue sweater.

"What on earth is going on here?" he asked, looking around at everyone.

Jack came up to him and put his hand on his son's shoulder.

"Your mother's been murdered, son, I'm sorry."

Jack looked at him for awhile as Garrett stared at the floor. He dragged his fingers through his messy hair and looked back up at his father.

"What? Where?"

"In the greenhouse," said Jack. "The inspector thinks Enoch did it."

Garrett wasn't listening, he was looking out the French doors and beyond towards the greenhouse. He walked briskly towards them.

"Garrett, no, wait," called Jack after him.

But Garrett was already out the doors and running towards the greenhouse. The French doors left open, James went over to them and closed them. Lady Marmalade came up to Gibbard.

"Don't you think you should interview everyone to determine their whereabouts before summarily charging someone?" she said in a quiet voice.

"Listen, my Lady, I've been policing for over thirty years, and believe me, Mr. Habbit is not innocent."

"He might not be innocent, but he might be innocent of this particular crime."

"We'll let the courts determine that."

Frances was getting a little frustrated, not for some time had she found a policeman to be so unwilling to help.

"Inspector, if you'll indulge me, I'd be ever so grateful."

Frances smiled at Gibbard with genuine warmth and touched his forearm. The inspector sighed and nodded his head.

"Very well," he said.

He took out his notebook and made some notes. Jack was at the bar refilling his and Meredith's drinks. She was whispering in his ear and she had her hand on his lower back.

"Mr. Forsyth, if you don't mind, I need to ask a few more questions."

Jack turned to look at him and Meredith did too. She took a slow sip of her drink. Gibbard walked up towards them accompanied with Florence and Frances.

"Who else has access to the shed?"

Jack looked down at his drink for a moment before answering.

"Well, Enoch has the key and he locks it up at night. Though James, our butler, has a spare just in case I ever need to get in there when Enoch isn't around. Enoch's here five days a week and I suppose that during the day he keeps it unlocked so that anyone might actually make use of it. Not like there's anything of value in there."

"Are there gardening tools kept in the shed, Jack?" asked Frances.

"There are, the main ones for the garden are kept in there, there is a smaller set, in both number and size which are kept in the greenhouse for that purpose."

"And the shovel you saw earlier, did that one belong in the greenhouse or the shed?" asked Frances.

"Well, it was a smaller shovel so I'd have to say probably in the greenhouse. Look, I'm not the gardener, Enoch is, and I don't believe he would have killed my wife."

Jack looked visibly upset again. He drank deeply from his drink.

"Is this really necessary, can't you all see how devastating this has been on him?" said Meredith.

"Yes, we certainly can, and we won't take up more of your time than is needed," said Gibbard. "Though I do have a couple more questions. Did your wife tell you when she was going out gardening?"

Jack nodded.

"Yes, I was reading the paper after lunch. It must have been around two or thereabouts. Yes, just after two I believe as I heard the clock chime twice. Ginnie told me she was going to the greenhouse to check in on the flowers."

"And were you at home this whole time?" asked Gibbard.

"Yes I was. I finished the paper and I was in my study, which is in the front of the house, by two thirty. I heard the clock chime once. I never left my study until James brought Enoch in with the terrible news."

"And that was around three thirty?"

"Yes."

"Was anyone at home with you, besides Ginnie?" asked Frances.

"Meredith was here, as was Garrett, though I saw him leave just after two thirty."

"Did he tell you where he was going?" asked Frances.

Jack shook his head.

"He probably went into town to run some errands. He'll take any excuse to drive his Alfa Romeo around."

"Was Meredith with you in the study?" asked Gibbard.

"Of course not, what sort of question is that? I was in my study working. That's what studies are for."

"It's okay, Jack, they're here to help," said Meredith.

Frances noticed that Meredith was not wearing any nail polish from the night before which she had been.

"And where were you dear, while Jack was in his study?" asked Frances.

Meredith looked at Frances over the rim of her almost empty glass.

"I spent some of that time reading right here in the living room before I decided to go and freshen up. From the upstairs bathroom I saw the police arrive. That's when I came down to see what happened."

"But you weren't here when we had arrived, you had gone back upstairs, had you not?" asked Frances.

"Yes indeed, but my dear Lady, this is not a conspiracy, I had not finished getting ready for the day, and after I heard the news there was nothing I could do other than support Jack, but I couldn't do that in my half undressed state."

"Did you see Garrett leave and did he tell you where he was going?" asked Gibbard.

"No, I was likely still here in the living room when he went off, I did remember hearing the door close though."

The coroner came back into the living room from the front of the house and spoke to the inspector.

"We're all done, Inspector," he said. "I'll ring you up when we have any news about the time of death."

Gibbard nodded and shook the coroner's hands.

"Thank you, Dr. Blackstone."

Seven

"Where is Garrett?" asked Inspector Gibbard. "He's been gone quite some time now."

"He went to the greenhouse when he heard his mother had died, perhaps he is still grieving," offered Florence.

"Yes, well, I'd like to be getting on. Crime doesn't take a break just because the police are," said Gibbard.

"I'll go and get him," said Florence.

As she turned around to walk to the end of the living room and through the French doors, she saw Garrett coming out of the greenhouse and back towards the house.

"Ah, there he is," she said. "Speak of the d..."

She stopped herself, realizing that such a phrase was perhaps not quite right under the circumstances. One of the constables came back into the living room just as Garrett came back in through the French doors.

"We're ready when you are, Inspector," said Leavens.

"Just a minute, you can go wait outside, I just have some last questions for the younger Forsyth on the Lady's insistence."

The constable left and Garrett walked up to his father who had sat back down on the same couch as he had been when Frances first entered the living room.

"What the hell was she doing in the greenhouse in the first place? She's not the gardener," said Garrett.

Jack looked up at his son and noticed his eyes were bloodshot and glassy. They were dry, but it was clear he had been crying.

"I don't know why, son, she said she wanted to go in and check on the tomatoes."

"Right."

Garrett looked at his father, his head was cocked to one side and his hands were on his hips. He ground his teeth together and thought for a moment.

"That's not why she was there. You know that."

"Listen Garrett, I'm just as upset as you are. I loved your mother and this ghastliness is not only senseless it's upsetting."

"Well, you had one hell of a way of showing it. If you'd just get yourself out of trouble and start working at the family business we might not even be in this predicament."

"That's enough. Not now! Our family affairs can be discussed after we've laid your mother to rest."

Garrett spun around and folded his hands in front of his chest and hung his head low. If he were a boy he would be pouting, but he wasn't a boy and this was different. He was angry and sad. But the anger and sadness had a depth to them that didn't seem to have come from this afternoon's news alone.

"I need to ask you a few questions if you don't mind, Mr. Forsyth," said the inspector.

"No, I don't mind. Call me Garrett."

Garrett looked up at the inspector with his hands still folded over his chest.

"We've heard that you went out this afternoon. Can you tell us where and when?"

"Yes. At around two thirty I went to town to have a few pints. I just got back."

"Where did you drink at?"

"The Wet Whistle."

Inspector Gibbard looked at Lady Marmalade and she nodded at him.

"Did your mother tell you she was going gardening?" asked Frances.

"No. As I said before, she's not a gardener. I don't know why she'd be in the greenhouse at all. That just wasn't her thing."

"So you've never seen her in the greenhouse before?"

"Well, yes, I have, but not to garden. I don't know why she'd go in there. I've seen her a few times. Probably just to smell the flowers. She's not in very long. No more than five minutes."

"Do you know who might want to kill your mother?" asked Frances, softly.

He looked at her for a moment and then broke her gaze as he looked off through the windows and into the garden. He slowly shook his head and fought back tears.

"No, she was a saint. She was really sweet. The glue that kept our family together in spite of everything he tried to do to bring chaos."

Lady Marmalade inferred the 'he' to be Jack Forsyth. She looked at the inspector for a moment.

"Inspector Gibbard has arrested Enoch. He thinks he might be the one to have killed her."

"He's as good as any. Sure he has a green thumb, but he's not all that he appears to be. I mean you've had a look at him. So no, I wouldn't put it past him if he killed her, a brute like that. But it'd be my father's fault in the end."

Frances and Florence looked at Garrett quizzically. Meredith and Jack stood up and went to the bar to refresh their drinks yet again. Seemed they were trying to find either solace or solutions in the bottom of a bottle. Lady Marmalade didn't hold out hope they'd find either. Jack poured their drinks and glared over at where Frances, the inspector, Florence, and Garrett were standing.

"Why do you think it was your father's fault?" asked Frances.

Garrett stared at the floor between the four of them, his face a twisted mask of anger and sadness. He slowly shook his head from side to side, his arms still clutched together in front of him.

"I've said enough. I'm just upset and angry, that's all." Then he looked up at them. "I don't believe my father killed my mother. He may be many things but he's not a murderer."

The four of them stood huddled together for a while in silence. Over the rims of their glasses, Jack and Meredith stood with blank stares, looking over at the foursome. Frances looked over at Meredith and Jack. There was something about the two of them that bothered her.

She had lost her husband and he'd lost his older brother. One could see how they might come together in a shared grief to console one another. But the way they whispered together, the small physical intimacies seemed to tell of something more. Frances turned to Garrett and smiled at him. She touched him gingerly on his forearm.

"I'm terribly sorry for your loss, Garrett. I just want to help bring justice and closure to this senseless crime."

Garrett looked up her, his eyes still wet and bloodshot, holding back the tears. He tried to peg a smile to the clothesline of his cheeks, but the tumultuous gale of grief blew it very quickly off his face.

"If you don't mind, Lady Marmalade, I have a man to take up to Blackpool. So I'll be off," said Inspector Gibbard.

Gibbard looked at her through his small blue eyes. They wobbled in their sockets as if they were loose. Gibbard closed up his notebook and tucked it into his inside jacket pocket. Frances had noticed he hadn't really been taking all that very many notes of late. Barely a scribble really. Didn't matter, she didn't need to take notes either, though in her case it was because she had a good memory and only focused on the one task at hand.

She couldn't say for certain if the inspector had either. Though she felt quite certain that this crime was unlikely to be his only concern. She smiled at him.

"Not at all, Inspector. Thank you so much for indulging me."

Gibbard started to turn around when Lady Marmalade put her hand on his arm. He stopped and looked at her.

"I hope you don't mind if I call you up tomorrow to see if you have any news from the coroner?"

The inspector's nose twitched and he pinched his lips before forcing a thin smile across his lips as if he'd just now tasted bile.

"As you wish. But mark my words, my Lady, by tomorrow we'll have this case all buttoned down."

"I'm sure you will."

Frances smiled after him as he left. Sometimes she wondered how some crimes got solved at all with the incompetence of some of the policemen she had met. Perhaps it wasn't just incompetence but an arrogant unflinching belief that was the problem. Not that she didn't think Enoch could have killed Ginnie, though her suspicions lay elsewhere. She turned to Florence. Florence smiled at her and raised her eyebrows.

"I'm afraid, my dear, I'm going to have to be a little indelicate. Be prepared to leave shortly."

Florence smiled.

"Ooh, sounds exciting," she said.

Frances walked up to the bar with Florence by her side. Jack gamely smiled at them as they came up.

"I'm going out," said Garrett as he left the living room.

"Would you like a drink?" asked Jack.

"No, thank you, Jack. Though I do have a question if you don't mind. An awkward one at that. But I feel it must be asked," said Frances.

Jack looked at her from the corner of his eye. Meredith also stared at Lady Marmalade while she sipped on her quickly vanishing drink.

"Um, how to say this. I guess the best approach is a direct one," said Frances. "Jack, do you know why Garrett might have wanted to blame you for your wife's murder."

Frances watched as Jack's face turned red. His eyes narrowed and he opened his mouth as if to speak. Then he thought better of it and finished his drink in one large gulp. He composed himself.

"I have no idea. Probably because he's upset. Aren't we all?"

"Yes, of course," said Lady Marmalade. "I'm terribly sorry for your loss. I can only imagine how deep your grief is."

Jack nodded curtly with Meredith like a statue by his side.

"Are you two having an affair?"

Frances knew she was being impolite, if not outright rude. But politeness be damned, she was investigating a murder and she didn't quite like the impression she got from the two of them.

"Well I never...how dare you!" said Jack.

Lady Marmalade's question had tipped him over the edge. He was upset and losing his composure. His veins on the side of his neck bulged like little snakes. His eyes narrowed and his thin mouth became a hot wire.

"My wife's dead body has not even cooled and you come into my house as a guest and accuse me of indiscretions. Do you have no shame!"

"I'm sorry...I didn't mean any..."

"I suggest you leave and allow me the peace and dignity of grieving alone."

"Yes, very well. I do apologize, I didn't mean to suggest...if I can help in anyway."

"You've done more than enough...please, just leave," said Jack.

He turned, blading his body towards Frances and Florence, trying his best to regain his composure and obviously wrestling strenuously with it.

Eight

At the end of the driveway, just as they turned onto the lane and started walking back towards Florence's home, Florence spoke.

"That was quite indelicate," she said, grinning mischievously. "What were you hoping for?"

Lady Marmalade turned and looked at her friend.

"Sometimes being indelicate in polite society catches people off guard, and when they're off guard you can oftentimes get a response that is quite telling."

"So what did Jack's response tell you?"

"That there is more to the story between him and Meredith than he cares to admit."

"Do you think? I just thought they were grieving a shared loss. You know, his brother being married to Meredith and now dead."

"Yes, I wondered about that myself, but it was something about them together that I didn't quite like. Something a little more...nefarious."

"Oh do tell."

Frances gazed down the lane, her mind like a locomotive gaining speed.

"I don't know for certain. But I think it will all come together in time. You know what we should do?"

Florence looked over at her as they walked casually towards her home. The sky was graying with heavy clouds, though blue patches of sky were still out as the sun started packing up its chores for the day and making it's way home.

"I think we should go to the Wet Whistle as you offered yesterday. No cooking tonight, let's go to the pub and have supper and drinks out."

"Sounds great to me, but I get the sense there's more to it than just that."

"My dear Flo," said Frances, "you know me too well. If there is someone who knows the workings of a community better than a barman, I have yet to meet him."

"Well, as it happens, I've developed a good relationship with the barman, Finley Moran. I'll make our introductions. This is so exciting, sleuthing around with you."

Frances smiled.

"Where is your bag you brought the marmalade in?" she asked.

"I left it behind. I'll pick it up another time. Tell me, Fran, do you think Enoch did it? He sure is big enough to have done it."

"No, I'm not certain he did. Did you see the size of the shovel used to knock Ginnie down?"

Florence nodded.

"Well, it was small, not something I'd imagine a big man like Enoch using..."

"But that's all that would have been available to him in the greenhouse," said Florence.

"In the greenhouse, yes. But why go to the trouble of using the shovel in the greenhouse and then taking it back to the shed to hide it. I would think he'd have just taken a shovel from the shed in the first place. In any event, I think the whole idea of Enoch using a shovel to knock Ginnie out before strangling her is nonsense."

"Why?"

"Well, look at the size of the man's hands. He could have strangled her with just one of them. No, I don't think he would have used a shovel to knock her out and then strangle her with his hands after."

"I suppose, though, he does seem a bit shifty, doesn't he?"

"Yes, I'm sure he's not an innocent man, but I'm not so sure he's guilty of killing Ginnie. Did you notice the footprints on the dirt floor of the greenhouse?"

"No, not really, it was the first time I've seen a dead body. It was awful actually."

"I know. Well, the footprints were of a variety of sizes. Some the size of men's feet and others the size of women's. None of them however, seemed to be as large as Enoch's."

"He could have brushed them away couldn't he?"

"He could have, but the dirt floor didn't show any signs of having been recently swept other than for the far end where the tomatoes were."

"Well, Fran, this is all very confusing to me. I don't know how you keep it all straight. I thought that when the inspector hauled Enoch away that he was our murderer. But if not him, then who?"

"That is a very good question. I have my suspicions, but we need to determine motive and we need to speak with more people in order to gather more evidence."

"I hate to be macabre, Fran, but I must say I'm thrilled to be a part of this detective work with you."

They stopped in front of Florence's gate as Florence opened the latch and they walked up the driveway towards her front door.

"I'll be thrilled when we catch the murderer?"

"Oh, me too. It seems so senseless to me why anyone would kill that poor innocent woman."

"Yes, sometimes it does seem all quite senseless. But you have to try and make sense of it from the killer's eyes before you can solve the crime. To madmen, my dear Flo, even their madness makes perfect sense to them."

Nine

The Wet Whistle is the only pub in Puddle's End and it's a large one. It was founded inside a house. A brick built house that is two story house. An addition was added at a later date that holds two rooms that can be rented by the night. The building's exterior was yellowed and old though the stability of the building was sound.

It was just after six when Florence and Frances made it to the pub, Florence parking her car right outside. Six in the evening was a good time to be at the Wet Whistle if you didn't much care for crowds and you wanted to be able to get a decent amount of the barman's attention.

Not being a smoker, Frances preferred less people in her pubs, if only because that meant there'd be less smoke around. It seemed all the rage lately, especially amongst the women, to be smoking. As to why, Frances had no idea.

Frances and Florence got out of the car and walked into the pub through the main doors which were two large wooden ones which opened surprisingly easily for their obvious heft. The Wet Whistle was at most, perhaps a third full. Off to a far side from the entrance was a comfortable booth made to fit four. Frances and Florence thought that'd be a good choice for them.

But first they made their way up to the bar. Behind it was the barman who had a dish towel draped over his left shoulder, on top of a black vest. He was wearing a dirty white shirt with the sleeves rolled up to bare hairy forearms that were thick and meaty. He was of average height but he was thick with it. He had a mess of gray hair over a pudgy face with a nose that looked like it had been stuck on his face by accident like a piece of putty. It was red and large.

Here was a man who had found his calling and took the time to savor it. His face was kind but he was not a handsome man. He leaned on a lower ledge from behind the bar. As soon as he saw Florence coming towards him he smiled and it warmed up his face and brightened his eyes.

"Ms. Hudnall," he said. His voice was crackly as if he spoke through the wireless. "So good of you to come. You never told me you had a sister."

Florence laughed good naturedly and Frances smiled at him.

"This is my dear friend whom I've known for, well, a few years. Lady Marmalade, Mr. Finley Moran."

Frances offered her hand which Finley shook in his big thick hand. A soft hand without calluses.

"My Lady, you'll be the first Lady I've had the pleasure of serving in my humble public house," he said.

"Please call me Frances."

He nodded and then looked back at Florence.

"Looks like you're here for more than just social visit," he said.

"We are, but social matters must come first. What do you recommend for supper tonight?"

"Well, Fiona has just finished up with what I humbly consider to be the best shepherd's pie north of the Channel."

"Sounds wonderful," said Florence, looking at Frances.

"I like it too."

"And to drink?"

"I'll just have a glass of white wine, I'm not fussy," said Florence.

"Two for two, Mr. Moran, I'll have exactly what my sister is having," said Frances, grinning.

"I don't believe you'll be disappointed, and please call me Finley" he said.

Florence opened up her purse to pay, but Frances wouldn't hear of it. She spoke sternly to Finley and instructed him in no uncertain terms not to take any of Florence's money. He reluctantly agreed and Frances paid for their meal.

"We'll bring it out to you when it's ready," he said. "Sit wherever you like."

Frances and Florence went and took their booth they had kept their eye on since they first walked into the Wet Whistle.

The pub was not dissimilar to any other pub in England. If they had been transported to one Blackpool or Manchester it might look eerily similar. The floor was hardwood and the walls were wood paneled and paintings were hung up here and there. It was dark inside until their eyes quickly adjusted to the warm glow of the sparse lights and the fireplace opposite where the two of them sat.

"It's a very cozy pub," said Frances. "I'm glad we came."

Florence nodded.

"I like it, I don't get out as often as I should. I enjoy my own time at home, but whenever I do get out here I always enjoy it. I think you'll like Finley, he's a very cordial sort."

"I like him already," said Frances. "And I hope he'll be a font of knowledge on some of the things we'll be asking."

They didn't have to wait long for the shepherd's pie to come out, which Finley brought to their table along with two glasses of white wine. He disappeared as quickly as he came and returned moments later with cutlery and cloth napkins which he placed on the wooden table. He stood at the end of the table and he had on a dirty white apron that covered his black pants just past the knees.

"So what brings you to Puddle's End?" Finley asked, looking at Frances.

Frances took some salt and pepper from the shakers that were already on the table and dusted the top of the shepherd's pie with salt as if she had a premonition of the upcoming rations. She looked up at Finley.

"Well, I came up to visit my friend Flo. However, things have taken a turn for the worse and now I find myself in need of your help regarding some of the good, and perhaps not as good, people of Puddle's End."

"I see," he said. "I am intrigued."

"I've always believed, and history has borne this out, that the barman of the local pub is perhaps most attuned to the goings-on of his community."

Finley nodded.

"You might be right. Some men and dare I say women, will treat us as they do a man of the cloth, though our cloth," he said, clutching at the towel over his left shoulder, "is of a different sort."

Frances took a bit of her shepherd's pie, she was famished.

"I'll let the two of you make some progress on your meals before I come back. I'll let Fiona know to keep an eye on the bar."

"Thank you, Finley," said Florence.

The two them sat in silence for a while, enjoying the food and taking in the atmosphere. An older couple were at a table with soiled plates in front of them. Bones were on both plates, his seemed like a cross made from lamb chops and hers were fish bones. His beer was half empty and her wine was all gone.

Frances imagined he was on his second beer while she had stuck with just one glass of wine.

They seemed to be a married couple. Comfortable with each other but by no means showing any warmth either. At another table was a group of four rough looking men. Not rough in the mean sense, they were rather laborers just got off from work. Mechanics perhaps, as their fingernails were black underneath, and their clothes although moderately clean held an oil stain or two.

"Have you got to know many of your neighbors around here?" asked Frances.

Florence nodded and finished chewing her food.

"I have a few of them. Actually I know a few of the people in here," she said. "That couple over there," and she pointed delicately with her fork at the couple with the soiled plates, "are married. John and Vera I believe are their names. Don't know their last names, but they're married, though from what I can tell, not very happily married."

Frances smiled.

"Yes, I could have guessed that myself from here."

"Those four men over there are the mechanics. The older chap is Reg who I've dealt with whenever I take my car for a service. Wonderful man, hardworking, looks rough but he's a real gem."

Frances took the last mouthful of her shepherd's pie and savored it.

"That was absolutely delicious."

"I hope so, you put enough salt on it for all the king's men, and their horses."

Frances laughed. She picked up her white wine and took a sip. She only had half of it left.

"Perhaps my taste buds are dying off as I get older."

"That fellow over there in the far corner by the window," said Florence pointing again with her fork at the back of a military man in dress uniform, "is someone I can't say I've seen before. Though lately there have been a lot of military men coming through. Can't say I like it."

"Eric feels the same. Not that he minds them, but he thinks it's an omen of dangerous times ahead."

Florence finished up her plate of food and laid her knife and fork down on its empty face. She dabbed at her mouth.

"You know, that's exactly how I feel too," she said. "I wonder if we won't be seeing another war."

"God forbid," said Frances. "We're not even over the first one."

Frances looked up towards the bar where Finley was busy serving a young man accompanied by an older man. They looked like they could be father and son. Perhaps the young lad was out for his first pint with his father. Frances had wished that for

Declan, but it hadn't come to pass, and that was quite a few years ago.

Frances watched the two of them take their beers and sit down in another booth across the large room. She saw the father lift his glass towards his son and they clinked. He made a toast, though about what or to whom Frances couldn't tell. All she could see was the older man's lips moving. She wondered if the son would be conscripted if they did in fact end up in another war. The thought was dreary as she wondered if he'd make it back home again to enjoy more pints with his father.

She looked away from them and down at the table. She'd been lucky, having Declan when she did. He was nine when the war started. The ugliest and meanest of wars as far as she had been concerned. And if they had another hot on the heels of the first, it would be meaner and uglier, she was sure of it. And Declan being thirty four would certainly be eligible for conscription if the Military Service Act of 1916 was any indication of things to come.

"Are you alright Fran? You look pale," asked Florence.

Frances looked up at her friend and smiled weakly.

"Yes, I'm okay," she said, fiddling with her napkin as she held it in her hand on top of the table. "Just this thought of another war is so disheartening. I was looking over at that young man over there," she looked over at the booth with the father and son laughing now, "and I wonder what's in store for him. And there's

Declan too, he'll be eligible for conscription if it comes to it. Oh Flo, I do get weary of all the murdering and misery and mayhem."

"Yes, I can understand that."

"Am I interrupting?" said Finley as he came up to their table.

"No, not at all," said Frances, "I was just starting to get morose about the possibility of another war. Let's talk of something else."

Florence moved up to the wall to give Finley space to sit on her side of the booth.

"Sit with us for a mo'," she said.

Finley eased himself into the booth beside Florence and placed his forearms on the table, his hands clasped together.

"War is never good, Frances you're right about that. But perhaps it can't be helped and perhaps if there is another war it will be the one that ends all wars."

"I hope you're right. Though they might have said something similar about the last one we had, if I remember correctly."

Frances smiled and Florence laughed. Finley smiled too, though it was a sad smile. He nodded his head sadly.

"I don't think I ever told you this," he said, looking at Florence, "but I lost my boy at Amiens in March of eighteen. Harold was his name, only nineteen years old. Thought he was going to change the world..."

Finley closed his eyes tight.

"He was supposed to be working with me as soon as he got back. But he never did."

He sighed and Florence put her hand on his hairy forearm.

"I'm so sorry," said Frances.

Finley took a moment and breathed deeply.

"It's a long time ago now, but the pain still pinches when I think about it. But you're right, we're better off talking about other things."

He smiled and looked at Florence and patted her hand which was on his forearm. Then he put his hands back together and Florence took hers off his forearm and held her wineglass by the stem and took the last long sip.

"So, how can I help you with something more cheery?"

"I'm afraid it might not be all that cheery," said Florence, "you probably haven't heard, but Ginnie Forsyth is dead."

He looked at her for a moment and furrowed his brow. Then he furrowed his brow deeper, tilling the soil of his mind, trying to make sense of what she had just told him.

"What do you mean she's dead? What happened to her?"

"Well, we believe, actually, we know that she was murdered."

"Good Lord, you can't be serious."

Finley looked at Frances, she nodded her head slightly, then he looked back at Florence.

"Yes, quite serious," said Frances.

"Shocking, absolutely shocking. What happened?"

Finley looked at Frances. Frances took the last drink of wine from her glass before speaking.

"She was found dead in her greenhouse by the groundskeeper, and that's what we want to talk to you about."

"The groundskeeper," said Finley, looking out towards the front entrance of his pub, in thought, not at anything in particular. "He's a bad sort. I told Jack not to hire him, not that it's any of my business."

"You're talking about Enoch Habbit?" asked Frances.

Finley nodded his head and then looked around the bar and leaned in towards Frances. Florence leaned in to. Finley's voice got lower.

"Yes, he's a bad sort, in with the wrong kind of people. I told Jack that when he hired him six months ago."

"Really?" said Florence.

Finley nodded.

"That's odd, Jack told us that Enoch had been working for him for some time. Was it three years?"

Florence looked at Frances. Frances nodded her head.

"He said 'over three years'."

Finley shook his head.

"No, that can't be right. It was just a little over six months ago when Jack asked me if I knew of any good men who might like grounds keeping. I gave him a couple of names and a few weeks later he came back to tell me he'd hired someone. I asked who, and he told me it was Enoch. Enoch Habbit. I told him he'd better look out, that Enoch had a reputation. Jack swore he trusted the man."

Frances pursed her lips into an O. Florence looked at Finley, her eyes wide open. She found this all very exciting.

"Who do the police suspect of killing her?" asked Finley.

"The very same Enoch you've just been telling us about," said Florence.

Finley hung his head in thought for a moment and then slowly shook it from side to side.

"Well, I guess nothing surprises me now. Who was the inspector?"

"A man named Gibbid...no, Gibbard I think he said," offered Florence.

"Ah yes, the highly esteemed Hank Gibbard. At least according to himself. I find him to be a bit hard to take, too arrogant for my liking, though he swears he gets things done."

"Yes, I found him to be testy," said Frances.

"I don't mean to press, but do you mind telling me how Ginnie was murdered?" asked Finley.

"She was hit over the head with a small shovel and then strangled. That's how it appears to me. We'll likely get confirmation tomorrow from the coroner but it appears the bump over her head didn't finish her off," said Frances.

"Thank you. The reason I was asking was because Enoch's a handyman in the sense that word has it he likes to use his hands to rough people up. Forgive me for saying this, and I can't be certain, but I'd imagine a man like him beating her to death with his bare hands, not gently hitting her over the head only to strangle her."

"What sort of a brute is this man?" asked Florence. "He must be a criminal."

Finley looked over at her again, nodding his head.

"Yes, I think he is. I've heard he's spent a number of years in and out of jail, mostly for violent crime. A story goes that he was once charged with murder but was acquitted. Apparently, the witnesses decided not to show up."

"Why on earth would Jack hire him?" asked Florence, looking at Frances with an astonished furrowed brow. "He must have known he was putting his whole family and especially his wife at risk."

"Yes, though to be honest, and to paint a fair picture of this man Enoch, I've never heard it said he's committed violence against women."

"Are you trying to say, Finley, that Enoch is more of a hired man for this sort of work. This violent work."

Finley looked at Lady Marmalade and then at Florence and nodded slowly.

"Yes, but I don't want to upset Florence, you're friendly with them," he said looking at Florence.

"I am, but more so with Ginnie and it's Ginnie's murder I want to help Frances solve."

"Very well then. Enoch works for a man named Lee Chan."

Finley's voice had gone quiet again and he looked around the room as he spoke and leaned in a little further still.

"I'll deny any of this if I'm asked, so please be discreet."

He looked from Frances to Florence and back to Frances.

"Frances is nothing if not discreet Finely, you can count on us."

He nodded his head. "Good," he said.

Slowly, more people were coming into the Wet Whistle. Finley looked behind him, towards the bar, but it appeared that Fiona had a handle on things for the moment.

"Lee Chan is a Chinese man who owns a restaurant in Blackpool. The Flying Chan I think it's called, for some reason that I don't know about. Anyway, attached to this restaurant is an opium den the he owns too. Mr. Chan also operates a gambling room, also attached to this restaurant and accessible from either the restaurant or the opium den."

Florence was hanging on his every word, she had never heard such scandals in all her life.

"Mr. Chan, so I've been told, is a generous man when it comes to offering loans to his clientele for either gambling or opium. He is not, however, as generous when these loans come due."

Finley looked around. They had some space between them and the other nearest tables. The four mechanics had left and had been replaced with two middle aged couples who had just started their first round of drinks. The father and son at the other side of the room had just been served their dinner. Looked like shepherd's pie for the young man and a meat pie of some sort for his father.

"I've heard that the interest on his loans is ten percent per month. Of course, men, and it is men mostly, who are under the influence of opium or gambling don't tend to think about the long term consequences of their actions. Anyway, what I'm really getting at, is that this Chan fellow is a dangerous sort and word has it that Enoch works for him as a hired man to insure that the loans are paid when due."

"Good heavens, never have I heard such scandal in all my life," said Florence.

"And what happens if the loan is called but the borrower can't pay?" asked Frances.

"That's usually when Enoch gets involved. I've heard he roughs them up, forces them to pay somehow. Makes them sell jewelry, any valuables, homes and cars even."

"And how do you think Jack fits into all of this?" asked Frances.

"I've heard it said that Jack is in debt to Chan for around ten thousand pounds."

"That's not a small amount for Jack," said Frances.

"It's not a small amount for most of us," said Finley, looking at Lady Marmalade.

"It's by no means a trivial amount for anyone," said Frances.

"So, Finley, do you believe that Enoch has been sent to extract his money from Jack by any means necessary?" asked Frances.

"Possibly, though it seems to me a bit odd that Enoch has been placed in service with the Forsyths. Usually, from what I gather, he pops by now and then to threaten, rough up and extract anything of value from those who owe Mr. Chan money. But perhaps this is a special case. I think there must be more to it."

"I see, what else could it be?" asked Frances.

"I don't know. I believe Chan is extending his reach into other nefarious activities, prostitution and smuggling is the last I heard."

"What is he smuggling?" asked Florence.

"People and gold is what I heard."

Florence's mouth went slack as she tried to comprehend the horror of what she was thinking.

"That's barbaric and cruel," was all she could muster.

"Quite, my dear Florence. There is another world out there that you and I are not aware of. A world that would cause us sleepless nights."

Frances nodded.

"Who's he smuggling and for what purposes?"

"Women for prostitution."

Frances pinched her lips and shook her head. The deeper she looked into the Forsyths and their dealings the muddier the waters seemed to get. She didn't like it.

"Good heavens, something must be done about this," said Florence.

"I agree," said Finley, "but it is up to the police to put a stop to these sorts of things."

Frances was looking at Fiona at the bar, but her mind was miles away. This whole hornet's nest was getting more complicated by the minute. Did Ginnie know about Jack's loan from Mr. Chan, and if she did, did she know the extent of it? And was that enough to get her killed. Frances found herself asking more questions than she had answers for. A position she preferred to get herself out of. And the prostitutes and the smuggling of women for that purpose.

Not only was that horrendous but how was Jack involved in any of that? The more layers of this rotten onion she peeled back, the more layers it appeared to have. She was beginning to see Jack as the rapscallion he was.

"Everything alright, Fran?" asked Florence. "You look lost."

Frances looked up at her friend and smiled.

"Lost in thought, and I find myself in a difficult position. It's getting harder to keep the whole thing together. All of this complicates matters and I find myself having great difficulty teasing out the motive for the murder of Ginnie."

Finley nodded. Florence looked at Frances in silence for a moment.

"It appears that there's more to Jack than we realized."

Frances nodded her head.

"Why gold, I wonder," said Frances, "what's the purpose of smuggling gold?"

Frances looked at Finley and he shrugged.

"I'm not sure. Some have said that Chan has ties to the Chinese government as well as mainland crime groups. I believe that some in the Chinese government believe that in the years, perhaps decades, to come that gold is going to be more valuable than currency."

"I suppose," nodded Frances. "The pound lost twenty-five percent of its value in thirty-. one after we came off the gold standard. Even still, the value of gold has been almost stagnant for many years, has it not?"

Finley nodded his head.

"You're quite right, from what I've seen gold hasn't even doubled in over a hundred years. I'm just sharing with you what I've heard about the Chinese plans for gold over the long term."

Frances thought for a moment.

"I suppose too, it depends what type of gold they're smuggling. Do you know if it's bars or coins, and if coins do you know which kinds?" asked Frances.

"I've heard that Chan is smuggling mostly gold coins but which kind I don't know."

"That's very interesting, Finley, you are sure a font of knowledge," said Frances.

"Well, you were right about us barmen. We lend our ears and people tend to use them."

"What can you tell us about the Forsyths, particularly Jack?" asked Frances.

"Well, they didn't come here very often. They seem to keep mostly to themselves. Ginnie was very pleasant. Didn't drink much and had a warm way about her. Jack on the other hand seemed hot headed and not very patient with her. Not really sure if he loved her actually. At least from how I saw him treat her."

"How so?"

"He was short and blunt with her. Sometimes unkind. I once heard him comment on the food she ordered here. I forget what it was, but he suggested that she not eat all of it as she was getting fat, and nobody liked a fat woman."

"I see," said Florence, "quite the gentleman."

Finley nodded.

"Not to excuse his behavior but he was...is a man of loose control. As mentioned, he was up to his eyeballs in loans owed to Chan, and from what I've been told, they consisted of both gambling and opium based debts. I imagine living a life like that is quite stressful. You're liable to treat others poorly."

"What about any other vices he might have had a weakness for?"

"Women too. I wouldn't be surprised if he made use of Chan's prostitutes. Not only that, but perhaps the worst part was what he was doing right under his wife's nose."

"What's that?" asked Florence.

Finley looked at Florence and sighed.

"I really don't think you want to know all of this, do you? I mean you're friendly with them."

Florence shook her head.

"Yes, well that seems like it was a long time ago. As I said earlier, I liked Ginnie more than Jack. There was just something about him that seemed a little greasy and oily."

"Very well. Right after Roger's death, Roger being married to Meredith and also being Jack's older brother."

Frances and Florence nodded.

"Well, it seems that Jack and Meredith got very close very quickly. On one occasion, Ginnie found Jack and Meredith in bed together. In her bed, the matrimonial bed."

Florence put her hand to her mouth.

"No," she said. "That's probably the most callous and cold hearted thing I've heard so far."

"He was a rascal and a knave. More than that, he seemed arrogant about it and without any compassion or sympathy as to his wife's feelings."

"I'll say," said Florence. "Do you think he would have killed her?"

"Possibly. Who can say for certain. She seemed to put up with it for years. But I had heard that she was thinking of a way out, of making a clean start. Maybe he was scared of that. Perhaps he didn't want his dirty secrets leaving with his wife."

"How do you know all of this?" asked Frances.

"I listen to people when they speak," he said. "As my grandmother once told me. She said, 'Finley, God gave you two ears and one mouth, and so you should listen twice as much as you speak'. It was good advice. It's kept me out of heaps of trouble."

He smiled and his face creased into warmth and his eyes twinkled.

"I like that advice," said Florence. "More people should heed it."

"I'll also give you a little secret, though perhaps the two of you, being bright and intelligent women might not find it to be a secret at all. The staff of the well to do visit my pub when they can, and they carry with them the keys to all the secrets that go on behind closed doors."

Frances nodded vigorously.

"Some in the upper classes seem to think that their staff standing in the very same room as they are not only invisible but deaf as well."

Finley chuckled, then looked back at the bar. The Wet Whistle was starting to fill up now.

"You couldn't imagine half the things I know about some of the upper classes around here. The guardians of culture and civility. Hardly, if you'll excuse me, but these men and women of soft hands are more often tainted with the deadly sins than those they employ."

Frances smiled at him, a small, kind smile.

"I don't doubt it."

"I should really get back to helping my wife. I think she's getting overwhelmed. Is there anything else I can help you two with?"

He slid out of the booth and stood to the side as he looked at them for a moment.

"I think not for the time being," said Frances. "You've been very helpful. Thank you Finley. Perhaps we can return if we have any further need of your assistance."

"You are always welcome." He paused and looked at Lady Marmalade with an eager face. "You will find the devil who did this to Ginnie, won't you? She didn't deserve it."

Frances nodded her head.

"You have my word, Finley, that I'll do my very best."

Finley nodded his head towards Florence and she smiled at him as he left. She looked at Florence.

"My God, Fran, I feel as though I'm in over my head."

"Aren't we all."

"Do you think he could have done it?" she asked. "Do you think Jack could have killed his wife?"

Frances looked at Florence and smiled, shaking her head just a little from side to side.

"At this stage, if I didn't have an alibi, I might even suspect myself."

She smiled and Florence laughed out loud.

"You know just how to relieve the tension," said Florence.

"Thank you, Flo. Though I do want to get to the bottom of this. For your friend's sake. She does seem to be an innocent bystander to Jack's philandering ways, which might be the reason she got killed."

"Thank you, Fran," said Florence, reaching out and grabbing Frances' hand and squeezing it gently. "I want us to find justice for her."

Ten

It was nine a.m. on Wednesday the 5th of April. Lady Marmalade sat in Florence's living room enjoying a pot of tea. They were heading up to Blackpool, leaving on the ten a.m. train out of Puddle's End. It would have them in Blackpool shortly after eleven all going well.

"So, Fran, you managed to get Inspector Gibbard to allow us to visit Enoch?" said Florence, cradling her teacup in her one hand, the other holding the saucer.

"I did, though he wasn't particularly happy about it, but I don't think he really had a choice. He said they had to release Enoch from their custody. The magistrate didn't seem to think they had much of a case against him. Much to Hank's protestations."

"Well, I could have told them that. In fact, didn't you suggest the same to him before he carted Enoch off?"

"I tried."

"I mean, really, what good are the police if they won't do a thorough investigation. Enoch might not be a choir boy, but nobody saw him with Ginnie at anytime around her murder."

"True," said Frances, "but there was the shovel tucking conveniently at the back of the shed."

"Do you think that's enough to get him hanged?"

"Depends on what kind of a barrister he can afford. It shouldn't be. As you heard Jack mention, the shed is left open pretty much the whole day when Enoch's around, in addition, Jack has a spare key that the butler keeps. That shovel by itself is hardly sufficient evidence to have Enoch found guilty. Though I must admit, Flo, as much as it pains me, that more innocent and better men have been found guilty on less."

"I'd rather not hear about that."

"I know, but it's true. Sadly, our justice is not as blind as she should be. Or rather, I've seen her turn a blind eye to the justice of the poor."

"A top up?" asked Florence, leaning in and picking up the teapot. Frances nodded and held out her teacup. There was a puddle at the bottom, no more than a sip really. Florence topped her up and Frances added in a lump of sugar and a splash of cream.

"You know," said Florence, settling back into her armchair, the teacup and saucer held delicately in her lap, "I've been thinking about what Finley said about service staff and how much information they no doubt overhear."

Frances nodded before sipping her fresh tea.

"In a way, I'm glad my housekeeper only comes in one day a week, and the gardener too. Being single, I don't need full time staff."

"And being single my dear Flo, they wouldn't hardly be privy to any secrets unless you have a propensity of talking to yourself."

Frances smiled at her friend. Florence laughed out loud.

"Yes, you're quite right."

"But you do make an excellent point. I often wonder what things Alfred and Ginny, my housekeeper, might have overheard that I'd rather they hadn't."

"I'm sure you and Eric are quite discreet."

Frances nodded.

"Yes, but one can't remain ever vigilant. Though I do usually take my calls privately and both Alfred and Ginny have the highest discretion."

Florence sipped her tea and looked down at it in her lap before she looked back up at Frances.

"What are you hoping to find out from Enoch anyway. He's a rough sort and I don't see how he's going to be happy talking with you."

"I know, that's the puzzle. I'm not sure what I want to find out from him. Perhaps I'll learn more about what he doesn't say than what he does. We'll see. Might end up a pointless trip. But we can always go shopping after and have tea in Blackpool before we head back home."

"I'm intrigued. How can you gather information from what isn't shared?"

"It's hard to explain, Flo, but if you keenly observe human behavior, if you watch how people move and adjust themselves when speaking you can often determine the truth from the lies and the misdirections. It's not exact, but sometimes it shows me a way."

Florence nodded.

"I see, you'll have to tell me more after we've had our visit with Enoch."

"Gladly. But back to your point about staff, I'm eager to talk with James and Agnus and see what sort of light they might be able to place over this murkiness."

"Who do you think did it?"

Frances gazed at her teacup watching the tan face swirl ever so slightly, inhaling the sweet floral bouquet.

"Can't quite say yet with any certainty, there's still a good case of suspects. Do you have any thought on the matter?"

Frances looked up at Florence who put her left hand to her chest as her right held the saucer and teacup.

"Me...good heavens Frances, I wouldn't suggest that I know who did it."

"I know, but you must have a feeling, and that's important, our instincts are often helpful in these things."

"Well, I don't know really, but if pushed I'd have to say I think Jack might have done it. There aren't many other suspects really."

"Who are the suspects?"

"Let's see, Jack admits he was home, so he's one, and the one I think might have done it. Meredith too, she also admits to being around the house when Ginnie was in the garden. And that's it, other than Enoch."

"What about Garrett?" asked Frances.

"Well, he was out wasn't he, at the pub?"

"Yes, but not all the time. Additionally, we don't know what time Ginnie was killed. She left for the greenhouse at about two, so we've heard, and Jack was informed she was dead by Enoch at about three thirty. Garrett only left, if he did indeed leave, we haven't confirmed that yet, at about two thirty. So there's a window of half an hour in which he could have killed his mother."

"Good Lord, you're right Fran. But I never would have suspected him of murdering his own mother."

Florence's forehead was furrowed in confusion.

"I'm not saying he did it. I'm only offering up the suspects. It's important not to let anyone off the hook until you can prove they didn't do it. And most of the time that is done through alibis. But there are other suspects too other than Jack, Meredith, Garrett and Enoch."

"Who else could there be?"

"James and Agnus, the butler and housekeeper. It's easy to overlook them, we oftentimes forget that our staff is there."

Florence nodded her head.

"I hadn't thought about them. You're right, we easily overlook them, don't we. But what sort of motive could they have?"

"I don't know, but that is something we need to find out."

Eleven

Florence and Frances stepped out of Central Station in Blackpool. It was busy. Over one hundred thousand souls called Blackpool home and that was without the influx of the millions of visitors from around the world, but mostly from the rest of Britain, who came for the leisure and beaches. The tourist season was not quite under way, May would see the start of the leisure seekers start to trickle in.

It was still cool in Blackpool and overcast, though it was not raining. Frances was wearing a red scarf over her neck and a red woolen jacket over her sweater. She buttoned up the top button of the jacket and shivered.

"The sea air is brisk isn't it?" she said.

Florence nodded.

"More brisk than I was hoping for."

Florence looked around for a taxi and found one sitting on the corner of the road. She went up to the driver's door and the driver rolled down the window.

"Where to?" he asked.

"The police station."

"You two in trouble again," he said chuckling to himself. "Get in."

The only items that Florence and Frances had with them were their handbags. This was only going to be an afternoon visit. As they drove along the promenade towards the police station, Frances noticed the looming Blackpool Tower, a mini Eiffel Tower, in the middle of town.

The green and yellow trams were active along the promenade too, but their double decks were not as full as they would be during the summer when they'd be bursting from the seams, full to overflowing with visitors. These trams did, after all, offer some of the grandest views along between the North and South Piers. The White Tower Casino, already quite a bit behind them was yawning no doubt, waiting for the tourists and their spendthrift ways.

Looking out the window and over at the beach, Frances was surprised by how many people she could see strolling along on what was such a dreary day. There weren't a lot, but more than one would have expected on a day such as this one.

They passed the War Memorial and Frances thought back to the Great War. There was nothing that she could think of that made it great other than the great number of dead and injured on both sides. Some had suggested that almost forty million were dead or injured by the war, which included both sides.

Her head and eyes followed the memorial as they passed by it and she wondered about the names placed there, the men and their families who still carried the gaps and emptiness of their loss. She wondered if another war would carve more names onto this memorial and the others like it found all over England and elsewhere. She sighed and looked ahead. The future was all the hope they had. The past was done, but could they learn from it?

A few minutes later and a few turns and the taxi pulled up to a stop at the Blackpool Police Station. Frances paid for the fare and they stepped out and walked into the brick building where a constable was as the front desk doing paperwork. He looked up at them.

"Can I help you, ladies?"

"Yes, thank you, we're here to see Inspector Gibbard," said Frances.

The constable looked at her for a moment and then picked up the telephone.

"Inspector Gibbard," he said to the switchboard operator.

They all waited for a moment until the constable was put through.

"Yes, sir, you have a couple of visitors...Right..."

The constable covered the voice receiver with his hand and looked up at Frances.

"Your names please?"

"Tell him it is Lady Marmalade and Ms. Hudnall."

"Lady Marmalade and Ms. Hudnall," he said into the telephone.

"Okay...yes, sir...Good bye."

The constable replaced the telephone and looked back up at Frances and Florence.

"If you'll please have a seat, my Lady, he'll be right out."

Frances and Florence sat on the hard bench off to the side. Being right out turned out to be extremely optimistic. They waited over five minutes until Hank Gibbard graced them with his presence.

"Nice of you to come," he said, though Frances had the impression he was being rather sarcastic. "Follow me."

They got up and followed Gibbard down the hall. He turned back to look at them just as they got to the cells.

"I think you're wasting your time. He hasn't said a word to us, and I doubt he'll be in the mood to speak to you two."

"We'll give it our best go," said Frances smiling at the ruddy inspector.

Gibbard nodded at the constable and he opened up the heavy metal door.

"I have him in one of our interview rooms," said Gibbard, walking down the end of the hall with Frances and Florence in tow.

On the left, Gibbard opened up a white painted metal door with a small square window in it. They entered in after him.

Enoch Habbit was sitting on a wooden chair, his hands and feet cuffed together. He was wearing prison overalls. There was a wooden desk in front of him that was bolted to the floor. Two chairs were placed on the opposite side of where Enoch sat.

"You ladies can sit here if you like," said Gibbard.

Frances and Florence sat down and put their handbags to the side of their chairs. Enoch looked at them through his heavy eyes.

"I 'member you two," he said.

Frances smiled and nodded.

"Yes, we were there when Inspector Gibbard arrested you."

Enoch looked over at the inspector who stood off to one side. In the room behind Enoch was a constable standing stiff as a board.

"You remind me of ma' aunt," said Enoch.

Frances smiled.

"I'm gettin' out of 'ere in a bit," he said. "Why'd you come 'ere anyway?"

Frances and Florence had their hands in their laps, they stood straight and a little nervous. Frances smiled at him thinly.

"I was hoping you might be able to help me find out who murdered Ginnie, Mrs. Forsyth."

"Wasn't me. I neve' done hurt a woman," he said.

Frances nodded.

"I know."

"Anyway I don' know who killed that nice lady."

"Do you know who might have wanted to hurt her?"

Enoch shook his head and looked at his hands in his lap before looking back up at Lady Marmalade.

"Look, you seem like a nice lady, but I ain't got nothin' to say with the copp'rs 'ere."

Enoch looked at Gibbard.

"Too bad," said Gibbard.

Frances turned to look at Gibbard.

"Inspector, would you please give us a moment to speak with Enoch alone."

Inspector Gibbard shook his head.

"I'm afraid I can't do that. He's a very dangerous man."

"Inspector," said Frances, "in fifteen minutes you have to let him go, we could wait until then but I'd rather seize the moment now. Surely you don't believe that Mr. Habbit is going to do anything to jeopardize his freedom?"

Frances and Gibbard locked eyes for a moment.

"Very well. I'll give you ten minutes and that's all."

Gibbard nodded to the constable.

"You keep an eye on things through the window. If Habbit even so much as twitches I want you in here and this interview is over."

The constable nodded his head.

"I understand sir."

"Don't try anything funny, Enoch," said Gibbard, looking at him harshly with squinted eyes. Enoch nodded slowly, and then Gibbard and the constable left. Frances turned to look at Enoch.

"I've heard that you don't often work within the law."

Enoch looked at her and smiled. He had a warm smile, but it was marred by his rotting and missing teeth.

"I ain't had a charmed life as some of you folks might say."

"I am certain of that, Mr. Habbit," said Frances.

"You can call me Enoch."

"Thank you, Enoch. Now I don't believe you murdered poor Ms. Forsyth. You might not be a good man, but I don't believe you're evil either."

Enoch stared at the table in front of him.

"A man is made how he is by circumstance ma'am."

"Please call me Frances, Enoch."

He looked at her and nodded.

"There's been things in ma' life made me bitt'r and angry. Things'll make you cry."

Frances looked at him as he stared at the table.

"A boy turns into a man an' a man has ta carry that baggage with 'im. Only now he's gott'n bigg'r and sometimes he gets tired of carry'ng that baggage."

He looked up at Frances then and Frances tried to smile at him. It was a hard smile, a difficult smile that felt awkward on her. Like someone had placed the wrong mouth on her face. But she understood in a way how he was. But she wasn't sure he was redeemable. A part of her liked to hope so, but a part of her had seen such men redeem themselves so rarely that you might as well pray for rain in the Sahara.

"I ain't done hurt nobody didn' deserve it. An' I ain't never hurt no woman."

He looked at her searchingly with his heavy eyes. Frances nodded.

"A man, even a bad man gots to have a code to live by, an' I gots a code, Frances, I try even as you don't believe it, I try to live by a code."

"I do believe it. I also believe that bad men can find their way to goodness again."

He looked at her earnestly for a moment before breaking her gaze.

"Do you think I killed Ms. Forsyth?"

"No, I don't, Enoch. But what I don't understand is why you're the Forsyth's groundskeeper. Your hands are rugged, scuffed and hardened but they aren't the hands of a groundskeeper."

Enoch brought his hands up and placed them on the table and looked at them for a long time. The fingers were intertwined like the roots of a tree planted in hard ground.

"I been doing a lot mo' gardenin' than I done in a long time with the Forsyths."

"Yes, but you're not a gardener are you?"

Enoch slowly shook his head.

"I like you, Frances, you 'mind me of ma aunt. But what you an' your kind don't un'erstand is that there's some bad people in high soci'ty. You look at me an' see a bad man, 'cause I got a mean face, I got scars and rough hands. But a gentl'min in a fine suit he could be rott'n to the core an' you can't see it. You won't see it."

"Are you talking about Mr. Forsyth."

"He's jus' one example."

"But he's the one I want to talk about. Why is he a bad man?"

Enoch unclasped his hands and lay them palm down on the table, all the fingers pointing to Frances.

"Ms. Forsyth deserv'd better n' that. He's a man who's going ta lose ever'thing to opium, women and gamblin'."

"I've heard you work for Mr. Lee Chan, is that correct?" asked Florence, who up until this time had been quiet as a mouse, but now found her courage and her voice. Enoch looked over at her.

"Mr. Chan is a businessman, an' like any businessman he expects to be paid his due."

"Enoch, I wish you'd speak more plainly with us. The police aren't here and they can't hear what's going on."

Enoch looked up at Frances and smiled. This made his eyes even smaller and the realization that he needed a dentist even more apparent.

"Mr. Forsyth owes Mr. Chan a lot of money. An' he's a addict an a wom'nizer an a gambl'r. I'm at Mr. Forsyth's 'cause he's tryin' to repay his debts. But it ain't going ta work out fo' him. He's a weak man an' a spen'thrift. His justice is comin' due."

"Are you saying that Mr. Forsyth is going to be killed?" asked Frances.

Enoch shook his head.

"No ma'am, Frances, I ain't sayin' that. A dead man pays no debts. But Mr. Forsyth 'as made more people angry an' upset than me and Mr. Chan."

"What do you mean?"

"I means ta say, that all the Forsyths is in a bad way. Mr. Jack 'as been ruin'ng the business, Mr. Gerald knows about it and Mr. Garrett has a temp'r you probably ain't seen the likes of."

"Are you saying you think they could've killed Mrs. Forsyth?" asked Florence.

"I ain't sayin' that. I ain't no d'tective but I reck'n that whoever kill'd Ms. Forsyth was part of that family. If I'd be guess'n I'd say it was Mr. Jack."

"Why?" asked Frances.

"'Cos Mr. Jack is a weak man. He's got no control over his probl'ms and he's going b'hind Ms. Forsyth's back with that Meredith, only they's in Ms. Forsyth's face 'bout it. An' she's not the only one Mr. Jack's with."

Frances looked down at Enoch's hands for a while. She was staring and thinking. Despite his lack of education, Mr. Habbit seemed to have a good grasp on human nature, perhaps having learned about it from the school of hard knocks.

"Thank you, Enoch," said Frances, "I don't think I have any more questions."

He nodded and looked at Frances as she and Florence got up.

"I lik'd Ms. Forsyth. She been good ta me. She deserv'd better 'n this."

Frances nodded.

"She did."

"She deserves justice, Frances, an' I hope you can get it for her."

"I'll try."

And Frances and Florence walked towards the door having picked up their handbags. They exited and the constable went back into the room behind them. They walked out the way they came. Inspector Gibbard was at the front entrance of the police station.

"Did you get anything out of him?" he asked.

"Well, he has his opinions as everyone else does, but nothing worth noting."

"But he did say..." said Florence.

Frances looked at her and put her hand on Florence's forearm.

"He did say," said Frances interjecting, "that he hopes we find out who the real killer is."

"So he's still protesting his innocence," said Gibbard.

"Well I think he's innocent of this too."

"What are you going to do now?"

"I'm going to speak with the Forsyth staff tomorrow."

"I guess it's your time to waste as you wish," said Gibbard.

"And how are you going to use your time," said Frances, ignoring his barbs.

"I will continue to dig for stronger evidence on Habbit. I'm certain he's the one who did it."

Frances smiled at him sweetly.

"Well, I suppose you can waste your time however you wish Inspector. Good day."

And then she and Florence walked out of the police station and hailed the first taxi to take them to Winter Gardens for some tea and lunch.

Twelve

The four p.m. train from Blackpool to Puddle's End was busier than Frances was expecting. Nevertheless, the two of them shared a first class compartment to themselves and they sat in it the whole way back home. Shopping at Blackpool had not turned out to be as successful as they had hoped. Neither Florence nor Frances were carrying any shopping bags. But the tea and lunch had been wonderful.

"Why didn't you want the inspector to know what Enoch had told us about his feelings regarding Jack?" asked Florence.

"Well, I don't have the most faith in the inspector, Flo, and I don't think it would have been helpful. It seems to me that Inspector Gibbard is set on charging Enoch and I doubt he'll be dissuaded otherwise. I'd rather not have Jack aware that he's a suspect in his own wife's murder."

"So you think Enoch might be onto something?"

"I do, but not necessarily about Jack. Jack may well have killed his wife but I'd rather not have word make it back to him about what Enoch thinks. And I'd rather not take the chance and have Gibbard send a constable down to make cursory inquiries that alert Jack to the fact that his misgivings are coming to the attention of the police."

"I see."

"Let me see if I can't explain better, Flo. If you let sleeping dogs lie, you can better inspect their lice."

Florence nodded and looked out the window as the green English countryside smeared by like wet paint. It was raining outside, or more accurately it was drizzling but there was very little mist. The day, although gray and dreary, was clear. Much as Lady Marmalade's mind was starting to clear from the fog. Though she was by no means certain as to who might have murdered poor old Ginnie, though she was beginning to whittle down her suspects.

"So you want to go to the Wet Whistle again when we get back to Puddle's End?"

"I do, I want to ask Finley if he saw Garrett at anytime during the afternoon yesterday."

"Oh yes, that's right, he said he had gone down to the pub for a drink."

"With all the information Finley shared with us yesterday, I forgot to ask him about Garrett," said Frances.

"I know, me too."

"This way we'll be certain of his alibi, I'm sure someone must have seen him at the Wet Whistle if he was in fact there."

Frances smiled out the window.

"Finley's good at that sort of thing. He can rattle off the names of just about everyone who's been at his pub over the last couple of days. Do you think Garrett might have been lying?"

"Not necessarily, Flo, but if Garrett was at the Wet Whistle he wasn't drinking anything other than tonic water."

"What do you mean?"

"Well, I didn't smell any alcohol on his breath when we were asking him those few questions yesterday. Did you not notice it?"

Florence pursed her lips together and brought her finger to her mouth. She looked out the window before turning back to look at Frances.

"You know, I can't say I noticed, Fran. Maybe he's a teetotaler?"

"Then he's an off again, on again teetotaler. He was drinking with the rest of us at the table on Monday night."

Florence laughed.

"You don't miss a thing do you, Fran? I can't say I had really paid attention to any of that, except for what I was drinking."

"No, I don't miss a lot. You can't afford to if you're trying to help solve a crime, especially a murder. I find the more I've been doing it, the more careful I am at observing things. It can get quite tiresome to be honest, Flo."

"I can imagine.

They sat in silence for a while, each to her own thoughts. Florence wondering who would have killed Ginnie and what kind of a brute was such a person. She liked the idea of Jack for it, even more now that Enoch had suggested the same. Florence looked over at Frances.

"What do you really think about Jack?" she asked.

"What do you mean?" asked Frances.

"As the murderer."

"You like him for it, don't you?"

Florence nodded.

"Enoch thinks he's good for it. And he's the one that keeps coming to my mind when I think about who could have killed her."

"Well, let's take a moment to talk about why. Why do you think he would have killed his wife?"

Florence shrugged and looked out the window.

"I don't know, maybe he'd had enough of her and wanted a fresh start with Meredith and he didn't want to worry about Ginnie and the pain of going through a divorce."

"That sounds reasonable. That's a decent motive, and men have killed their wives for reasons such as you suggest. But there could be more too. Perhaps he had taken out insurance on his wife and needed the money to pay off his debts."

"But we don't know that."

"No we don't, but it's worth finding out if we're going to be thorough. Maybe Ginnie had found out about his debts and his business problems. It seems that he's running the business into the ground. She might be haranguing him about it. He could have had enough of the pestering and killed her just to shut her up."

Florence nodded.

"I suppose there are a variety of reasons why he might have done it, if he did indeed do it."

Frances nodded.

"And they're all good motives. Not condoning any of this obviously, but you'd be surprised, sadly, what reasons some people find to be enough to kill one another."

"That depresses me just to think about it."

"As it should. Man's inhumanity to man seems to find no bounds. Look at the atrocities committed by both sides during the Great War."

Florence nodded sadly. Thinking back to those awful times, she was glad for not having married and not having had any children.

"But what bothers me about the motive you offered for why Jack could have killed Ginnie, namely, that he wanted a fresh start. Well, I think back to what Enoch said and how Jack appears to be quite the philanderer. And if that is the case, would he really want to settle down with anyone again. I'm not convinced he would."

"You make a good point, Fran. But it could be a reason, could it not? That he used it as an excuse. You never know, perhaps

Meredith is the woman to turn Jack around into an honest upstanding citizen."

Florence chuckled at her own thoughts. Though stranger things had happened.

"Not out of the question, Flo. Some women keep hoping they'll change the men they're with, and some men do change. Perhaps he was about to straighten out and fly right. Though we won't know for sure until we interview them alone."

"Are you going to do that?"

"Yes," said Frances, "not before I've spoken with James and Agnus though. I could really use a little bit of clarity on this case. At least I want to try and find a clearer path through this. I think there's more to it than meets the eye."

The train started slowing as it pulled into the station, the wheels started squeaking a little more regularly and the engine groaned and moaned.

"I'd like to know what James and Agnus were up to too. Everyone has to provide an alibi if we're to eliminate them as suspects."

"And Meredith too, she was at the house the whole time apparently," said Florence.

"Quite right, Meredith too. How many suspects do you think we have so far?"

"Five," said Florence, "Meredith, Jack, Garrett, James the butler, and Agnus the housekeeper."

"Don't forget Enoch," said Lady Marmalade.

"I thought you said you didn't think he did it?"

"I did, but one mustn't turn one's feelings into blinders. We have no strong evidence to the contrary that he didn't do it. You heard of his whereabouts. He was off eating lunch alone. So until we have strong evidence that someone else murdered Ginnie, I'm afraid, my dear Flo, that we have six candidates vying for our attention."

Florence laughed.

"I suppose that's one way to look at it."

The train came to a stop and the conductor announced the station. Frances and Florence got off the train, taking with them their handbags which is all they had taken with them to Blackpool, and all they had brought back. Florence's car had been parked at Puddle's End station when they first arrived, and like a good steed it waited for them as they returned.

It was just after five thirty when they climbed into the car and Florence drove them off to the Wet Whistle. Almost a repeat of the evening before to the hour. And like the previous evening, the Wet Whistle was only about a third full at this time. Though Frances noticed that there was a dart tournament happening at eight.

"I think we came at a good time, Flo, there'll be throwers tonight at eight. Did you see the sign?"

"Do you want to stay and watch?"

"Not particularly, not unless you do."

"I'm not bothered one way or the other," said Florence. "Do you not like the game."

"Oh, I like it well enough, but not so much as a spectator. I've watched Eric a few times throw darts with some of his friends, but it's much more fun when you're throwing them yourself."

"So you've played then?"

"Just a couple of times. It's not normally seen as a lady-like thing to do."

"To hell with that, maybe I'll enter the tournament myself and give these chaps what for."

Frances laughed and tapped Florence's forearm.

"You know, Flo, I think I'd actually pay to see that."

"Me too."

The two of them walked up to the bar where Finley was holding himself up, leaning on the ledge behind the bar. He might not have changed and if he had, he was wearing identical clothes to those he had on the night before. Even his sleeves seemed to be rolled up just like they were, just below the elbow. He grinned at them as they came in.

"My two favorite customers," he said, with a twinkle in his eye.

"Hi Finley," said Florence.

"Are you here for chow or conversation?" he asked.

"Very American of you," said Frances.

"Well, we've had our share of American sailors over the years, especially during the Great War. I picked up a few extra words from them."

He grinned and went to wiping the bar in front of them. It didn't need cleaning but it was a gentlemanly gesture nevertheless.

"I think Frances and I will share an order of both," said Florence, looking at Frances who nodded in agreement.

"What do you recommend for tonight?" asked Frances.

Finley finished up wiping the counter and put the cloth down on the ledge that was behind the bar. He grabbed the dish towel over his shoulder and wiped his hands with it.

"Tonight we're featuring fish and chips. The freshest cod and the best chips you've tasted north of the Channel."

"Those are big boots to fill."

Finley smiled at Florence.

"You'll see, I stand behind my wife's cooking."

"Good enough for me then too," said Florence.

"And if you're feeling particularly thirsty, as I know you might be having just come back from Blackpool, I'd suggest quenching your thirst with a pint of Smithwick's. Goes very well with the fish and chips."

"Sounds exactly like what I need," said Florence.

"Me too," said Frances.

"Okay, just give me a few minutes and I'll bring out your food and drinks and we can have a course of that conversation you ordered too."

He winked at Florence. Frances and Florence went over to the booth they had sat in the night before. It now felt like their booth. Looking around, Florence saw a group of ladies, four of them, in the booth across from her, where the father and son had been previously. A couple of officers, in their navy blue dress uniforms, were sitting at another table and a middle-aged couple seemed to be enjoying each other's company at yet another table closer to the sailors.

"Oh God, Fran," said Florence as she sat down in the cushioned seat opposite Frances, "I think I might stay here all night."

"It has been a busy day hasn't it?"

Florence blew air out of her mouth across her face, it was a big sigh.

"You've got me running all over hill and dale," she said smiling, "I can't remember the last time I've been out and about as much as I have today. Not that I'm complaining though."

"Good, because we aren't quite done yet. It'll be a couple more days I daresay when things are wrapped, if they are wrapped up."

"That doesn't sound like the Frances I know. Are you doubting your abilities?"

"No, that's not what I mean. I meant if this case is wrapped up as quickly as that. Who knows? Might take longer. By the way, remind me to ring up Inspector Gibbard before we leave."

"Might be too late, why don't we wait until we get home in the coziness of my home. Why do you need to speak to him anyway?"

Frances looked at her watch, it was coming on five to six.

"You're right, it might be too late. I wanted to ask him if the coroner had determined time of death for Ginnie."

"I think, Fran, that you should phone the coroner directly, you might have better luck with him than with the inspector. He hasn't warmed to you yet."

"At least with the inspector we've made each other's acquaintance, I haven't yet met the coroner."

"True, but perhaps your reputation precedes you? You never know Fran, he might hold you in higher esteem than you realize."

Frances laughed heartily.

"Oh, Flo, you're too much. I'm just a meddling little old lady, I doubt the coroner of Blackpool has heard of me at all. The only reason I get away with as much as I do with Scotland Yard is because Eric pulled some strings and spoke to the Commissioner. And I suppose I'll admit that Inspector Pearce and I have warmed to each other over the years."

"I think you're being too modest. I'll prove it."

With that, Finley came by bringing a big pile of chips and a large piece of battered and fried cod on each plate. He carried them along with two pints of creamy Smithwick's on a large tray. He placed them down in front of each of them.

"Do enjoy, and if you don't I'll have a stern word with the missus."

He chuckled.

"I'll let you eat and then I'll be back for our visit."

"Before you do," said Florence, "can you settle a question for me quickly."

"Certainly," he said, clasping the tray behind his back.

"Frances doesn't believe that her reputation precedes her. So I wanted to ask you, did you know about Lady Marmalade the detective before I ever mentioned her to you?"

Finley looked at Frances and smiled.

"I most certainly did. You're quite the celebrity it seems, at least in these parts, what with your solving of the vicar's murder in Ambleside and others you've solved in London. I think that's why Inspector Gibbard might not be as warm to you as he would otherwise be. I think he feels threatened."

"See what I mean?" said Florence.

Lady Marmalade smiled.

"You're too kind," she said, and if you looked closely you might see she was blushing.

Finley touched her on the forearm.

"But it doesn't hurt that Florence sings your praises from the rooftops."

He grinned at her.

"Would you like anything else with your fish and chips?"

Frances looked at the table and not seeing what she needed, she asked for it.

"Some vinegar would be nice, please."

"Right away," and with that he left and was back in a matter of moments.

"I told you," said Florence.

"Yes, you did, Flo, you're a very dear friend. But that doesn't mean that the coroner has heard of me."

Florence took a bite of her fish and chewed before answering.

"I still think it's worth a chance."

"Agreed."

Lady Marmalade dashed salt all over her fish and chips. Then she did the same with the pepper and lastly she emptied most of the bottle of vinegar onto her chips. At least that was the impression she gave. She took the lemon wedge and squeezed it against her fork and dribbled the juice all over her fish. She took her first bite.

"You know, Flo, I have to say, this public house of Finley's has some of the best cooking I've tasted in the country."

"It is good isn't it. And he didn't lie about the fish and chips, did he?"

"He certainly didn't."

"You should tell him that."

"Tell him what?" asked Frances, biting a thick chip in half.

"How good his wife's cooking is."

"I will."

They sat in silence then for several minutes. Florence was the first to finish, leaving several chips on her plate. Frances was a close second though she left half her chips behind.

"That was a lot of good food," she said, dabbing at her mouth with her napkin. "Too much for me to eat though."

Florence laughed.

"I know, I think they gave us the men's portion."

Finley came by and took their emptyish plates away. Then he came back quickly and tucked himself into the booth on Florence's side.

"Please give your wife my compliments," said Frances. "As I was telling Flo, your wife cooks some of the best food I've tasted in the country."

Finley looked at Lady Marmalade for a moment and smiled.

"Really?" he asked.

"Truly."

"Well, I will certainly let her know, and I'm delighted you think so. Thank you."

"Thank you, for two nights in a row now, you've treated us to wonderful suppers. I fear I may already have put on five pounds in my short stay in Puddle's End so far."

Finley chuckled, looking at her.

"Well, if you don't mind me saying, you have room for it on you slim frame. Well, what was it you wanted to chat about?"

"We wanted to ask you about Garrett," said Florence.

"Yes, terrible temper that one, I heard his last girlfriend left him because of it."

"Was he violent?" asked Florence.

Finley nodded.

"I'm afraid so, I heard he slapped her a few times over the months they were together."

"Like father like son, I suppose," said Florence.

Finley shook his head and looked at her.

"No, that's one thing I can say about Jack. I've never seen or heard mention of him hitting anyone, let alone his wife. Can't say where Garrett picked up that atrocious behavior."

"Did he ever hit his mother do you know?" asked Frances.

"No, I don't think so. Something like that would have made its way here. From what I have heard, he dearly loved her."

"Sometimes that's a reason to murder," said Frances.

"Really?" asked Finley.

"Yes, inasmuch as murder is so often a crime of passion that the victim is usually known to the murderer, and oftentimes intimately."

"We'll, I'll be, I'm going to have to keep an eye on the missus," said Finley.

"Well, she does have the knives in the kitchen, doesn't she," said Florence.

Finley chuckled.

"Yes, well, I suppose that's why I'm so well-behaved."

"I was wondering, Finley, if Garrett was here yesterday?" asked Frances.

"Yes, he was, after you left."

"Not before?"

"No, why?"

"Well, he said he was, at least during the times when his mother was in the greenhouse. Between two thirty and about four thirty."

Finley shook his head and furrowed his brow.

"No, certainly not at that time. He was only here after nine until about midnight. Drowning his sorrows, he seemed very upset."

"About his mother's death no doubt?"

"No, apparently not. Well, I should say not only about his mother's death. I overheard him mumbling to himself something about his sister."

"Did you hear anything specific about his sister?" asked Frances.

"No, other than he kept talking about his 'bloody sister' something about ruining everything."

Florence looked at Frances.

"He doesn't have a sister that I'm aware of, does he?" she asked looking back at Finley.

Finley shrugged.

"I didn't think so. But James was here with a couple of the other butlers from around Puddle's End and he said something about the poor lad finally finding out about his sister. I didn't hear anything else about it. Perhaps it was a secret they'd kept from him all these years."

"Interesting," said Frances, "so if he wasn't here, where could he have been?"

"Not too far," said Finley, "at least if you say he left around two thirty and was back by four thirty."

"That's the time the witnesses said he left and we saw him back in the house at around then, didn't we Flo?"

Florence nodded.

"I remember hearing the grandfather clock chime once before he arrived, so yes, it must have been shortly after four thirty."

"Well, in his Alfa Romeo he might have been able to get as far as Liverpool and back in a couple of hours. Blackpool or

Lancaster and back in the north and Manchester to the south east. Not many other bigger towns he might have gotten to in that time."

Finley looked up towards the ceiling.

"Though I suppose he might have made it to Halifax and back in that time if he were in a rush."

Florence looked at Frances and raised her eyebrows.

"I suppose we have to decide who or what might be out there in those cities that Garrett wanted to visit. And why would he lie to us and more importantly the police about it?" said Frances.

"The plot, it thickens," said Florence.

Frances smiled.

"There was something else I wanted to mention to you now that you're here."

Frances and Florence both looked at Finley eagerly.

"What is it?" asked Florence.

"Doctor Garnet was here last night too."

"Luther Garnet?" asked Florence.

Finley nodded.

"We met him on Monday night," said Florence looking at Frances. Frances nodded.

"Well, he was here with a colleague, I presume, part of their conversation I overheard was about building up a practice together. Anyway, Luther was adamant he couldn't at the moment because his money was tied up with Jack's business. Luther as you might now is Ginnie's brother."

Frances nodded.

"I think that might have been mentioned on Monday night."

"It appears he lent Jack a substantial amount of money to keep his business afloat and it sounds like this was several months away. He sounded upset and assured his colleague that he was going to get his money back one way or another, 'come hell or high water' was the term he used."

"Do you know how much was lent?" asked Frances.

"No, but it seemed substantial. He was upset and he seemed to suggest that Jack had been using the money for other purposes and not for the business as it was lent. Luther has a temper too, you know what they say about redheads."

Finley smiled.

"It seems I'm not really helping, am I? If anything, this might be making things that much more complicated."

Florence nodded, smiling.

"I'll say."

"At the moment, certainly. This whole Forsyth scene is like peeling an onion, there's layer upon layer of deceit and misdealings it seems," said Frances.

The pub was getting busier. It was coming up on seven and the crowds for the dart tournament were filling up the back of the pub where the darts were. But the front, where Frances and

Florence were sitting was getting busier too. And with the busyness came an increase in the ambient noise. And Lady Marmalade preferred quieter environments, not that she had the luxury of enjoying them as often as she'd like.

Finley looked around. This was the second night in a row that he had left his wife to hold down the fort so to speak. She was getting exasperated at the bar, and she had to take care of the cooking too. She had help in the kitchen, and that's where she preferred to be.

"Is there anything else I can help you ladies with?" he asked. "It's almost seven and I should start preparing for the tournament."

Frances nodded.

"I think that's all. Thank you so much, Finley, we won't keep you, and I hope I don't have to pepper you with any more questions."

Finley smiled and climbed out of the booth.

"Not at all, I'm always your ever humble servant. Please do return if only to say goodbye when you leave. I'd love to introduce you to my wife."

"I will," said Frances.

"Cheerio," said Florence.

And with that, Finley walked back to the bar and Frances watched as his wife smiled in relief.

"Well, should we go?" asked Florence.

Lady Marmalade nodded and they got out of their booth and walked out of the pub into the darkening night.

Thirteen

Frances plopped herself onto the couch and Florence sat down in her armchair.

"Would you like a pot of tea, Fran. Everything's better with tea," said Florence.

"I think a cup would be just perfect."

"You know what else I was thinking? You should ring up the coroner."

"I don't know, Flo, it's half past seven, I'm sure he wouldn't still be at work at his late hour."

"Oh, go on, give it a try. I'm just dying to find out and I can't wait another night to learn what we can from the coroner. If he's not there, then so be it. But perhaps he's a busy man and works late sometimes. Please do call. I'll fix the tea while you speak with him."

"If he's there," said Frances.

"Yes, if he's there."

"Very well, for my dearest friend, but I doubt he'll be there. Mark my words."

"They're marked," said Florence, grinning.

Frances picked up the telephone and asked for the Blackpool coroner's office. The phone seemed to ring for an eternity. Frances was just about to put it down when a man answered it.

"Hello?"

"Oh, hello, sorry to bother, I was hoping to find the coroner," said Frances.

"And who is this?"

"Never mind, I'll ring back tomorrow."

"Who is it?" The voice was more testy this time. "You've reached the coroner."

"Oh dear, I am so sorry to be catching you this late, Dr. Blackstone. This is Frances Marmalade, I'm trying to help out with the Forsyth investigation."

"The Frances Marmalade, Lady Marmalade?"

The voice had thawed now and warmth like honey came from the coroner's voice.

"Yes, this is Lady Frances Marmalade."

"Good heavens," said Dr. Blackstone, "why didn't you say so, my Lady. I was just finishing up and about to head out when the phone wouldn't stop ringing."

"I do apologize for calling so late, doctor."

"Nonsense, it's my pleasure to speak with you Lady Marmalade."

"Please call me Frances, doctor."

"If you'll call me Levi."

Frances chuckled on the other end of the phone.

"Very well."

"So how are things going with the investigation? I didn't know the Forsyths, but I'm always saddened by the apparent senseless death of a young woman."

"It's turning out to be more of a puzzle than I had imagined, Levi. More suspects than I can count and I don't believe I have all of the information related to her murder yet either."

"So you don't think Inspector Gibbard found his culprit in Enoch Habbit then?"

"No, I don't believe so, Levi. Whatever else Enoch Habbit might be, I don't believe he's the murderer of Ginnie."

"I'm glad you said that, because I agree, and the evidence suggests he didn't do it."

"Can you explain?"

"Ginnie died from strangulation. Now the blow to her head was quite a bit more severe than it looked like at first glance. I believe that she might have died from those injuries alone if she hadn't received medical attention. In any event, that's a moot point because she was strangled."

"So why do you believe that she wasn't strangled by Enoch?"

"Because the strangulation marks indicate she was strangled by hand, and the size of those hands were on the smaller size."

"So you're saying a woman might have done it?" asked Frances.

"Not necessarily. A woman might well have done it, or a man with small hands. I'm extrapolating from the bruising and it's not an exact science. It's not like a glove, it's a generalization. All I can say is that whoever strangled her had smaller hands than someone like Enoch. Smaller hands than your average man but a little larger than your average woman. So I'm afraid Frances, you're looking for a man with smaller than normal hands or a woman with slightly larger than normal hands. I'm sorry I can't be more helpful."

"Not at all, Levi, this does help, if only to eliminate Enoch as my suspicions suggested. All I have to try and understand now, is why. If I can determine why she was killed that might lead me to the who."

"And are you getting clearer about it?"

"Slowly I think I see the dawning light of day clearing out the fog of confusion. But it's too early to help."

"Well, I hope you can get to the bottom of it. Between you and I, I don't hold Inspector Gibbard in the highest esteem."

"I understand how you feel, Levi, though I'm sure he must be reasonably competent to have made inspector."

"If only I shared your enthusiasm."

Levi laughed heartedly on the other end.

"If I may, Levi, can I ask if you've determined the time she was murdered?"

"Unfortunately, that aspect is not yet an exact science either. I'm afraid I can't offer a narrower window than you already have. Just a moment."

Lady Marmalade heard some papers shuffling on the other end.

"I see from what the inspector told me, she was alone between two and three thirty. Is that what you understand?"

"Yes, that's my understanding."

"That would appear to be the time frame in which she was killed. In fact, I'd have said between two and four, but since she was found at three thirty I'll have to acquiesce to that. Sorry I can't be more specific."

"Not at all, Levi, I just wanted confirmation."

"Happy to be able to help in some small way, Frances."

"Well, Dr. Blackstone, thank you so much for taking my inquiries. I shan't keep you any longer."

"Not at all. I've heard a lot about you and my faith in finding justice for Mrs. Forsyth has been renewed. Please keep me informed, Lady Marmalade."

"I will."

And with that they said their goodbyes and Lady Marmalade hung up the phone and stood by it for a moment. Levi had been more helpful than he had realized. Frances could feel herself getting closer to uncovering the killer. If she could just find out the reason why, it should be all buttoned up within the next day or two.

"Everything all right, Fran?" asked Florence, coming into the living room and noticing Frances still as a statue standing by the phone. Frances looked around and saw her friend and then smiled absentmindedly.

"Yes, yes, everything's quite alright."

Frances came over to the couch and sat down. Florence placed the tray with the teapot, teacups, and accoutrements on the table between them.

"We should let it steep a few minutes more. Do tell what the coroner said," said Florence.

"You were right, my dear Flo, you were right about two things. The first is that apparently, in some quarters my reputation does precede me, and the second thing is that he was there and willing to take my call."

Florence smiled.

"Well, go on, what did he say?"

"He said something very interesting. He said that by itself the blow to her head could have caused her death in time, but that she was strangled and it was the strangling that killed her."

"So it could have been someone like Enoch with enough strength to do the job."

Frances shook her head.

"No, I don't think so. I believe any man or woman with a good swing could have caused enough damage with that small shovel and the evidence appears to bear me out."

"How so?"

"Well, the clincher, Flo, was that Dr. Blackstone said that whoever strangled Ginnie had small hands. A man with small hands or a woman with slightly larger hands."

Florence picked up the teapot and started pouring them each a cup of tea through the strainer. Each white teacup had a pink rose painted on its side.

"Well, I don't know if you noticed, but both Jack and Garrett have dainty hands, if you can say that about a man's hands."

Frances nodded as she squeezed a wedge of lemon into her tea from a plate of lemon wedges Florence had brought in on the tray.

"I thought you might prefer lemon tonight," said Florence.

"You know me too well. I did notice that about Jack's and Garrett's hands. Did you notice James' and Agnus' hands?"

Florence looked up from stirring her tea. It was creamy and there was sugar in it too. She smiled at Frances.

"No, I didn't notice their hands."

"Well, Agnus has large hands for a woman and although James' hands seem average for a man, I believe they're too big for having strangled Ginnie. Not that I'm certain, we still need to speak with him, and Agnus, but that's my suspicion."

"The evidence continues to mount in my favor, Fran, for Jack as the culprit."

Florence smiled, and there was a twinkle in her eye.

"It certainly does look that way, but I have to disagree."

Florence sipped her tea.

"Okay, Fran, enough already. Who do you think murdered Ginnie then. I need an answer, you can't keep me in the dark if you know something," said Florence grinning.

Frances picked up her teacup and held it in one hand, cradling the saucer in her other. She took a long, slow sip.

"Wonderful tea, Flo, thanks so much."

"Oh, Fran, you are simply incorrigible. You're welcome for the tea, but you won't get any more if you don't spill your beans."

Frances smiled at her friend.

"I'm just teasing with you."

Florence laughed.

"I know, but you must be fair, I've kept saying I think its Jack and you keep saying you don't think it's him. So then, who is it?"

"I haven't ruled out Jack with absolute certainty, but you're right, Flo, I don't think it's him. I'll give you a hint. Did you notice Meredith's hands?"

Florence shook her head.

"She has larger hands for a woman her size. I think, my dear Flo, that she did it."

"Good heavens, Fran, are you serious? I've never heard anything so chilling in all my days."

Florence put her teacup and saucer in her lap and looked at Frances with a mixture of bewilderment and shock.

"I am serious, Flo. I think she's the one, I just need to find out why?"

"But what caused you to believe that she might have done it?"

"That's a good question. I noticed a few things that started me towards thinking she might be the killer. When we first went to the greenhouse and saw Ginnie, one of the tools was missing. I knew it was a small tool and perhaps not up to the job of finishing Ginnie off with one blow."

"I see."

"And women, generally, in my experience, don't often murder with a lot of blood and violence. You see, if Jack and Garrett had done it, I think they might have kept using the shovel multiple times. You see, Flo, I think this is murder of passion. In other words, the killer got quite worked up about something."

"Go on."

"And yes, Jack's and Garrett's hands are small enough to have strangled her, but I don't think that is how they would have done it. So that left Meredith."

"What about Agnus or James?"

Florence had recovered her shock enough to take another sip of tea.

"As I mentioned previously, I think James' hands are too big and Agnus, well, I can't seem to fathom a reason for why she would have done it. I'm not ruling her out, we must speak to her and see if there is some reason for motive. In my opinion, I have seldom come across staff who have murdered their employer without very good reason. It happens, but they're not usually as emotionally invested in the relationship as people are when there emotional attachments."

"That sounds reasonable, but is there any evidence?"

"I hope to find motive in the greenhouse. I think there's something about the greenhouse that is important. I'm not sure what yet, but everyone agrees that Ginnie wasn't much of a gardener, so I think there's some other reason why she was in the greenhouse."

Frances looked at Florence and Florence raised her eyebrows and shook her head. She had no idea what might lie hidden in the greenhouse other than tomatoes and other plants both edible and aesthetic.

"Maybe she was starting to garden as a sort of therapy. You know, having to live with her philanderer of a husband."

Frances smiled wistfully.

"I don't think so, Flo. I can't put my finger on it, but there's something about that greenhouse that I think holds secrets."

Frances took a sip of tea, absentmindedly as she gazed past Florence, her thoughts wandering and revisiting the greenhouse. Then she shook her head and focused back on her friend.

"In any event, did you notice how well dressed Meredith was when she came back downstairs shortly after we arrived?"

"Yes, she mentioned that she was just finishing up getting ready when she saw the police arrive, from her bedroom overlooking the driveway I imagine."

"That's right. She smelled wonderful, she had put on her makeup and she was dressed for the rest of the afternoon. But there were two things out of place that I think gave her away."

"What's that?"

"Her nails. She had applied makeup and yet hadn't done her nails. Her nails were painted from the night before when we were all at dinner. They weren't chipped or cracked either."

"What was the other thing."

"There was a scuff on her one shoe that she hadn't managed to wipe off. Her shoes were clean, but I noticed as she crossed her leg that there was a scuff of dirt, same color as that in the greenhouse, that she had missed."

"I can't say I had noticed any of that," said Florence.

"I know, it's the small things, the little details that often give the murderer away."

"I'm impressed, Fran, you don't miss a thing. When are you going to tell Gibbard?"

"When I'm certain it was her. The one missing piece of this puzzle is motive. If I can find that, which I believe is hidden in the greenhouse, then I believe I have it solved. You see, Flo, I believe that when Meredith killed Ginnie, she must have gotten her fingers dirty while strangling her on the on the dirt floor of the greenhouse. That's why she likely scrubbed her fingers clean but forgot to paint them again. And her shoes would've gotten scuffed and perhaps she was too hasty cleaning them when she saw the police arrive and thus missed a spot that gave her away."

"Seems good enough to me, Fran."

Frances nodded her head and took the last sip of her tea.

"I'm happy with it, I'd just like to button it down tight with a motive."

"Well, Fran, I'm incredulous with your insights and attention to detail. I have no doubt you'll find the motive."

Frances smiled and nodded at her friend.

"You're really a big help, my dear Flo, with your insights and conversation."

Fourteen

It was a thin spoiled milky day as Frances and Florence sat in the living room enjoying their last cup of tea. It was thin because the sky had a diaphanous veil of clouds across its face. Perhaps still in mourning at the loss of Ginnie Forsyth. It was milky because the sun burned through, offering hope for a brighter day, but this milkiness was spoiled because the sun was losing the battle. The gray hung onto the sky's glower like the pallor of an old man stained from years of smoking.

Frances was looking forward to visiting the Forsyths again. She wanted some clarification on a few things. She wanted to explore the greenhouse in greater detail to see if she couldn't uncover its secrets held within. She also wanted to speak with James and Agnus not only about their whereabouts but about anything else they might be able to shed light on, and she'd like to speak to both Jack and Garrett.

Garrett about his lying ways and Jack about his philandering. Though that subject needed delicacy. She wanted to know how much Ginnie really knew, and whether Meredith was privy to that.

"I hope, Flo," said Frances, "that today I get some clarity on this awful murder. Maybe, if all goes well I can actually speak to Inspector Gibbard about closing this case."

She looked at Florence over the rim of her rose painted teacup as she took a sip. Florence took a last sip of hers and put the teacup and saucer back on the tray on the table between them.

"I'm sure you will. You know who killed Ginnie, all you need know is to figure out the motive and that should put the whole case to bed."

Frances nodded. The two of them were dressed, almost as twins in long gray dresses that fell well below the knee, their tops covered with thick gray cardigans. The only difference were the patterns. Florence was wearing an Aran style off white cardigan and Frances was wearing a cable knitted off white cardigan.

Frances hadn't brought with her a large assortment of clothes, and certainly nothing in black as she wasn't expecting to wear the colors or attend a funeral. Florence felt gray was appropriate and decided to join Frances in sympathy. Although, where Frances wore a plain navy silk scarf around her head, Florence was adorned with a gray snood.

Frances took the last sip of her tea and put her cup back down on the tray next to Florence's. She looked up at Florence.

"Well, that's that, I guess I'm ready to go."

"Do you think we should ring them up first?" asked Florence.

"I'd rather not. I'd rather surprise them. When people are surprised their defenses aren't up and you can often get a more honest response from them than you would otherwise. I hope you don't mind, Flo."

"Not at all, the person I cared about most in that family is dead and the more I learn about Jack and I suppose Garrett too, the less I like them."

"Shall we be off then?"

"Certainly, I just want to pop out into the garden and cut some flowers."

"That's very kind and a very good idea too."

Florence and Frances left the living room through the French doors and Florence went to the small shed up against the back of her house. She came out with a short length of twine and gardening shears.

Frances watched as Florence looked for her best daffodils and crocuses, snipping them at a good length and arranging the clump so that the blues and yellows were in an aesthetically pleasing and varied pattern. She tied them off, not too tight and handed them to Frances to hold onto.

She went back into the shed and put away the shears. When she came out, Frances handed the bouquet back to her and they reentered the house through the French doors and walked out again through the front. Frances had chosen to leave her handbag behind. As had Florence. It was to be a short visit and they were coming straight home after.

The two of them walked along the gray dirt road with the thickness of the gray veiled sky as their canopy, dressed in gray, their thoughts leaning to the maudlin as Frances contemplated how the first time they had come visiting the Forsyth it was for a fun supper.

The second time was supposed to be fun, bringing around the marmalade, but that visit had turned rather dour and here they were on their third trip. A trip made in mourning but she comforted herself in the fact that she knew now, almost with certainty who had killed Ginnie Forsyth, and she felt that the clues to the motive were hidden somewhere in the greenhouse.

She looked over at the bright colored faces of the flowers in Florence's hand. They were bursting with enthusiasm as their heads burst open with bright petals. Little did they know they had been snatched from the ground only to die drying upon a tabletop as an offer of sympathy.

"So what do you want to do first when we get there," said Florence, looking over at Frances as they walked along in step.

"Well, I imagine that James is likely to answer the door, I'll ask him if I can't have a moment with him and Agnus. Then I'll want to peek around in the greenhouse before speaking with Jack and Garrett. If they're home. Though they should be, I can't think of why they wouldn't be. At the very least they'll want to be planning the funeral I'm sure."

Florence nodded as they trod up the driveway towards the Forsyth's estate. Their steps heavier than they had been the first and second time they had come visiting.

Frances knocked on the front door and waited a long time. She was just about to knock again when she heard slow footsteps echoing towards them from inside the home. James answered the door, unsmiling. He looked ten years older and worse for it.

"Hello, James, we're here to see Jack and Garrett if that's all right?" said Lady Marmalade.

James nodded and stepped aside as Florence and Frances walked in. Florence smiled at him as she passed but he wasn't looking at her. His gaze was upon the floor.

"Everything alright, James? You don't look so well." said Florence.

He shook his head slowly.

"No ma'am, the police were here at three this morning. Mr. Forsyth has been murdered."

Florence put her hand to her mouth, her eyes wide and startled. Frances was taken aback too.

"Jack or Garrett?" asked Frances.

"Mr. Jack," said James hardly holding Frances' gaze.

"Good heavens," said Florence, and that was all she managed to say for several moments.

Frances put her hand on James' shoulder and looked at him kindly.

"I'm sorry, James. This is a terrible time for the Forsyths. Who is here then?"

James closed the door and offered to take their cardigans though it was cool enough inside to keep them on so they did.

"Mr. Garrett Forsyth arrived not long ago. You just missed Mr. Gerald Forsyth and Dr. Garnet. Garnet left around eight this morning and Mr. Gerald Forsyth left just after nine. Ms. Church has been here since shortly after the police arrived."

In the living room the grandfather clock chimed once, sadly as if losing its voice.

"Where is Garrett now, James?" asked Frances.

"He's in the study, my Lady, but I wouldn't disturb him just yet, he's in a very foul mood."

"Very well, is the greenhouse open, James?"

"It should be, my Lady, Enoch arrived back this morning at eight and he usually opens it."

"I'm going to inspect it if anyone is wondering where I am."

Frances grabbed Florence by the forearm. Florence looked back at James as Frances started off with her, and she handed him the flowers.

"Please put them in a vase, James. I'm so sorry."

"Yes ma'am."

They made their way past the study where Lady Marmalade could hear the grumbling of Garrett inside, cursing about something or someone, behind the partially closed door. She couldn't see him.

They walked into the living room and through the French doors that opened out into the back garden. Frances and Florence walked in silence towards the greenhouse. She saw Enoch and Agnus talking by the side of the shed diagonally across from the greenhouse at the very end of the garden. As she entered the greenhouse, she noticed a couple of cars parked oddly at the far side of the house. That was why she hadn't seen any cars when she and Florence walked up the driveway.

The door to the greenhouse was open and it was in a mess. Planters had been overturned all over the place. Florence, to her horror, couldn't see a spared plant.

"Looks like someone's been here before us," said Florence.

Frances nodded and surveyed the scene. At the far end of the greenhouse the tomato plants had been overturned as well. About a half dozen planters were overturned and the tomatoes upended. Frances walked down towards them. Florence followed her.

All around, small and large planter boxes had been emptied and nothing was left except overturned plants, their roots clinging to stingy clumps of soil that had been left after the violence.

"Somebody was looking for something in here and they were in a hurry it seems like," said Frances.

"Or maybe a few people were in here looking for something," offered Florence.

"You could be right," said Frances. "But what?"

She and Florence looked around. It was hard to make sense amongst all the mess. Everything had been turned upside down. Frances couldn't see anything from where she was standing. She slowly walked around the greenhouse looking for clues. She didn't find anything of note. Any plant that had just the day before been sitting comfortably in a box was now upended.

The planter boxes were empty and everyone she had a chance to look at held no clues. If there was something in one of these boxes, it was no longer there. She walked towards the back of the greenhouse, coming full circle and saw something that looked out of place.

Where the tomatoes had been before they were upended was not smooth dirt. But this was unusual, the rest of the greenhouse's dirt floor was scuffed and held the prints of many shoes, but the three foot by five foot patch of dirt where the tomatoes had once been had been carefully smoothed.

Lady Marmalade kneeled down and took a closer look. There appeared to be a length of loose wood just off the side. Only the smallest splinter of it was showing.

"Do you see any gloves I could use Flo?"

Florence looked around and saw a pair of green and white gardening gloves that she handed to Frances. Frances put them on and then tried to flick the piece of wood away. It didn't move, but the dry dirt brushed away, showing more wood.

On closer inspection it looked like a thin piece of wood was covering an area of about two feet by three feet. Frances brushed more of the dirt off the wood and it did indeed reveal a rectangle of about that size.

"What on earth is that?" asked Florence, as she knelt down next to Frances to take a closer look.

"It looks like a plane of wood under this dirt. Which seems strange."

Frances knocked on the top of it and a hollow echo sounded.

"I think there's a space underneath it. I might just have found what I was looking for. Can you get me a gardening fork or small shovel, Flo, I need to try and lift this up."

Florence got up and went to the front of the greenhouse which held the small tools attached to the wall. Frances inspected the wood more closely, there was no lever or handle with which to hold the wood and yank it off its base. Though it was seated flush against the rest of the floor but not terribly snugly.

Frances took the small shovel from Florence and slid it into the small space around the edge of the wood. Using it as a lever she pulled the shovel towards her with one hand and the wood lifted up over the lip. Florence took a corner of it.

"I've got it, Fran," she said.

"You should have put gloves on," said Frances.

"I didn't see any."

Frances took the other corner with her free hand and lifted it up higher. The wood wasn't terribly heavy and they lifted it up and slid it back towards the upended tomato planters.

Frances looked inside. The only thing in the shallow hole was a wooden box measuring about a foot by a foot and a half. Frances leaned in and took it out. She stood up and placed the box on one of the tables nearby.

"I'm intrigued," said Florence, "what on earth could be in there."

The box was solid wood and about six inches tall. There was a keyhole with which to lock it securely, however, the top of the box and been forced open, leaving splintered and smooshed wood just above the keyhole where the lid closed on the top.

Frances opened up the lid and it lay back against its hinges, a gaping mouth, screaming its secrets.

"Very interesting," said Frances.

Florence went to put her hand inside.

"Not yet, Flo, we need to take a closer look."

Inside were three pieces of paper folded, along with one hundred pounds in a variety of notes.

"There seems to be something missing," said Frances.

"What do you mean?"

"Well, if you look at the papers, they've been replaced carefully, but there is a slight discoloration on most of them from the dirt and dust that must have gotten in here over time. However, this third of it looks as though the paper is brand new."

Florence looked and indeed, it did seem that one third of the top paper was unblemished.

"And also, if you look at these two sides here," said Frances pointing to the right corner of the box that was away from them. "The wood on these two sides is much brighter and newer looking compared to the rest. The rest seems stained by dust and dirt."

"Well, I'll be," said Florence. "I would have never thought of that, I was too eager to get looking at the papers."

Frances nodded.

"I know, that's how I was once, when I started, but as I've said before, it's the details that are important. I wonder what might have been there?"

It was a rhetorical question, the answer to which Frances wanted to find. Florence didn't say anything. Anything she might offer would be pure speculation. France took off her gloves and picked up the three pieces of paper. She opened up the first one.

"Dear Daddy,

I've been looking a long time for you and I've waited patiently all these years to find you. My mother was Maude Daubney and she died giving birth to me. I've spent my whole life living in one form of destitution or another.

So imagine my surprise when I found out how rich you were. I want to receive what is rightfully mine. You've never been a father to me and I don't care for one. But you owe me or I'll ruin your life.

Meet me at the Fighting Cocks, Southport at noon, March 25th. If you don't show up you'll get your comeuppance.

Yours,

Lottie Daubney"

The letter was dated Wednesday the first of March.

"That was last Saturday," said Florence.

"I know. It appears that Jack has been a rake for much longer than we might have thought, if this is indeed true and he does have an illegitimate daughter."

"Do you think she might have killed Ginnie, or heaven forbid, Jack?" asked Florence.

"I don't know," said Frances shaking her head. "This complicates things, though I don't think she would have killed Ginnie."

Frances opened up the second letter and she and Florence read it together.

"My Darling Jack,

Oh, how I've missed you. You promised that we'd be together at the beginning of this year and now it is March already and I still don't have you to hold and love.

I know you said that money is tight but that you were still committed to saving enough for us to move to Argentina together. But when will this be. I wait and wait patiently in Liverpool, but each week without you is an eternity that breaks my heart.

You aren't cheating on me are you? I know that sounds silly but I'm already terribly jealous that Ginnie is with you daily.

Please Jack, let me know we'll be together, soon, forever. Or I'm afraid I might have to tell your wife. I know you don't love her, but then why do you still make me wait?

With all my heart and soul,

Rachel Badcocke"

Frances carefully folded the letter. This one too, was dated the first of March. She placed it back inside the box carefully.

"My dear Flo, that letter is exactly what I was looking for. That is the reason I believe that Meredith killed Ginnie," said Frances pointing to the letter she had just placed back into the box.

"I don't understand. Wouldn't she be mad at Jack rather?"

"The heart can be a petty and fickle pouting child. You'd think she would be more angry at Jack, but sometimes loves blinds you to the real culprit and you lash out instead to others. But I don't believe she actually got to see it."

"Then why would she kill Ginnie?"

"I think I'll explain that later, Flo. I want us to put this back quickly. We've been out here a while and someone will suspect something soon."

Florence nodded and glanced up at the front door, it was almost closed, just a sliver of it open to the garden. Frances opened up the third piece of paper which was not like the others. It was a coarser piece of paper that looked like it might have been handmade. She read it silently with Florence leaning over her shoulder.

"Eagles to Flying Chan. Good Friday. Noon"

It was written in a very elegant hand. Just those seven words. Florence looked up at Frances and frowned.

"That's an odd bit, isn't it?"

Frances nodded.

"Yes, but it is the clue as to why I think Jack was killed."

"Oh do tell," said Florence, smiling.

"In due time, my dear Flo, in due time. We must put all of this back into the box and place it back where we found it. I don't want anyone to know we've uncovered this. This must be our secret until we've sorted it all out and we have the police on the trail of the murderer."

"Who is?"

"Not quite certain, but we'll find out soon enough."

Frances rearranged the papers in the order she had picked them up from inside the box and lay them back down in the same manner. She put on her gardening gloves again and closed the box. Then she placed the box into the hole beneath the greenhouse and covered it with the wood.

Florence took the small shovel and began to spread dirt over its face until it was covered and almost impossible to see. Frances smoothed it out with her gloved hands and then they stood up and looked at their handiwork.

"I don't think anybody will know it's here unless they're looking for something like it specifically."

Florence nodded.

"Where did you find these gloves, Flo?"

"Just over there on that table," answered Florence pointing towards the middle of the greenhouse at one of the tables littered with upturned planters and potting soil. Frances took the gloves off and placed them back.

"I think we should get back."

As they exited the greenhouse, Frances looked off towards the shed at the opposite corner. Enoch and Agnus were no longer there. As she and Florence walked towards the house, Frances dusted off her dress by the knees. She couldn't get all of the dirt dust off, but enough of it that you could hardly tell there was any there.

Fifteen

They were alone when they first entered the living room. But moments later James came in, still looking tired and as worn out as these days had been long. He smiled his best at them and asked if he could get them anything to drink. James was just about to leave when Frances spoke again.

"James, is Agnus around?"

"Yes she is, my Lady."

"Good, I'd like to have a word with her. But first, I'd like to ask you some questions if you don't mind?"

"Not at all."

"Please sit down if you'd like. I know you must be tired."

James sat stiffly in the couch and Frances sat in one of the armchairs while Florence stood by her side.

"Before I ask you about Ginnie's passing, the news you recently shared with us is quite shocking. Did the police say where Jack had been murdered?"

"They did, my Lady. They said he was found at Albert Dock in Liverpool shortly after two in the morning."

"Did they say how he had been murdered?"

"They said he'd been shot."

"Did they mention anything else?"

"They wanted to speak to Garrett and Meredith but they weren't available so they said they'd be back sometime today and to let Garrett and Meredith know."

"Thank you James, I know it must be terrible news. But your help might be instrumental in helping us solve these terrible crimes."

James nodded and looked at her with sad almost vacant eyes.

"I do hope so, my Lady."

"No doubt the police have asked you this, but where were you between two and three thirty?"

"They didn't ask me specifically, my Lady, but you might recall that Agnus called us for supper at two, and I ate with her until three. Enoch left us at two thirty and only returned his plate at three. Between three and three thirty I was back in the house. At three I called upon Mr. Forsyth, if he needed anything. He didn't so I went to the kitchen to help Agnus."

"Yes, thank you, James, I remember the conversation you had with the inspector. Between three and three thirty did you see Meredith?"

"No my Lady. I only believe I saw her later when she came down when the police were here."

"Did you see her before then, during your supper?"

"No, we were inside the living area of our quarters and I didn't see anything, my back was to the window. Agnus was sitting opposite, she might have seen something."

"Can you tell me anything about the relationships in this family, James?"

"Well, with due respect, my Lady, I prefer not to gossip about my employers."

James continued to sit stiffly on the edge of the couch, his hands in his lap, his back straight as a board. He looked down at his hands and fidgeted with them for a moment.

"I understand, James. But anything you might be privy to could be awfully helpful in trying to determine who committed either of these ghastly crimes."

What Frances really meant to say was that he was as good as unemployed now. Seeing as how Ginnie and now Jack were both dead. Dead men tell no tales but those who knew them should. If only to serve justice. James glanced up at her and his eyes were wet and distant as the sun seemed through the gray clouds.

"She was a good lady," he said. "She never had a stern word for me or Agnus."

James reached inside his pocket for a white handkerchief and he dabbed at his eyes.

"You could honor her in death, James, if you help bring closure to this," said Frances.

James nodded and carefully folded his handkerchief back up into a small perfect square before putting it back in his inside jacket pocket.

"Yes, my Lady. I'll try answer as best I can."

"Could you tell me what the relationship was like between Ginnie and Jack?"

James looked down solemnly for a moment, collecting his thoughts, before he looked back up at Frances.

"It was never particularly good since I can remember, and I've been with them for twenty years now."

"How would you describe it?" asked Frances.

"Distant and cold with angry eruptions now and then."

"Why is that?"

"Uh, Jack is a man of..."

"Weaknesses?'

James nodded.

"Yes, indiscretions I was going to say, but perhaps, not meaning to be disrespectful of the dead, but yes, weaknesses. It was no secret to anyone who spent much time here that he was a womanizer, a gambler and an addict."

"How do you know all this?"

"It first came to my attention during a fight between Mr. and Mrs. Forsyth many years ago when the troubles with the business first came to light. It seemed, from what I overheard, that he was pilfering funds from the company's profits to gamble."

"Where did he gamble?"

"I'm not certain my Lady, but I overheard them fighting about someplace in Blackpool, I think it might have been called the Flying Man or something like that."

"The Flying Chan, perhaps?"

James nodded.

"Occasionally he'd also disappear for a few days at a time, and when he'd come home they'd fight about his drug habits. She accused him of being an opium addict to which he never did deny it. And looking back now, I can say that he was almost anesthetized on quite a number of occasions when he came back from Blackpool. He seemed almost vacant for the first day he was back."

"And what about the womanizing?" asked Frances.

"That was an ongoing problem. He often came back from Blackpool smelling of cheap perfume. And there were no ends to the fighting then."

"What about Meredith?"

James glanced back down at his hands and he started knitting them together again. Perhaps he was trying to knit a noose with which to hang himself from. He was clearly nervous.

"What is it, James?" asked Frances.

He looked up at her, taking a break from his knitting.

"It's one thing to speak ill of the dead, my Lady, but I'd rather not speak ill of the living. I still need to work around these parts."

Lady Marmalade leaned in and patted him on the knee.

"I understand, James, I really do. And what you say is strictly confidential. Only between the three of us. I promise you that."

He looked into Lady Marmalade's eyes, searching for a crack or any misgivings. He didn't find any. So he nodded his head again as if the silent searching for truth within her eyes was a contract they'd just verbally agreed to.

"Ever since Mr. Roger Forsyth passed, God rest his soul, some three years ago or thereabouts, Mr. Forsyth and Meredith got close. I guess in sympathy or shared pain. You see, while Mr. Roger Forsyth was around, things stuck together pretty well. He was the glue that kept the family and business working. He was also the nicest of the three of them."

"Which three?" asked Florence, finding her voice.

James looked up at her standing next to Frances.

"The three Mr. Forsyths, Roger, Gerald and Jack. Mr. Roger Forsyth was the oldest and kindest. When he passed, things started to quickly turn worse. Not to say the company wasn't in trouble before then, it seems to have been. You see Roger was a careful businessman, but from what I gather he was a pushover for his brothers, especially the youngest, Mr. Jack Forsyth. I've overheard that Roger allowed Jack more discretion with the company ledger than he should have allowed."

"So Jack and Meredith weren't together while Meredith was married to Roger?"

"It appears that way. I guess Meredith was the one woman out of reach for Jack. Jack really loved his oldest brother and you could tell Meredith was madly in love with Mr. Roger Forsyth, and I might add, it was a returned love."

"And when Roger passed, Meredith and Jack got together?" asked Frances.

"Yes, and she changed, and it wasn't for the better. She became jealous, and moody and temperamental. She also started drinking quite a lot too."

"And did Ginnie know?" asked Frances.

"Not at first. Not for the first couple of years. I mean, she knew that Jack wasn't faithful and that was an ongoing problem, but it wasn't until she found them together some months ago that thing started a turn for the worse."

"How so?"

"I believe that Meredith planned it that way. I can't say for certain, but I don't think Meredith knew about Jack's other womanizing, and she was extremely upset that he wouldn't leave Ginnie."

"How do you know that?"

"I overheard them having a row about it over a year ago. I suppose that at first their casual relationship worked for them both. But about a year ago or more, Meredith wanted to have

Jack to herself. In any event she told him that he had to come clean and divorce Ginnie or she'd tell Ginnie about the two of them. Jack said she didn't have the courage. And he was right, she didn't. At least not outright."

"And so you're suggesting that she created a situation where the two of them would be found together?" asked Florence.

"Yes, ma'am. And that's when things really started to get nasty. Meredith would start to flirt and become affectionate with Jack right in front of Mrs. Forsyth. You could tell it upset her deeply. Ginnie and Jack argued about it for a long time and Mrs. Forsyth would threaten to leave if he didn't call it off."

"But she never did, did she?" asked Florence.

"No. But I believe she was planning to. One of the last arguments was about a daughter and gold. Mrs. Forsyth said she was leaving and he could have his sinking ship all to himself. She said she knew about his illegitimate daughter, how she wasn't surprised, but that it didn't matter anymore because she knew he was storing gold and she was going to take what was hers and leave."

"Meaning the gold?" asked Frances.

"I believe so, my Lady. But Mr. Forsyth warned her very sternly not to go anywhere near it. It wasn't his, it belonged to some very bad people that he was trying to pay off. Mrs. Forsyth laughed and said how stupid she had been all these years, when she was blind to the cad he was. She told him he'd get his due."

"Did you ever see any of this gold?" asked Frances.

"No, my Lady, I don't even know if it was true, other than what I overheard in the arguments."

Florence looked up and off into the garden through the French doors. She touched Frances on the shoulder and when Frances looked up at her she nodded towards the end of the living room.

Frances looked up and followed her gaze. Outside, Garrett was marching determinedly towards the greenhouse. As he entered, he looked around carefully to see if he was being watched. Then like a thief he snuck in quietly into the greenhouse and closed the door behind him.

Frances looked back at Florence and smiled, then she looked back at James.

"How did Ginnie know about the illegitimate daughter?"

"She said, in one of their arguments, that she had found the letter in his study. Mr. Forsyth got angry about that and told her it was none of her business and she shouldn't be snooping around in his private study anyway."

"Did anyone else know about the gold or the daughter?" asked Frances.

"Quite a few. I remember her mentioning it to her brother, Dr. Garnet as I was passing around tea and crumpets on one occasion. Their voices were very hushed and they stopped speaking when I came near, but I did hear her mention gold and Jack."

"Any others?"

"On one occasion during dinner, my Lady, Mrs. Forsyth decided to mention it to her son. She was quite sarcastic about it, saying something to the effect that while Mr. Forsyth was ruining the company his father had built, he was storing gold. Garrett inquired about it and Jack denied it. He added that even if he were, he didn't have any at that time and that he was just a middleman and the gold was not theirs anyway. A very weak denial."

"How did Garrett respond?"

"He got very upset. The two of them, he and his father, yelled about it for a while as Garrett felt he should stop this nonsense and be done with it, that he owed his mother better than this."

"He was alluding to his father's debts and other misbehaviors?"

James nodded.

"Yes, I believe he knew about that. He also told his father to break it off with Meredith or he'd fix it."

"What do you think he meant by 'fix it'?"

"I can't say, but for a moment I thought they might come to blows."

"Did you hear them argue at other times?"

"On one occasion, Mr. Garrett was in his father's study which he wasn't allowed to be in. Mr. Jack came storming in demanding to know what he was doing in there. Garrett said he was looking for a book, but Jack didn't believe him."

"What did he say?"

"He said, 'you've been looking at my calendar'. Mr. Garrett didn't respond, he came storming out. I don't know why he would have been looking at Mr. Jack's calendar, though I did overhear Gerald and Garrett talking once about Liverpool."

"What about Liverpool?"

"It was hard to say but Gerald said something about Liverpool was their best chance at winning. I can't say I knew what they were talking about, it might have been football, but they started talking about Garrett's car when they saw me."

"Going back to that argument they had at dinner, James, who else was there at the time?"

"Other than Garrett, Mr. Forsyth and Mrs. Forsyth, there was Mr. Forsyth's older brother Gerald."

"I see," said Frances, looking at Florence. "So it appears that a number of people knew about this gold. The only thing that gives me pause is that gold hasn't become that valuable lately. Rather, it's been quite stagnant."

"What do you mean?" asked Florence.

"A hundred ounces of gold wouldn't be worth even a thousand pounds. That's not a lot of money to kill someone over and it certainly wouldn't be easy to cart all of that around. That's a little over six pounds."

"Yes, but didn't Finley say to us that the Chinese expect a surge in gold prices in the coming decades?"

"Yes he did, but that still doesn't explain why someone would be interested in six pounds of gold which is barely worth a month's salary for most of those who knew about it."

"Perhaps, but we know that money was likely tight here at the Forsyth's over the last little while. Perhaps the facade hiding a burgeoning poverty."

Frances nodded thoughtfully.

"If I might," said James.

Florence and Frances both looked at him.

"Yes, please, go ahead," said Frances.

"I believe that the financial matters here at the Forsyth estate are much more dire than perhaps most realize. For the last year, more than that really, but especially during the last year, my pay has been intermittent at best."

"What do you mean?" asked Florence.

"I've been paid half of what is owed me, ma'am, with promises and assurances for the rest which never seems to be forthcoming. A hundred pounds is not easy to live on."

"And that's half of what you're owed?"

James nodded, looking back at his hands.

Frances looked outside and saw Garrett leaving the greenhouse. He was visibly upset, muttering something under his breath and shaking his head. His hands even at this distance could be seen covered with dirt. He paused, leaned over and rubbed them over the grass trying to get rid of as much of the dirt as he could.

She heard him re-enter the house from the front door, but he didn't come down to the living room where Frances, Florence and James were. Frances suspected he was back in the study if she had to guess.

"So if I've got this correct," said Florence, "the people who knew about the alleged gold, were Jack and Ginnie, both of whom are dead, Garrett, Dr. Garnet and Gerald?"

"Don't forget Ms. Church," said James.

"How did she know?" asked Florence.

"She overheard Ginnie speaking of it to her brother and then I heard her confront Mr. Forsyth about it."

"What did he say?"

"I wasn't privy to the whole conversation, ma'am, I do try and remain discreet and respectful. They were in the study and what I did overhear was he saying something about trying to clear his debts so he was doing a couple of favors to do that. He said he was only doing it so they could have a fresh start."

"They being Jack and Meredith?" asked Florence.

James nodded looking at her.

"She seemed happy about that again when I saw her after the conversation. He also promised this was his way of getting out of gambling and opium."

"She didn't know about the women?" asked Frances.

"She might have suspected but I don't believe she wanted to believe it. Though on Monday morning, I heard Ms. Church and Mrs. Forsyth have a terrible argument."

"What was it about?" asked Frances.

"From the snippets I could gather, Mrs. Forsyth was telling Ms. Church to leave her husband alone. Ms. Church wouldn't hear of it, so Mrs. Forsyth said that Mr. Forsyth was nothing but a philanderer and womanizer. I remember one part she said in particular was, 'he's cheating on me with you, isn't he?'."

"And what did Meredith say about that?"

"She said something about her relationship with Mr. Forsyth being different. The last bit I heard was Mrs. Forsyth saying she had proof that he was cheating on the both of them. She told Ms. Church to meet her outside in the greenhouse and she'd show her."

"Did Meredith say anything after that?"

"She said something to the effect that she wasn't interested and didn't believe her. That Mr. Forsyth was going to leave Mrs. Forsyth and that would be the end of that."

"So the six of them knew about the gold. Has anyone actually seen any?"

James slowly shook his head.

"I can't say my Lady. I don't believe so. I've never seen any and I never heard anyone say they saw any either. Mr. Forsyth might have been making up a tale about that. He wasn't always the most reliable gentleman when it came to his word."

Frances looked at him and shifted in her seat. She sat back a little more comfortably.

"Can you offer an example, James?"

"Well, he would lie or even downplay the state of the business. Whenever Mrs. Forsyth or anyone else for that matter asked him about how the business was doing, he'd say it was fine, when in fact, I wouldn't be surprised if it closed by the end of the year, except that Mr. Gerald Forsyth might save it now."

"Surely he must've known things had been bad for quite some time?" asked Frances.

"I'm afraid not. Up until recently he had been hands-off, involved in some side businesses that I don't know about. But I heard Ginnie implore him to get more interested in it a few months ago if he wanted to have any hope of keeping the business afloat. I think that must have gotten him interested because he started badgering Mr. Jack Forsyth about the business often after that point."

"In person or over the telephone?"

"Both. You could always tell when Mr. Forsyth had spoken to his brother by phone because he'd come out of his study, visibly upset and angry at everyone. The last time I heard them speak would have been last Friday. Gerald had come by to talk business and they'd gone into the study. Even though the door was closed you could hear them down the hallway."

"What was Gerald's main concern?"

"He wanted Jack to hand over the reins to the business to him."

"And was he agreeable?"

"No, my Lady, in the strongest terms he wasn't. So Gerald threatened him and said he'd get rid of him from the business one way or the other."

"Did he threaten his life?" asked Florence.

"No, ma'am, not directly. He stormed out of the study then and left the home in quite a hurry I might add."

"All because of mismanagement and deceit," said Frances to no one in particular.

Then she looked back at James.

"Is there anything else you might like to share with us, James, before I ask you to let me speak with Agnus."

James looked out the window into the garden. You couldn't see anybody out there from where the three of them were sitting, and they could see most of the garden.

"It's that Enoch chap, my Lady. I don't know why Mr. Forsyth hired him. He's not like any groundskeeper I've seen. He's rough a sort too. I don't care for him and I can't say I was upset when the police carted him off. I should've thought he'd done it, but he's back now."

Frances nodded at James and smiled warmly at him.

"I don't think he'll be around for much longer, James. You're right, he's not a proper groundskeeper as you'd expect. But I don't believe you have anything to worry about as far as he's concerned."

"Thank you, my Lady."

James got up.

"I hope I've been helpful."

"You most certainly have, James. Thank you for your honesty and forthrightness."

"Can I bring you anything to drink now?"

"No, thank you. But if you could get Agnus to come speak with us, I'd be terribly grateful."

"Certainly."

James bowed and left the living room.

"I don't know about you," said Florence, "but this whole thing has just become as opaque as the Prime Minister's office."

Frances laughed out loud and grabbed at her friend's hand.

"Oh Flo, you are too much. I love your way with words. It does seem a little opaque, doesn't it. Though honestly, I think things are coming into place quite nicely."

"I have no idea how you can see through any of this mess."

Florence went over to another arm chair and dragged it closer to Frances. She sat down into it.

“Well, I think a lot of it has to do with the gold. And perhaps those letters in the box which I believe are related to the gold somehow.”

“If you say so, though I can’t seem to make hide nor hair of any of this, even Ginnie’s murder.”

“Ginnie’s murder is definitely clearer for me now. All will be explained in time, my dear Flo. The question we must ask ourselves is what was Jack doing at the docks last night and who might have been with him?”

“I have a suspicion that you might already know the answers to most of that.”

“I have a hunch that this is all interrelated like some incestuous family.”

Sixteen

Agnus Van Buren walked softly into the room and curtsied to Lady Marmalade and Florence. She wore the classic black dress of her profession with a frilly and thick white collar. The arms of her dress went all the way to her wrists where they met white cuffs. She had on a white apron. The dress was not becoming on her and ended just a few inches above her ankles.

"You wanted to see me, my Lady?" she said, barely making eye contact with Lady Marmalade.

"Yes, thank you for joining us, Agnus. Please sit down, I know you must get tired standing on your feet all day."

Frances pointed to the couch that James had just recently sat in, and Agnus took a seat in it. Though she looked as though she were sitting on a porcupine.

"Am I in trouble, my Lady?"

Frances chuckled.

"Good heavens, no," she said, "but I hope you might be able to help me in finding out who murdered Ginnie or Jack."

Agnus clutched her bosom with her big hands.

"Something terrible has befallen this home, my Lady," she said.

Frances nodded. Agnus was middle aged and of average height. Her hair was tucked up and out of the way, covered in a white bonnet, and what you did see of it was mostly gray, She either didn't care to or couldn't afford to color it. She had a pleasant face which was by no means pretty. Her nose was too large and reminded one of an eagle's beak.

"James had been most helpful to us already and he suggested that you'd be just as helpful as well. Was he correct?"

Agnus nodded. Her hands were now in her lap and she was sitting bladed towards Lady Marmalade, her left side towards Frances and her legs pointing to the far corner of the living room.

"He did not lie, my Lady. I'll do whatever I can to help."

"That's exactly what I thought," said Frances. "Can you tell me what you and Enoch were speaking about earlier when I saw the two of you down by the greenhouse?"

Agnus looked out through the windows at the end of the living room and out into the garden. Nobody was out there. The grass was green and the sky was gray but it shed no rain for Jack's death. She looked back at Lady Marmalade.

"He was asking me why so many people had been coming and going from the greenhouse the last few days. I said I didn't know why."

"Did he have any idea?"

"No, but he kept asking me if I'd heard anything about the greenhouse. I told him I hadn't. I don't think he quite believed me. He told me that this morning he'd seen Dr. Garnet leave the greenhouse just before eight and then Mr. Forsyth leave the greenhouse at just before nine. He's an odd sort, my Lady, that Enoch, I don't quite care for him. He sticks to himself mostly unless he wants something and he's not much of a groundskeeper neither."

"I understand. I don't think he'll be around much longer, so you needn't be worried. Did he mean Gerald or Garrett Forsyth?"

Agnus seemed visibly relieved by that. She glanced back outside again and Frances followed her gaze. Enoch could be seen kneeling over the patch of tilled ground at the end of the garden.

"He was speaking of Mr. Gerald Forsyth, my Lady."

"Have you been in the greenhouse, Agnus?" asked Frances.

"No, my Lady. It isn't part of my duties and I've never had reason to be in there."

"What about James? Have you ever seen him in the greenhouse?"

"No, it isn't part of his duties. The only ones I've seen are Mr. and Mrs. Forsyth, Mr. Garrett Forsyth and now I suppose seeing as Enoch says Dr. Garnet and Mr. Gerald Forsyth have been in, I guess them too."

"But you haven't seen them go in have you?"

Agnus shook her head.

"No, my Lady."

"You and James and Enoch were having lunch together on Tuesday. Did you see anyone enter the greenhouse then?"

"Yes, my Lady. Now that you mention it, it was just before Enoch left us to go and eat by himself. I guess that would have been about two thirty, I saw Mrs. Forsyth enter the greenhouse and she was followed a couple of minutes later by Ms. Church."

"Do you know why they might have been interested in visiting the greenhouse together?"

"No, though I didn't get the impression they were together."

"And you didn't see Enoch enter the greenhouse?"

"No, my Lady. He went to eat his supper by the shed so he said, though I didn't see him after that."

"Did you see Meredith or Ginnie leave the greenhouse later that afternoon?"

"No, my Lady, but I was washing up our plates before three and then I was back in the house at three to start afternoon tea. I only heard Ms. Church when she came down when the police had arrived."

"Why do you think Enoch was so interested in the greenhouse?"

"I can't say, I guess he felt maybe it was part of his responsibilities and he didn't much like others interfering with what he was supposed to be taking care of. Though he did say something strange to me."

"And what was that?" asked Frances.

"He asked me if I'd seen any gold in the house at all. I told him I hadn't and that I wouldn't say if I had, not to his kind. I told him he shouldn't be speaking like that?"

"How was he speaking?"

"I think he was thinking about robbing Mr. and Mrs. Forsyth if he could. And I wasn't about to encourage it."

"Did you tell him that?"

"I said if anything went missing I'd be sure to tell the police about this conversation we'd just had and he told me to mind my own business."

"Did he say anything else after that."

Agnus shook her head and fiddled with her fingers in her lap.

"No, my Lady, I think he was upset at me then, because he huffed off into the shed and I haven't seen him."

"So you think he was planning on robbing the Forsyths now that they're both dead?"

Agnus nodded and looked earnestly at Lady Marmalade.

"I do."

"I want to ask you a personal question Agnus, and I'd appreciate your honesty."

"Yes, my Lady."

"Have the Forsyths been regular with your salary?",

"No, my Lady, they've only paid me half what I'm due over the past year. But Mr. Forsyth promised it was just an accounting error and that he'd catch me up soon."

"Do you know much about the Forsyth's business affairs?"

"Nothing more than what I've heard the rumors saying which is that their business is in bad shape."

"Do you know if this affected Jack and Ginnie's relationship at all?"

"I'm sure it must've but whenever I overheard Ginnie and Jack fighting it was about Meredith or his gambling or opium."

"When was the last time you heard them argue?"

"It was last week. Might have been Wednesday or Thursday, I think. She said she knew about his daughter and his mistress and that was the last straw. She was going to leave him."

"What did he say?"

"He said it'd be the last thing she did. She wasn't going to get a penny of his. She said she didn't need it anyway she'd found his secrets out."

"Do you know what she meant by that?"

"No, my Lady, but the last thing he said as she left was that it wasn't his and she'd better not if she valued her life."

"I see. Do you really think he'd kill her?"

"I wouldn't have thought so, but now that she's dead, maybe he did."

"How was Garrett's relationship with his father?"

"He hated his father, that was well known. Mostly he hated him for being weak and treating his mother so poorly, but I know Mr. Garrett was aware of how his father was ruining the business."

"Did you hear anything the two of them might have said about any of these matters?"

"Once they had a fight about it and I thought Mr. Garrett was going to strike his father, but that was when I entered and they stopped."

"What gave you the suspicion that Garrett was going to hit his father?" asked Frances.

"Well, my Lady, he had his fist up as if he was about to box him."

"What had they argued about?"

"They had been arguing about Mr. Garrett wanting his father to stop going around with Meredith and to clean up his gambling and drug problems, and if he didn't then he, Mr. Garrett, said that he and Mr. Gerald Forsyth would have him removed from the company."

"And how did Gerald and Jack get along, can you tell me about their relationship?"

"Theirs was very strained too. I heard Mr. Gerald and Mr. Jack talking once, actually they were arguing, and Mr. Gerald told him to get his act together and straighten out. He said that he wasn't going to lose everything because his brother was so lily-livered and weak. He said he'd taken out insurance on him for one hundred thousand pounds and if Mr. Jack didn't get it together he'd get his share one way or another."

"What did he mean by that?"

"That's what Mr. Forsyth asked his brother, Mr. Gerald, and Mr. Gerald said that he and Meredith and Garrett, and even Dr. Garnet who had lent Mr. Jack a large sum of money would be paid out one way or another. That's all he said."

"I see. Did you hear anything else about the conversation?"

"A little bit more. You must understand, my Lady, it was hard to be deaf to it, their voices were loud and carried almost throughout the entire house."

Agnus looked at Lady Marmalade a little nervously. She didn't like telling on her employer. It made her uncomfortable, but she supposed that with them both being dead now, perhaps she was doing more good than harm.

"I understand, Agnus, please carry on. This is all very helpful you know."

Those few words were just the encouragement she needed.

"Mr. Jack Forsyth said that he couldn't get him out of the business, and Mr. Gerald said he could. In fact, he said there were two ways. One was if something unfortunate happened to him. And Mr. Jack said something to the effect that Mr. Gerald wouldn't dare to which Mr. Gerald said he had money on it. And the second way was that Mr. Gerald would speak with the board of directors and tell them about Mr. Jack's wicked ways, those were the words he used, and he'd be sure they'd relieve him of his duties."

"Thank you, Agnus. That's most helpful."

"Now earlier, you mentioned Ginnie finding out about Jack's daughter and mistress. Do you know about this daughter? Because Garrett is Ginnie's and Jack's only child, correct?"

Agnus nodded her head and fiddled with the hem of her apron.

"Yes, my Lady, as far as I know, Mr. Garrett is the only child to Mr. and Mrs. Forsyth."

"Do you know who this daughter might be? Have you met her?"

"No, my Lady, I haven't met anyone saying they're Mr. Forsyth's daughter. I think this is new, as Mrs. Forsyth only seemed to have found out about it late last month."

"Did Jack deny having a daughter?"

"No, he didn't. Mrs. Forsyth had said she'd seen the letter, so maybe someone had written to tell him. What he did say, is that it was a long time ago, when he was young and stupid."

"And how did Ginnie respond to that?"

"Well she said she'd found out about his mistress and his plans to go to Argentina. I forgot to mention that. I heard her say that during the argument with Mr. Forsyth."

"How did she know about Argentina?" asked Florence, quite enjoying playing the part of Frances' Watson.

"Like I said, ma'am, she said she'd seen the letters."

"I'm confused, Agnus, this mistress, is she Meredith, and if so, why would they be writing to each other when they could just talk in person or over the telephone?" asked Florence.

"I got the impression that Mrs. Forsyth wasn't talking about Meredith. It felt to me that this was another woman."

"How so?"

"Well, she said something like 'does Meredith know'. And I think she was talking about the mistress and not the daughter as she said that after they'd spoken about the daughter."

"I see," said Florence.

"Agnus," said Frances, "have you ever heard Jack or Ginnie talking about Argentina before?"

"No, my Lady. They've hardly spoken of holidays together for a long time."

"And these secrets that Ginnie mentioned. Did they say anything else about that at all?"

Agnus looked down at her lap, still fidgeting with her hem before she looked back up at Lady Marmalade.

"I didn't hear them say anything else about it. I just assumed the secrets were the things they had just spoken about, the daughter and the mistress."

"Have you seen Jack with anyone else other than Meredith?"

"Well, my Lady, I don't wish to speak ill of the dead."

"It's quite alright, Agnus, this is very important and helpful."

Agnus nodded her head.

"On occasion, Mr. Forsyth would leave, vanish for a few days and when he got back he'd smell of cheap perfume, he looked disheveled and he'd act strangely."

"How would he act?"

"Almost like he wasn't really himself, he seemed very slow and vacant almost. I overheard Mrs. Forsyth cursing him a few times whenever he came home like this. She said he'd been out whoring in Blackpool, if you'll pardon my language, my Lady."

Frances smiled at her.

"It's quite alright."

"I want to ask you, Agnus, if you were awake this morning and late last night when the police came?"

"I was in bed sleeping when James woke me around three. The police had come to our quarters round back, not getting any response from the main house."

"So was there nobody at home at that time then?"

"I guess not, my Lady, though there should have been."

"Who do you think should have been home?"

"Well, Mr. Garrett, Mr. Jack, and Ms. Church most likely as she'd been staying around the house a lot lately."

"But none of them were here then?"

"No, James and me got up and spoke with the police and they told us that Mr. Forsyth had been shot at the docks in Liverpool. Then they asked us to open the house so they could speak with whoever was home. We opened the house and there wasn't anybody home."

"What did the police do?"

"They looked around for a bit and then left telling James that they'd be back later to speak with everyone and that we were to tell them, especially Mr. Garrett and Ms. Church, not to go anywhere. So we stayed up and made a pot of tea. Ms. Church came home shortly after the police left."

"Did you tell about Jack?"

"I did, my Lady, I offered her some tea but she said she'd just be going off to bed. I suppose that's where she still is now."

"How did she seem when she came home?"

"She seemed tired and she looked as if she'd been crying."

"And when you told her Jack had been murdered?"

"She sighed and nodded and her eyes teared up and she went upstairs and I haven't seen her since."

"Do you know where she might have been so late at night?"

"No, my Lady, it's not my place."

"Of course not."

"When did you see anybody else come home?" asked Frances.

"I stayed in the kitchen. I was really tired so I kept nodding off at the kitchen table. I heard other men's voices. I believe Dr.

Garnet was here after seven. James said he was in the study and didn't want to be disturbed. Then he went out into the garden and into the greenhouse where Enoch saw him leave again, at about eight I think he said."

"What about Gerald, you told us that Gerald was here too, at least from what Enoch said?"

"Yes, my Lady. I heard Mr. Gerald arrive not long after Dr. Garnet. He also rummaged through the study. I heard him that time, then he too left the house for the garden and went into the greenhouse."

"And what time did he leave again?"

"Must have been a little after nine, I remember because I heard the clock chime. Just a couple of minutes after he left I heard the front door open again and I thought he must have forgotten something but it was Mr. Garrett instead."

"And he's been here since then, hasn't he?"

"As best as I can tell."

"You must be very tired," said Frances.

Agnus nodded and smiled a thin smile that showed no teeth.

"I am," she said nodding.

"Would you know why Dr. Garnet and Gerald might have been round this morning?"

"I don't, my Lady, but they were probably here to see Mr. Forsyth, they obviously don't know what's happened to him."

"And they're usually allowed to wait in Jack's study?"

"No, that's the odd thing about it. I heard James trying to keep them out of Mr. Forsyth's study but they were absolutely determined about waiting for Mr. Forsyth in the study. They were quite mean to James about it too, and what could he do?"

Agnus looked at Lady Marmalade with a pained, searching expression.

"I understand. Where do guests usually wait for Jack?"

"He prefers they wait in the smoking room or the living room."

"I suppose you wouldn't have any idea where Garrett was last night instead of being here?"

Agnus shook her head from side to side, slowly as if feeling the weight of it.

"I don't know where he was. He's often out and about spending time with friends."

"What about a girlfriend?"

"I've never known him to have a girlfriend, my Lady."

"Thank you, Agnus. Is there anything else that you think is important?"

She looked into her lap and fiddled a bit and shrugged.

"It's probably nothing."

"Go on."

"I heard a strange conversation last week sometime in the afternoon when I was washing dishes. It sounded like Dr. Garnet and Mr. Gerald were talking outside the kitchen window. It was hard to hear what they were talking about."

Frances waited for Agnus to compose her thoughts.

"I think I heard Dr. Garnet say something about the docks and that Jack would be getting gold. Mr. Gerald asked if it was safe and was he certain it was a good idea. Dr. Garnet said it was Jack's problem anyway and they were due. That's all I heard."

The clatter of shoes could be heard in the hallway, it sounded like they were coming towards the living room.

Seventeen

A moment later Garrett entered and then stopped and looked at the three of them.

"What's this?" he said.

"I'll be off, my Lady, if you don't mind," said Agnus, standing up as quick as jackrabbit. She didn't look at Garrett as she stepped past him carefully.

"What are you two doing here?"

Garrett walked over to the bar and took a glass tumbler and poured three fingers of Scotch into it. He walked back over to where Frances and Florence were still seated. He leaned on the high, back end of the couch.

"We came to offer our condolences and Florence brought some flowers that James is likely putting in a vase."

"I see."

"Why don't you sit down, Garrett, you look terribly disheveled and tired."

Garrett looked down at himself. His dark brown pants were creased and had a smear of gray from on the outsides of the thigh where he had tried to brush off the dirt. His white shirt wasn't looking as crisp and white as it should. A corner of it was sticking out in the front which he tucked back in, but that did nothing for the wrinkles. His brown jacket was equally in need of some starch and ironing.

He sat down and Frances noticed some paper barely sticking out of his trouser pocket on the right side. Garrett took a long sip of the Scotch.

"I feel remarkably good actually," he said.

"Tell me, Garrett," said Frances, "have the Forsyths always chosen lies as a first recourse."

Garrett looked at Lady Marmalade sternly. He furrowed his brow and clenched his teeth. His eyes smoked but he got control of himself.

"That's quite impertinent," he said to her, his voice hot from his mouth.

"At least you're alive to feel the dull thud of impertinence. I'm here to help solve your mother's and, now it would seem, your father's murder."

"And you think you can do better than the police?"

He looked at her out of the corner of his eye and leaned back into the couch. He crossed his legs in front of him, his left one over the right. He draped his left arm over the ridge of the couch and casually held his tumbler in his right hand while he swirled the golden liquid inside.

Someone unaware of the severity of the situation might mistake the three of them as old friends visiting and chatting about the controversial Fred Perry's move to the United States. And in some ways, perhaps this conversation was much like the start to a tennis match. The volleys back and forth to test one's opponent.

"All I want, Garrett, is to bring justice to your mother and father."

"That would be nice for my mother," he said, "as for my father, well I think he got what's coming."

"That's a little cold, isn't it?" asked Florence.

He looked over at Florence with a squinty stare.

"Is it?" he asked. "You who knew my father so well."

The sarcasm came out of his mouth as biting as the Scotch had gone down.

"Tell us about that," said Frances.

"Tell you that my father was a philanderer, a drug addict, gambler, and all round cad. Surely you've figured all of that out by now."

"Yes, we've come to learn about your father's indiscretions..."

"Indiscretions, ha!"

"Tell us about why you think he deserved to die?"

Garrett took a long last swig of his Scotch and then stood up and walked back towards the bar. He looked back at them.

"This is going to take a while."

He poured another thick three fingers of Scotch and he wasn't using his somewhat slender fingers as guides. He came back, walking with a swagger, holding his tumbler out in front of him as the golden liquid licked the sides of the glass up and down. He sat down and leaned back.

"My father would sleep with any woman who'd give him the chance. Looking back now, I realize this has been going on for years. More than that, this whole life I've lived is a lie."

"How so?"

"Because I'm practically destitute now because of him. Or rather, I now realize I've been destitute all along because of him. This life, this upper crust life that I thought I was born into has slowly been whittled away and now remains barely a stick upon which to hang my coattails."

"Can you not salvage the business now?" asked Florence.

Garrett took a sip of Scotch. It had started to loosen his tongue.

"That's what I thought. That's what Gerald and I thought when we first confronted him about it. But I've had a look at the records he's kept in his study. Forsyth Motor Manufacturing is not worth the buildings that house it. We're going to have to sell of the company and hope that will appease the creditors. If not, I'll be spending the rest of my life in debtor's prison."

"There haven't been debtor's prisons in this country for over fifty years," said Florence looking at him with worry stitched into her forehead.

Garrett leaned forward resting his elbows on his knees, his tumbler threatening to relinquish the Scotch upon the carpet. He shook his head.

"God, I was using it metaphorically. I'll be in court trying to extricate myself from all the debt. The last thumbscrew good old father left me with was to name me the heir to his business. Instead of that being a blessing, it's a bloody curse."

"We've heard rumors that your father was storing gold," said Frances. "Do you know if there was any truth to it?"

Garrett steadied his gaze on Lady Marmalade, the tumbler still weighing the decision about whether to rid itself of the golden liquid.

"Yes, I heard about it. Mother dearest spilled the beans at dinner one night. Though I don't know if it's true. And if it's true I haven't found evidence to back it up. That's what I was looking for in the greenhouse. But there's nothing there."

"Why on earth would there be gold in a greenhouse?"

Garrett hung his head and shrugged his shoulders. Then he sat upright and stared out into the hallway.

"What the hell do you want?"

Eighteen

Meredith walked into the living room and sat down on the second couch which was at right angles to the couch that held a now stiffened Garrett. Frances and Florence looked at the two of them as they stared at each other.

"Could you be a dear, Garrett, and fetch me a drink?"

"Certainly not, haven't you bloody well done enough?"

"Now, now, Garrett, I'm only here to commiserate in shared pain."

Meredith got up and walked over to the bar and mixed herself a Tom Collins in the proper glass. She looked back and offered one to Frances and Florence. The grandfather clock off to the side looked sternly down at the bar disapprovingly. It was not quite eleven. The hands on the clock looking like a squinting eye. Frances and Florence declined.

Meredith came back with her cloudy drink in the tall round glass, the cherry was missing, but that was hardly the point of the drink. She took a long sip.

"That's exactly what I needed."

"I'm here to try and help bring justice to these terrible murders," said Frances, trying to feel the temperature of the room.

Meredith winced a smile.

"Father got what he deserved, like I said," said Garrett.

Meredith looked over at him and knitted her eyebrows together.

"Your father was a good man, better than you I might add. At least he worked for a living."

"Oh, I see, that's what we call it now. Working for a living. When you ruin a productive business handed to you by your father and spend the money on whoring, opium and horses, that's called working for a living is it?"

Garrett threw his head back and laughed. It sounded more like the cackle of a jackal. He took a sip from his tumbler and then turned back towards Meredith.

"I suppose so long as you got your way he was a good man. I'll have you know he wasn't just stepping out on my mother with you, but with a whole bunch of women. He was even going off to Argentina with one apparently, and unless your name's Rachel, it wasn't with you."

Garrett reached into his pocket and took out a couple of pieces of paper. He opened the one and read it. Then he crumpled it up and threw it at Meredith.

"I don't believe it for a minute," she said.

"Then why don't you take a read for yourself?"

Meredith leaned over and picked up the crumpled up ball in front of her with her free left hand. She opened it up and straightened it out on her leg. Frances watched her eyes zig zag as she read the contents.

"I didn't believe it," she said under her breath.

"I beg your pardon?" asked Frances.

Meredith looked up at Frances and shook her head.

"I mean, I don't believe it. Not a word."

"Stupid cow," said Garrett, spitting out the words, "no wonder he chose you. You're so damn gullible. Probably like the rest of them."

"Please, can we keep it civil and polite at least. I understand the two of you didn't care much for each other, but for the sake of trying to find justice, can we not at least pretend?" asked Frances.

Garrett looked away and stared into his drink. It was already halfway gone and he was already thinking about his third. Meredith sipped her Tom Collins and reached up into her sleeve for a tissue which she used to dab at her wet eyes.

"Where were you on Tuesday, Garrett, between two and four thirty?" asked Frances.

"I already told you that when the police were here. I went out to the pub to have a drink with some mates."

Garrett didn't look at Frances as he spoke. He stared into his drink and then took a sip.

"Why are you lying? What are you trying to protect?"

"I'm not lying," he said, again with his flittering eyes not looking directly at her.

"That's interesting, because we spoke to Finley just the other day?" said Florence.

"Finley who?" said Garrett starting to feel a little nervous and hot under the collar.

"Finley, the barman at the Wet Whistle."

"I didn't kill my mother!" he said emphatically.

"I know that," said Frances.

"Then why are you hounding me about where I was?"

He looked at Lady Marmalade, his bite had softened, the spirits had started soothing his temperament. Thankfully he was not a mean drunk from the look of things.

"Because I want to know why you're protecting her?"

Garrett looked at Frances quickly before breaking eye contact.

"I have no idea what you're talking about."

"You do, Garrett, and you're knotting yourself up in a tight bundle of lies that isn't going to help. Tell me where I can find Lottie. Lottie Daubney?" asked Frances.

Garrett took the last finger of Scotch in a big gulp and got up to pour himself a third.

"She's got nothing to do with it," he said from the bar.

Meredith looked from Garrett to Frances and then to Florence. The edge of her glass was balancing on her lip. She couldn't decide if she wanted a taste or she wanted to think about what had just happened. Her eyes searched the faces in her field of vision but the puzzle wasn't coming together.

"Who's this Lottie?" she finally asked.

Garrett finished pouring his third drink and walked back to the couch.

"Not who you might think. She's not one of his whores."

"Why don't you tell her," said Frances.

"Yes, tell me," said Meredith.

Garrett sat down and stared at his drink, not quite sure what to say so it seemed.

"Lottie is..." said Frances.

Garrett looked up at Lady Marmalade, a cross look all about his face.

"I'll tell her," he said, and his words were harsh and biting.

"Lottie happens to be my half sister."

He looked at Meredith and sat back into the couch, crossed his legs over each other and did the same with his arms, leaving the right one holding the drink in front of the left so he could sip it at will.

"I see," said Meredith.

"Where is she, Garrett?" asked Frances.

"I shan't tell, I think it's best for everyone if we leave her out of this."

"I can get that information from the police you know, Garrett," said Frances.

"Then that's where you'll have to get it," he said. "Listen, Lady Frances, Lottie has nothing to do with this I swear it."

He leaned in saying that as if to give emphasis or reassurance to his words.

"That is not something I'm fully convinced of yet," and then Lady Marmalade looked over at Meredith who was watching her and Garrett. "Where were you, Meredith, last night?"

Meredith brought her drink down to rest in her lap and looked into it, as if the answers could be fished out of it like the cherry that should've been in the Tom Collins.

"I was here last night," she said looking up at Frances.

"I meant before the police arrived."

"Good God, Frances, are you spying on us now?"

"I've earned my title honestly, Meredith, I'd appreciate it if you used it."

Meredith didn't say anything. She and Frances stared at each other for some time until Meredith broke the gaze.

"I was out," she said into her drink, not wanting to use Lady Marmalade's title.

"I see," said Frances, "and I suppose that Jack's car happened to drive here by itself sometime last night?"

Meredith didn't look at Lady Marmalade, she swirled her drink instead, perhaps hoping to create a vortex that might suck her in.

"The police will be here any minute and I'm going to suggest that they search both the cars. Imagine what they might find."

"Better not," said Garrett.

Meredith got up to leave.

"I suggest you stay right where you are if it's all the same."

Meredith hesitated and then sat back down. Garrett shifted uncomfortably.

"Do you know how Jack died?"

Frances looked from Garrett to Meredith and back again. Neither of them would meet her gaze.

"He was shot, so I've been informed."

"Yes, we bloody well know that. James informed us to," said Garrett.

"And I'm sure the police will be able to tell me if Jack had any pistols." Frances paused for emphasis. "And I bet they'll know if you have any pistols registered to you Garrett."

Frances looked at him, but he just stared into his drink.

"This is silly, of course Jack had a pistol," said Meredith. "When you live out here and you've been through the Great War, one wants to take the necessary precautions to protect oneself. That's not a crime you know."

Frances looked at Meredith and smiled.

"That wasn't so hard was it? How do you know Jack had a pistol?"

"He showed it to me for heaven's sake."

"And like father like son, Garrett?" asked Frances.

Garrett finally looked up and took a drink. He shrugged his shoulders.

"So I do, and what of it?"

"Nothing," said Frances, "but I find it odd, don't you, that Jack was in Liverpool and shot by a gun, we don't know yet what kind, and the two of you don't want to answer a simple question."

"It's been a long, trying night, Lady Frances," said Meredith, "you can't know what it's like, we're just tired is all."

"I can see that," said Frances. "Tired because I think the two of you know more than you're letting on. I'd even suspect you were in Liverpool too, the both of you."

Frances looked at them carefully, Garrett's eyes danced around the room and he took a good swallow of Scotch. Meredith blinked her eyes several times even though it wasn't all that dry in the living room.

"Good heavens, that's the silliest thing I ever heard," said Meredith, uttering a false laugh and looking at Garrett, but he wouldn't return her look.

"The truth will come out eventually," said Lady Marmalade. "Someone will be willing to talk. And if not the two of you then I suspect someone else."

"Why don't you just go back to London and leave it to the police to figure it out?" said Garrett with only half the threatening tone he had hoped to muster.

"Because, Garrett, you're very nice and dare I say, almost saintly, mother brought me into her home as a stranger and fed me and treated me well. The least I can do is try and bring some justice to her unfortunate end."

"And I'm grateful for that, my mother deserved more, but I'm sure the police will have a handle on it."

"She's also doing it as a favor to me," said Florence. "And frankly, I want to get at the truth now that I've met you two. You should both be ashamed of yourselves. You," she said looking at Meredith, "for carrying on with a married man, and you," looking at Garrett, "for not offering as much help to Lady Marmalade as you can and should."

They heard James walk towards the front door, his steps echoing back more quietly with each step. There had been a knock. An impatient and belligerent knock if you could call it that. They all sat on the edges of their seats as James opened the door and welcomed the guests into the home. They heard the voices and then several pairs of shoes echoing down the hallways, coming towards them, louder and louder like a judge's gavel.

Nineteen

It didn't take long for James to enter the living room, bringing with him two policemen.

"Lady Marmalade, Inspector Gibbard is here."

James bowed.

"If I might offer tea?" asked James.

And as if hearing him, the grandfather clock struck eleven. Lady Marmalade nodded and James bowed again.

"So now you've taken to ordering my butler around?" asked Garrett.

"Well, my dear Garrett, he asked and I responded. Are you likely to be keeping him around? He's owed wages in arrears. Half of what he should be paid to this point."

Garrett ignored Lady Marmalade and looked over at Inspector Gibbard. It didn't look like he had changed his suit, yet it was in better shape for it than Garrett's.

"Good morning, inspector," said Garrett.

Inspector Gibbard nodded.

"I'm glad to find the two of you here. I need to ask you some questions. You'll remember Constable Warren Leavens."

The four of them nodded at the constable as he stood to the side of the door, his hands clasped behind him and his posture as stiff as a rod. It appeared, though you had to look carefully, that he might have nodded back. Inspector Gibbard walked towards the four of them seated almost in a square. He came up to the left side of Lady Marmalade, standing between Meredith and Frances and opposite Garrett.

"I imagine you know why I'm here."

Nobody said anything, Garrett swirled his drink, sitting back in the couch with his left arm flung over the back of it. Meredith kept her Tom Collins close to her mouth, sipping it now and then. Florence had adjusted herself to look at Inspector Gibbard more easily. Frances found craning her neck to see him too much effort and she was more interested in keeping her eyes on Garrett and Meredith.

"Last night, at around two a.m., so the coroner informs me, Jack Forsyth was shot once in the chest at Albert Dock in Liverpool. He died at the scene."

Inspector Gibbard looked around and his eyes finally fell on Frances.

"Do you have a man looking in the cars parked outside, Inspector?" asked Frances.

"We do."

"Good, because I think these two know more about it than they're letting on."

Gibbard looked at both Meredith and Garrett, steadying his gaze on each one in turn.

"Do you have anything to say?" asked Gibbard.

Meredith took a dainty sip of her drink, Garrett stared at his, swirling it around seeing how high up the rim he could get the golden liquid.

"I was there," said Meredith, though it was more like a whisper. Garrett looked up at her and frowned ever so slightly. She didn't look at him.

"I beg your pardon madam?" said Gibbard.

"I said, Inspector, that I was there."

Her voice carried better this time and everyone could hear her. Lady Marmalade smiled just at the corners of her mouth. Now they were getting somewhere. At least Meredith could tell the truth when it suited her.

"You were where, Ms. Church?" asked Gibbard.

"I was with Jack last night in Liverpool."

"I see, go on."

"Well, that's all there is to it, I was there."

"Ms. Church, if you don't speak with me plainly now, I can take you down to the station where we can have all day to talk about it. Who shot Jack?"

Inspector Gibbard's voice was loud and authoritarian, cutting through the room as cleanly as the clock's chimes. Meredith looked up at Garrett and he squinted at her as if to tell her something, but he didn't open his mouth.

"We have to say something, Garrett," she said.

"You bloody well keep me out of this!" he yelled.

"I believe they were both there, Inspector," said Frances.

Gibbard nodded and stared at Garrett and then at Meredith, giving them both, in turn, his stony glare.

"Get on with it, Ms. Church."

"I was with Jack, we left here just before one. You have to understand, Inspector, he was in with the wrong sort, this was going to be his last trip to the docks."

"And what happened?"

Meredith's hand was shaking slightly so she flattened it against her thigh and took a long sip from Tom Collins. She looked up at Gibbard nervously.

"We arrived at the docks at about twenty to two. He parked the car out of the way and told me to wait for him in the car. This was all supposed to be so easy, he was just going to pick up a few things from a ship and then we were supposed to leave. Instead..."

Meredith took her tissue and dabbed at her eyes again.

"What happened, Ms. Church?" asked Gibbard, he was clearly becoming impatient.

She looked at him and blinked her eyes a couple of times then dabbed them one last time. She looked over at Garrett.

"I'm sorry," she said.

"Don't!"

Meredith looked up at the Inspector, her eyes still welling with tears.

"Before Jack could get to the ship he was stopped by..."

She looked over at Garrett, he was shaking his head and his face was a scowl. She looked over at Gibbard and he nodded for her to continue.

"Garrett was there with some woman, he stopped Jack and they had an argument."

"How do you know they were arguing, could you hear them?" asked Gibbard.

Meredith shook her head.

"No, but you could tell they were arguing. They were gesticulating back and forth, I could see by the expressions on their faces that they were shouting at each other. At one point Jack pushed Garrett to get him out of the way and I saw Garrett pull out a gun and he pointed it at Jack..."

"This is preposterous, I'm not going to sit here and listen to these slanderous accusations," said Garrett as he started to get up from the couch.

"Constable," said Gibbard, and Constable Leavens stepped forward and Garrett thought better of it and sat back down with a sigh.

"Inspector, please, this woman is a backstabbing cow who cheated on my mother with my own bloody father. You can't take a word she says seriously."

Gibbard put up his hand to stop Garrett.

"Let her finish."

Then he looked over at Meredith and nodded at her. Meredith took the last sip from her Tom Collins with a trembling hand.

"And then I heard a loud bang and Jack fell to the ground. Garrett and this woman he was with just stared at him lying there for a minute, the gun still pointing at where Jack had stood. Then they ran off and I haven't seen him until this morning."

"And I take it you have a gun, Mr. Forsyth?" asked Gibbard, looking at him sternly.

"Inspector," said Garrett, trying to put on a brave face with a smile that kept slipping off like a bad toupee. Garrett held out both hands towards the inspector, palms up, the tumbler in his right. "I have a Webley, but you must believe me, I didn't kill my father. I didn't shoot him."

"We'll see about that. Ms. Church, did you see anyone else in the vicinity when Jack was shot?" asked Gibbard.

Meredith shook her head.

"No, I didn't..." she paused and then looked off to the side. "Actually, Inspector, now that you ask there was someone else."

"Who?"

"I could have sworn it was Gerald, Jack's brother. I thought I saw him running from the dock after I heard Garrett shoot Jack. And then I distinctly remember him driving off in his car shortly after."

"You're sure?"

"Well, I'm sure it was his car. I only saw him running away from behind some containers at the dock. It certainly looked like him, but I can't be certain. It was definitely his car though, that drove off."

"Inspector," said Lady Marmalade. "If I may?"

Gibbard looked over at her and nodded.

"How did you know that your father was going to the docks, Garrett?"

"Well, my mother told me last week. She had overheard him on the telephone, complaining to whomever was on the other end and telling them that this would be his last. He wrote the address and time on the pad of paper by the phone and my mother saw it through the indentation left on the sheet beneath."

"Did you tell anyone else about it?"

"Well, I spoke with my uncle Gerald about it. I told him I was going to confront my father about this nonsense as a last ditch attempt to get him to straighten out. I swear, Lady Frances, I didn't shoot him."

"But, dear boy, you were confronting him with a gun. How do you explain that?" asked Frances.

Garrett hung his head low, his elbows resting on his knees, and he shook his head slowly and sadly, like a tired old dog.

"I know," he said. "It looks bad. But you see, my father wouldn't listen to me. He thought I was lazy and no good. I took my gun, and I know it was stupid now, but I took it just to try and scare some sense into him and get him to listen to me."

"You need to be honest and forthright, Garrett," said Frances, "if you sincerely want my help. Why were you confronting your father with a young woman by your side, your half-sister, Lottie, I'm assuming."

Meredith took the opportunity with all eyes off her to get up and mix herself another Tom Collins. It was the only man in the room with whom she felt comfortable. Constable Leavens kept a careful watch on her until she came back down and took her seat.

"Yes, you're right. I was with Lottie, I also wanted to confront him about his daughter. I didn't tell Gerald about that part, but I really wanted him to take responsibility. We were going to try and find out where this gold was. I wanted to give it to Lottie, she hasn't had an easy life you know. And he owed her. He owed her!"

"What's this gold all about?" asked Gibbard.

"I believe that Meredith might have the answer to that, Inspector," said Frances.

Inspector Gibbard looked over at her. At the far end of the living room, another constable, and if Lady Marmalade remembered correctly this was Constable Dobson, came in through the French Doors.

"I'm waiting," said Gibbard.

Meredith looked up at him and then over at Lady Marmalade, avoiding looking at Garrett at all.

"Jack was involved with the wrong sort. He was supposed to pick up a couple of young women and some gold, he said, which he had to take to Blackpool on Friday."

"And who was he going to deliver these women and gold too?"

"He didn't say," said Meredith.

"A man by the name of Lee Chan," said Lady Marmalade. "He owns a restaurant in Blackpool called The Flying Chan. He deals in prostitutes, opium and gambling. Mr. Forsyth owed a substantial amount of money to him."

Gibbard looked over at Lady Marmalade and raised his eyebrow.

"I see, and how do you know all of this?"

"I've made inquiries, Inspector, and Enoch Habbit mentioned some of this to me."

"And you believe him?"

"I do," said Frances, turning to look at Meredith. "What did he say about the gold, dear?"

"Not much, other than he was just going to pick up a few coins of it. He said they were extremely valuable."

Frances nodded her head. Gibbard beckoned over the constable. The constable came over. In his left hand he was holding two Webley revolvers, identical.

"I found one in each of the cars," he said to Gibbard.

"Good, go and put them away as evidence."

"It's not looking good for you, Mr. Forsyth," said Gibbard. "But I'd like to know, Ms. Church, why you left a dying man in the docks and drove all the way back here without alerting authorities?"

Meredith took a long drink from Tom Collins, her hand still trembled.

"I was scared, Inspector. When Jack got shot I was in shock. I couldn't believe what I had just seen. Then I saw Garrett and that woman run off and Gerald too. I got out of the car and grabbed Jack's gun which he had left in the glove compartment with me. I went up to him, but he was already dead. I heard some men coming to see what was going on. They looked rough, I don't know, I got back in the car and drove here. I've never seen anything like this, Inspector, you have to believe me I was scared out of my wits."

"So you're saying to me, Ms. Church, that we won't find Jack's gun to have been fired?"

"Yes, Inspector, I didn't shoot him. He was shot in the front, I was watching him from behind."

"You won't find my gun has been shot either, Inspector. I'm telling you, someone else was there, and I felt the bullet whizz past my right side," said Garrett.

"Convenient," said Gibbard. "And this woman, Lottie, was she the one with you?"

Garrett nodded his head sadly.

"And I suppose she can corroborate what you're telling."

"Yes, she will. Honestly, she will."

"Something we need to do, Inspector," said Lady Marmalade, "is to speak with Gerald Forsyth."

"Thank you, Lady Marmalade," said Gibbard sarcastically, looking down at her as she sat next to him. "But I'm quite aware of how to do my job."

"Yes, Inspector, I have no doubt you imagine yourself quite competent. But what you don't know is that Gerald had recently taken out a substantial life insurance policy on Jack."

"And what do you consider substantial?"

"One hundred thousand pounds."

"Really?"

Inspector Gibbard stopped for a moment and looked at Frances for a long while. She stopped looking up at him. Her hair was in brunette curls. Her scarf was now around her neck. After some time thinking about what she had just said, he looked over at Garrett.

"Did you know about this?"

"No, Inspector, I did not know about this."

He turned back to look at Lady Marmalade.

"And how do you know about this?"

Frances looked up at him and smiled simply.

"You ask the right questions of the right people and you get the answers you're seeking."

Gibbard turned away from her.

"I'll look into this further and I plan on speaking with Gerald Forsyth at the first opportunity. But right now I'm quite satisfied with the evidence. Garrett Forsyth, you'll come with us. You're under arrest for the murder of your father Jack Forsyth."

Garrett looked up at the inspector, his eyes big as eggs.

"But I didn't do it, you've got to be joking."

"I'm quite serious, Mr. Forsyth. Don't make this harder for yourself than it has to be. Constable."

Constable Leavens stepped forward. Garrett stood up as stiff as a pole and drank the last of his Scotch. He handed the empty tumbler to Florence who took it reluctantly. He turned to Lady Marmalade.

"Please, you must speak with Lottie, she knows who did it, I'm sure she does. I swear to you, I'm innocent."

He started to walk out with the constable right behind him.

"What's her address?" asked Frances.

"Twenty-one King Street," he said as he left the living room. Inspector Gibbard started out behind them.

"Inspector," said Frances, "if you don't mind."

He stopped and turned around, raising an eyebrow at Lady Marmalade. He wasn't the happiest to be entertaining her inquiries.

"Has the coroner determined what kind of gun was used to kill Mr. Forsyth."

"He has, it was a Webley revolver just like the two we found in Garrett's and Jack's car."

"And from what I understand, that's quite a common revolver in England is it not?"

"Yes, I'd say it was."

You could tell Gibbard was getting impatient.

"What are you after, Lady Marmalade?"

His voice was testy and his tone sharp as if she'd just given him a lemon to suck on.

"If it wouldn't be too much trouble, I'd be most grateful if you'd find out if Gerald Forsyth and Dr. Luther Garnet own any revolvers of the same kind."

Inspector Gibbard sighed and rolled his eyes.

"If you insist."

"I do, Inspector, yes I do."

"Very well, but the case is as good as closed. Everybody knows Garrett held no love for his father. He's as guilty as the Cheshire cat's grin."

"If you say so, Inspector."

"I do."

He turned and walked out after his constable and Garrett. Though he left with shoulders slumping more than usual. Lady Marmalade had a way of weighing him down with fool's errands. Or so he thought.

Agnus came in carrying a tray of scones, whipped cream, strawberries and tea. She lay it down in front of Lady Marmalade and Frances. Meredith moved over to the couch where Garrett had just sat. It was still warm from his body.

"Sorry it's late, my Lady. I didn't want to interrupt the inspector."

"Not at all. Thank you for bringing it."

Agnus offered a small curtsey and turned to walk out again.

"Agnus," said Frances.

Agnus stopped and turned around to look at Lady Marmalade.

"Yes, my Lady."

Frances looked up at her and smiled.

"Please let James know that I'll be making sure you and he are both paid your wages owing."

"Thank you, my Lady, but that's not necessary. It's not your concern."

"I know Agnus, but you should be paid for the work you've done."

Agnus curtsied again and offered her thanks. She also offered Lady Marmalade one of the biggest smiles Frances had seen in quite some time during these trying events. And she walked out with what might even have been a skip in her step.

Not wanting to be rude. Lady Marmalade and Florence sat for another thirty minutes drinking tea and eating scones. When the clock struck noon, they excused themselves, leaving Meredith to her ghosts and Frances and Florence to their important work.

"We must waste no time, my dear Flo, in getting to Southport. That must be our first order of business," said Frances as she and Florence walked down the driveway towards Florence's home.

Twenty

Southport might be south of the Lake District, but the journey there and the small sleepy town itself still offer some of the best scenery in England. At least that's how Lady Marmalade thought of it. But then old Blighty had always held a wonder and beauty to her that she had not seen bettered anywhere else in her wide travels.

And as they headed towards Southport in Florence's red Alvis Speed 25. On either side of the engine were two spare wheels in red covers, their silver spokes blinking like jewels in the sun. The roof was down and Frances had her scarf round her neck. It wasn't warm, but now that the sun had burned through the veil of gray clouds Frances was warm enough with the exhilaration of the wind through her hair.

The two of them grinning in the car like a couple of school girls as Florence drove, edging the Alvis up to sixty miles an hour on the thin English country roads. Traffic was light and the car was low to the ground and the green and brown countryside blurred past like wet smeared paint.

"You know," said Florence, yelling above the whistling wind, "they say this car can get up to one hundred miles an hour. Though I've never had the courage to push it past sixty five. Do you want to give it a go?"

Frances looked over at her friend and grinned, nodding.

"Why not, we're on a straight road without any traffic. But don't you dare tell Eric."

Florence laughed.

"Not a word."

She dropped the Alvis into third gear and the car gave a throaty roar as it leapt to life like a sleek leopard. She was soon at a little over seventy miles an hour with the car starting to get angry under the third gear. She changed to fourth and watched the needle edge up slowly but surely. It wasn't long before she was seventy five and then eighty.

Florence's knuckles were white on the steering wheel and Frances' eyes were streaming from the wind. Frances was also holding onto the top of the door for dear life with her left hand.

As they got to ninety, Florence started to get worried. She eased off the accelerator and let the Alvis come steadily back down to fifty.

"Almost," she said.

"You had me terrified. I swear I think my heart is in my throat. Absolutely exhilarating. This is such a wonderful car, Florence, I must have Eric get me one."

"Nonsense, you're not as much as a daredevil as I am."

"True, but it was fun."

"I lost my nerve at ninety," said Florence, looking over at Frances as tears started drying down her cheeks.

Frances reached into her handbag and took out two tissues. She offered one to Florence and they both dabbed their eyes dry. Although there were no speed restrictions on these roads leading into Southport, Florence had enough of high speed and the remainder of the journey they took at the relatively leisurely speed of fifty miles per hour.

It was more relaxing at that speed, and Frances could enjoy her English scenery and the rolling hills and greenery of these fair isles. As they got closer to Southport the sun was bobbing and weaving in and out of the clouds like Joe Louis. It had not yet won its bout for the day. Southport was a mix of sun and clouds and you could feel the difference in temperature as soon as the sun disappeared behind a bruising cloud.

King Street wasn't far from the coast, but it wasn't considered a desirable part of Southport for holidayers. It was a stretch of street that held a mix of business with heaping red bricked flats on top of them. Florence found a place to park just outside along the street. It was a quiet day on King Street.

The holidayers hadn't arrived yet, it was too early, and the residents were mostly at work. Frances and Florence got out of the car and inhaled the fresh salty Irish Sea air. Then they walked across the street to the main entrance. Inside the building they found number twenty-one with the name Lottie Daubney on it.

"I hope she's in, Flo, I hadn't considered that before we left."

"Well, it is Good Friday tomorrow, she might have taken extended leave from work."

The two of them climbed the flight of steps to the first floor. The building was clean and well kept. Though the hallways were dim and the carpet on them wearing thin in places. They found number twenty-one. It was a white door, like all the others.

"Here goes something, I hope," said Frances as she knocked politely on the door three times.

"What do you expect she's like?" asked Florence.

"Not a clue. I wouldn't have expected Garrett to have been born of Ginnie and Jack. Where he got his looks from I have no idea."

Florence chuckled and nodded in agreement.

"Who is it?" came the polite and upbeat voice from behind the door.

"It's Frances Marmalade and Florence Hudnall, we're here as friends of Garrett Forsyth."

"Just a minute, please," said the young female voice on the other end.

"Why didn't you use your title?" whispered Florence.

Lady Marmalade shrugged.

"You've seen this place, these are good honest, working people and I don't want to put on any airs and put the poor dear out. She's probably been through a lot the last day or so."

The door opened and behind it stood a tall young woman in her early twenties. She stood eye to eye with Florence. She had long blonde hair, not natural, that fell just below her shoulders in slow heavy curls. She was as pretty as her half-brother Garrett was handsome. She had a full mouth painted with red lipstick and bright blue eyes. She was well manicured and had taken up the recent fashionable habit of plucking her eyebrows.

"Is everything alright with Garrett?" she asked, not quite letting them in right away.

"Well, that's what we'd like to talk to you about, dear, if you don't mind," said Frances.

Lottie looked down at Frances absentmindedly for a moment.

"Oh yes, sorry, please come in."

Her voice had class to it, but every so often it cracked and the slightest hint of her Cockney would come through which she quickly shoved back down her throat. Frances and Florence walked in and waited in the hallway as she closed the door behind them.

"Please come this way," said Lottie as she led them into the living room which was one big room that also held a small dining room table at one end and a galley kitchen just off of it.

Frances and Florence sat down in two seater couch covered at the back with a crocheted blanket. Lottie sat down opposite them in a well worn cushioned chair with worn wooden armrests.

"That blanket was from my grandmother," said Lottie pointing to the blanket that Frances and Florence were sitting against.

"It's lovely, dear," said Frances. "Just to be certain, you are Lottie Daubney aren't you?"

Lottie got up from her chair and came over to them and offered them each a delicate hand which they shook. Her hand was small and slender for her height and seemed as fragile as a bird and as warm.

"Silly me, when you said you were friend's of Garrett's I quite forgot my manners. Yes, I am Lottie Daubney."

"Nice to meet you," said Frances, "I'm Frances Marmalade and this is my friend Florence Hudnall."

"Marmalade like the jam we put on our toast?" said Lottie, a little awkwardly.

"One and the same," said Frances. "Florence and I just made a batch of marmalade. We should have brought one, perhaps next time."

Lottie hadn't sat down again. She was wearing a white dress that fell below her knees, red high-heeled shoes the color of her lipstick and a red and white polka dot blouse.

"I should offer you some tea, would you like some?"

"That would be lovely, dear," said Florence. Frances nodded in agreement.

"Then if you'll excuse me, I'll just be a minute. I hope you don't mind, I don't mean to be rude, but I hardly ever have visitors."

She stepped away into the galley kitchen and Lady Marmalade and Florence sat quietly alone to their thoughts. The living room, like much of the flat that Frances had been able to see was sparse. The carpet was a firm weave and a deep red. The walls were white and there were two prints on them. The whole theme was trying, unsuccessfully, to look modern and Art Deco.

On the dark wooden table that stood stolidly like a sentinel next to the chair Lottie had recently sat in, was a wireless and an ashtray. On the lower wooden table in front of the couch where Frances and Florence sat was a single glass ashtray, the twin to the one next to the wireless, and a small rectangular crocheted cloth that covered about half of its face.

It didn't take Lottie long to bring out a painted white wooden tray that held a teapot, small milk jug, a bowl of sugar cubes, a plate with three lemon wedges and three teacups. The teacups held an assortment of blue, pink and yellow flowers on both the cup and saucer. Lottie placed the tray on the table in front of Frances and Florence.

"I don't know how you like your tea so I brought out everything."

She smiled broadly at Frances and Frances couldn't help but feel some compassion for the young woman.

"Should I make some sandwiches?" Lottie asked, looking at both Frances and Florence.

"No thank you, dear, I think we're quite alright."

Lottie nodded her head and her wavy hair, heavy with bouncing curls towards the end swayed slightly. She went and sat down.

"We should probably let the tea steep a minute or two more," she said.

"Good idea," said Frances.

Lottie looked a little nervous. She fiddled with her fingers in her lap and looked up at Frances and smiled a smile as weak at the tea might have been to that point.

"Is Garrett okay?" she asked at last.

"No, I'm afraid he isn't, my dear, and that's why we've come to speak with you."

"What's happened?"

"Well, you might well know what's happened, Lottie, and it's a very serious matter," said Frances.

Lottie looked down at her hands and wrung them white, as if she could wring out the memories from last night.

"Oh bother," she said. "Garrett had nothing to do with it."

"I'd like to believe so, but the police have arrested him and I'm trying to help find out what his actual role was."

Lottie looked up at Frances and stared at her for a while, then feeling self conscious she let her eyes fall onto the ceramic teapot.

"Am I in trouble?" she asked.

"Garrett doesn't think so."

Lottie looked back up at Frances and tried on a brave smile, though it wasn't as sticky as she might have liked. It kept slipping off and she had to put it back on a couple more times before it stuck.

"I think I know you," she said. "Weren't you in the papers a while back for having solved that horrible murder of Lady Bromson?"

Lady Marmalade smiled and nodded her head just a bit.

"Yes, I suppose that was me."

"It's such a pleasure to meet you, my Lady, I don't know what to say. Do I need to curtsey? Let me get some biscuits."

Frances put her hand up.

"That's quite alright, my dear, please just call me Frances and let's do away with the pomp and ceremony."

Lottie was excited now. She leaned in on the edge of her seat.

"I've never met a celebrity before. Nor royalty, nor a real detective."

Lottie was smiling broadly, perhaps even naively under the circumstances that she found herself in.

"Not royalty, dear, I'm not a member of the royal family. Nobility would be the appropriate term. And if you were curious about formality I'd be called The Most Honorable The Marchioness of Sandown." Lady Marmalade chuckled. "It's all quite silly really, and so I usually don't bother with that formal title and prefer Lady Marmalade to The Lady Marmalade, as if there could even be others."

Frances smiled, trying to ease the awkwardness she was feeling. Lottie was riveted. "But I'd still much rather you call me Frances."

"That is quite a mouthful, my Lady...I mean Frances. I've never met a Marchioness before. Sounds important."

Florence was sitting quietly next to Frances, quite bemused by it all.

"Yes, but that's not why we're here, Lottie. We need to hear about last night and what happened. You do want to help Garrett, don't you?"

"Yes, most definitely, he's been very good to me."

"Good, then let's start with tea," said Frances reaching for the teapot. Lottie shot up out of her chair like a sprinter might from her blocks.

"Please, Frances, that sounds strange to call you by your first name," said Lottie self-consciously, "let me pour the tea."

Lottie took the teapot and poured it into the three teacups without spilling a drop of the floral scented rusty colored tea. Frances took a wedge of lemon and squeezed the juice into her tea with her fingers and spoon. A small pip fell in. Frances looked at it for a moment and fished it out onto the saucer.

"Sorry about that, I suppose I should've taken the pips out first," said Lottie.

Lottie and Florence poured cream and two sugar cubes into each of their teacups and stirred them to the color of salmon.

"When did you know you were related to Garrett?" asked France, coming quickly out of the gates.

Lottie sipped her tea and then looked up at Lady Marmalade.

"It was when I started making inquiries about who my father was."

"And when was that?"

"I only started to look into about six months ago I think it was."

"And how long had you known that your father was actually Jack Forsyth?"

Lottie looked off to her right and out the window. You might have imagined her looking out and across the beach to the expansive blue of the Irish Sea. But you'd be wrong. Lottie didn't live in a flat like that. All the flat looked out onto was a similar complex across the road.

Lottie wasn't from money. She had a rich father, or she had once had a rich father who had, in the last several years completely ruined his company and everyone along with it. Lottie looked back and looked at Frances, though her stare was vacant, lost in the mists of time.

"I found out not long ago, when I made inquiries regarding my birth certificate. You see, my mother passed when I was born. It was a hard labor on her and I was a big baby. It took me a long time to forgive myself for my mother's death."

Lottie paused then and blinked her eyes. They were wet and she dabbed at her left eye with a finger, trying to cauterize the pain. Frances reached into her purse and pulled out another tissue. She offered it to Lottie. Lottie took it with a pained smile.

"Ahh, I wish I'd known my mother better. She was a good hard working woman if a little naive. You see, she thought that Jack was a good man, an upstanding man who would take care of his responsibilities. But alas, she learned the hard way that he was not such a man at all."

Lottie dabbed at her eyes some more with the tissue. She folded it up and tucked it into her right hand. She took her teacup and sipped more tea.

"You see, Frances, my birth certificate always said that the father was unknown. I suppose, in those days, that was the best a woman could manage. But after I lost her and after all the foster parents and orphanages I'd been through I wanted a real family."

Lottie paused and looked over at Lady Marmalade. She smiled and her blue eyes were bright with pain, sadness and lost dreams.

"I understand, my dear," said Frances.

"I eventually claimed some personal items from the government. It wasn't a lot really, a box of assorted knick knacks of my mother's that had been in storage almost twenty years. The box contained some letters that my mother had written to a man named Jack Forsyth."

Frances nodded.

"What did those letters say?" asked Florence.

"They started off quite romantic, talking about undying love and their futures together, but the last couple were of quite a different tenor. My mother informed him that she'd become pregnant. You can hear the joy in her voice as she writes to him..."

Lottie took a moment and cleared her throat. She looked outside, through the window to steal her strength.

"He wrote back and said he'd found a doctor who would take care of it for her."

"It being the pregnancy?" asked Florence.

Lottie looked outside again and nodded. She bit her lower lip, took the tissue and dabbed at her eyes.

"Her last letter to him was pleading almost. She went on about how madly in love they were and how he'd promised he would marry her and they'd have a family. It was almost pathetic. His last letter was short and cruel. He told her he never loved her, never wanted to have a family with her and that she'd be better off if she ended the pregnancy."

"That must have been difficult to read," said Frances.

Lottie nodded and took a deep breath. Frances sipped her tea.

"It was. I lived with those letters, that last letter of his really, for a long time. I was angry and I was sad and I didn't know what to do about it. Finally I got the courage to write to him about six months ago."

"What happened?" asked Florence.

"What you might expect from a man like that."

Lottie looked into her teacup expecting she might be able to read the tea leaves for a brighter future, but the tea leaves had clung like desperate children to the teapot.

"He didn't write back at first, so I sent him a second letter and told him if I didn't hear from him I'd come and visit him. He responded then. His tone was mean and blunt. He wanted to know what I wanted."

"You hadn't told him that you were his daughter?" asked Florence.

"I had, but I think he meant what sort of money I wanted to go away. I told him I didn't want anything, that I just wanted to talk to him and understand why he'd been so cruel to my mother."

"He told me not to bother, nobody would believe that I was his daughter and I'd better watch my mouth and drop this whole 'silly' affair. That's what he called it. A 'silly affair'."

"But you didn't?" asked Frances.

"No and he didn't respond when I sent him my penultimate letter. So about a month ago I sent him another one telling him he better come and visit me or he'd be sorry."

"Did he respond to that?"

"No, I'm still waiting for a response, but I doubt I'll get one now, seeing as how dead he is."

Frances sipped her tea and looked at Lottie for a long while. Lottie met her gaze but then dropped it into her tea without making a splash.

"I've read the last letter you sent. You sound very determined, and also, what's the word," she looked at Florence for a moment.

"Greedy," said Florence.

"That's a little strong, but I got the impression you were trying to blackmail him."

Lottie shook her head.

"No, no, not at all. You have to understand, he wouldn't meet me, I just wanted to talk to him, I didn't want his money, but he wouldn't speak to me. He wouldn't write, I had to force it. I wasn't really going to tell his wife, and son."

"How did you know he had a family?" asked Florence.

"I investigated him before I sent my first letter. Anyway, he wouldn't talk to me, that's why I had to threaten him."

"This brings us to the crux of the matter, Lottie. If you weren't after his money, why were you with Garrett last night, when he killed his father, trying to find out where the gold was?"

Twenty One

Lottie looked up in shock and leaned towards Lady Marmalade.

"No! You've got it all wrong. Garrett didn't kill him. He was only trying to get his father to reason with him. To talk with him. The same problem I was having with Jack Forsyth, Garrett was having too. He was a belligerent and self absorbed man. It seemed the only way you could get his attention was through threats."

"We have a witness who saw Jack shoot his father," said Florence.

Lottie looked over at Florence and her face turned hard like stone.

"Let me guess, probably that mistress of his, Meredith, Meredith Church?"

Florence nodded.

"I figured as much. He would have brought her along to the pickup."

"Are you denying then, that Garrett shot his father?" asked Frances.

"I most certainly am," said Lottie.

"And are you denying that Garrett had a gun with him last night that he was pointing at his father?"

Lottie placed her teacup and saucer on the table next to her that held the wireless. She fiddled with the damp tissue in her hands.

"No, that's true. I told him it wasn't a good idea to bring a gun. It was too dangerous, I said. But he wouldn't hear of it. He said he wasn't going to use it but that it was the only way to get Jack to listen to us."

"I'd like to go back a bit if you don't mind, my dear. You admit you were at the docks last night. You admit that you and Garrett were there to talk to Jack and you admit that Garrett had a gun and pointed it at his father. Am I correct so far?"

Frances held her teacup to her lips and took a sip. In her left hand she held the saucer which still carried the lemon pip like a boil on its face. Lottie was looking at her tissue and fiddling with it still. She nodded.

"Yes," she mumbled, "that's correct."

"What you haven't told us, Lottie, is why were you meeting Jack, what were you hoping to talk to him about?"

Florence took the last sip of her tea and put cup and saucer back on the tray on the table. Lottie finally looked up at Frances.

"It was Garrett's idea," she said.

"Which brings up my other question. How did you and Garrett meet?"

"A few weeks ago he found the last letter I sent to Jack. He sought me out. He came down to Southport and found out where I lived. It's not hard, it's a small tight community here and I work at the Irish Air Hotel. He visited me and we spoke for the whole afternoon."

"About what sorts of things?"

"Mostly about Jack. At first, Garrett didn't believe me and he asked why I was making more trouble for him and his family. But then I showed him the letters and he believed me. He remembered his father taking a few trips down to London when he was just a boy. And that's where Jack and my mother, Maude, met. Garrett's several years older than me and he remembers his father coming back from these trips when he was around six or seven."

"I see, please go on."

"He confided in me that his father had practically ruined the company and that there was no money to be had. I told him I didn't want the money, I just wanted to understand why he left my mother so horribly."

"And what did Garrett say?"

"He thought about it for a moment, and then he decided that there was a way we could get Jack to pay. He told me he had heard about some gold that his father was supposedly stashing away and that he was coming to the docks to pick up some new gold. At least that was what Garrett suspected. I told him I wasn't interested in gold, but he said it would also be an opportunity to confront my father and get the answers I wanted."

"And that's what you had in mind?"

Lottie nodded.

"Yes, I just really, really wanted to understand who this horrible man was who treated my mother so poorly."

"And what about the gold?"

"Well, Garrett insisted that I should get half the gold. He didn't know how much was coming but he said it wouldn't be a lot but it was really valuable. It didn't make sense to me but he said they were American eagles that could fetch a high price. We only needed a few of them and our money problems would be over."

"How did he know about these coins?"

"He said he had seen his father having a conversation with his groundskeeper. The groundskeeper handed him a piece of paper and he heard his father say something like 'Chan wants the Eagles by Good Friday'. Then Garrett said he had remembered reading an article in the paper which said that a few years ago some American gold coins were stolen or lost. So he put two and two together. I guess."

"Did you see any of these gold coins?"

"No, it sounded a bit too fantastical to me, but Garrett was convinced. He was certain that it would be his chance to head out on his own and make a fresh start regardless of his father ruining the business."

"Did you have a chance to talk to Jack about any of this before he was shot?"

Lottie looked out the window again as a host of sparrows flew by, all smartly dressed in their brown suits.

"That was the first thing Garrett asked when we confronted Jack. Jack said he wasn't here to pick up gold, that the gold was back at the house, but he'd never find it and nor should he. He said they were dangerous people who wanted the gold and that Garrett shouldn't mess with them. Garrett said he didn't care, that Jack owed him and I for all the horrible things he'd done to his family over the years. Jack swore he was changing now, that this was his last pick up and that his debts would all be paid and he'd be making a new start. I didn't believe him, there was something about Jack, I think he was just saying all that to calm us down. Garrett didn't believe it either. That's when Garrett pulled out his gun and threatened his father. He said that he was serious, that he was going to take the gold and that he'd find it himself but if Jack wanted to live then he'd tell us where it was."

"Did he?"

"No. I think he was about to but then he got shot. His last words were 'the study'. Then he died, we got scared and ran off."

Frances tipped her cup to her mouth and took the last sip. She put the teacup back on the saucer and placed it on the tray next to Florence's.

"So, my dear, you weren't able to ask the questions you wanted?"

Lottie shook her head slowly and sadly.

"No."

"Did you see who shot Jack?"

Lottie looked up at Frances.

"Not exactly. I heard the shot first and then I was in shock for a moment as I realized that Jack had been shot. I looked over at Garrett and he was staring at his father who was now lying on the ground. I looked past Garrett and saw a man in a dark suit run off away from us, on our right. I caught a good glimpse of him under a lamp and I saw that he held a gun which looked similar to the one that Garrett was holding."

"Did you get a chance to look at his face?"

Lottie nodded.

"I did. Just as he was under a lamp at the docks he turned to look in my direction for some reason and I saw his face. He was jowly, had a bulldog sort of face...Actually, now that I think about it, he reminded me of Winston Churchill. He was older though and his hair was thin and gray. It's hard to say, now that I think about it, he might have been older, maybe a similar age. I only saw him briefly under the lamp. I couldn't be certain."

Frances looked at Florence and Florence nodded at her and raised her eyebrows. Lottie looked perplexed, she knitted her eyebrows.

"Do you think you know who did it?"

Frances nodded.

"What about Garrett's gun, are you absolutely certain he didn't shoot his father?" asked Frances.

"Yes," said Lottie, nodding, "I know for certain because I told him he was mad to take a gun to confront his father with. He said it wasn't even loaded. He showed me the..." Lottie made a circle with her finger to indicate the cylinder, "the circle thingy that holds the bullets and they were empty, you could see right through them."

"The chambers inside the cylinder were empty. Are you sure?"

"Yes, that's right, the cylinder didn't have any bullets in them. He showed me and I could see right through the...chambers?"

Frances nodded.

"Interesting, then the police will likely find that the revolver they took from Garrett is empty," Lady Marmalade said to Florence.

"Indeed," said Florence.

"Lottie, dear, did you see anyone else at the docks?" asked Frances.

"Yes, there was Meredith, I think, it must have been her in Jack's car waiting for him. As Garrett and I left I saw another man run off. I asked Garrett who that was when we got into the car. He said it was his uncle Gerald. I asked him why his uncle was here and he said he'd told his uncle that he was going to confront his father at the docks that night."

"Did he say why?"

"He said because he and his uncle were going to try and wrestle the company away from Jack and salvage it. Garrett thought it might have been too late already and that's why he wanted to get the gold as a backup plan."

"Did he mention anything about Gerald and Jack's relationship?"

"Not specifically but he thought Gerald was mad to be there. He said he was going to deal with it, but maybe Gerald didn't quite trust Garrett. I asked Garrett why Gerald would be crazy to be there and he said because he'd taken out life insurance on Jack. I asked how much and Garrett said one hundred thousand pounds."

"Are you sure it might not have been this other man, identified as Gerald, who shot Jack?" asked Frances.

"I'm pretty sure. He was going in the other direction to the other man I saw running away with the gun. I didn't see a gun on Gerald, and he was wearing a lighter suit, a gray suit I think it was. He also didn't look like the other man. I didn't get a good look at him, but he was wearing a bowler's hat and he seemed a bit smaller than the man who shot Jack."

"Thank you, Lottie, this is most helpful," said Frances.

"Lottie," said Florence. "Did Garrett see the man who you say shot Jack?"

Lottie looked over at Florence and shook her head. Her blonde curls shook ever so slowly and slightly as if they might have been cut from brass.

"No. I asked him. I said 'Garrett did you see that man who shot your father?' He shook his head and said no. I said I saw him, he looked right at me. Then we sped off out of there and Garrett brought me home and he slept on the couch that you're sitting on. He left shortly after eight this morning."

"Did you see the woman, who you think was Meredith, do anything before you left the area?" asked Frances.

"I saw her get out of the car, I think she was Meredith because that's the name Garrett used when we drove by. She crept up to Jack's body. She was quite upset you could tell. Her head was darting this way and that and she held a gun in her hand. A gun that looked exactly like Garrett's only you could tell she didn't know how to use it. It was sort of just hanging limply from her hand. She went up to Jack and kneeled over him. She put her hand on his cheek and then looked at his chest where he had been shot. She looked towards us as we drove by and brought her hand up to her mouth. That's the last I saw of her."

"Thank you, Lottie, for your honesty. Is there anything else that you might be able to offer that could be helpful?" asked Frances.

"You must believe me, Garrett didn't kill his father. I swear it. You will help him get out of jail won't you?"

"I believe we can, especially if the gun was empty, I'm sure the police will let him go right away. He might even be home by the time we get back to Puddle's End."

"I didn't want his money either. I would have taken it, that's true, if Garrett had managed to get the gold, but I wasn't seeking it. I just wanted to understand what kind of a man Jack Forsyth was. He wasn't a nice man, I can tell you that, but he didn't deserve this."

Lottie was earnest in her expression. It seemed to Frances that she really wanted to impress upon her that she wasn't that kind of a woman. The kind of woman who would take advantage of easy circumstances. Frances wasn't convinced. Not that Lottie seemed malevolent, but she didn't strike Frances as the type of young woman who would turn down an opportunity at some easy money.

"You do believe me, don't you? It wasn't about the money."

"That's not important now, dear. What's important is that you told the truth, and that will help both you and Garrett."

Lottie smiled a thin smile and looked over at her tea. It had become discolored, the cream from the milk settling a little on the top like badly painted whitewash. It was cold and she didn't feel like the rest of it.

"I'd really appreciate it if you could come out to Puddle's End tomorrow for noon. I'm gathering everyone at the Forsyth estate to identify the murderer of both Ginnie and Jack. Florence will pick you up from the station at noon."

Florence nodded. So did Lottie.

"If you recognize the man who shot Jack when you come over tomorrow, don't give it away unless I ask you," said Frances.

Lottie nodded.

"Is it the same person who killed them both?" asked Lottie, her eyes wide with anticipation.

"You'll find out tomorrow," said Frances smiling

Twenty Two

They were nearing Puddle's End. It was just after two thirty and the drive back in Florence's car had been slow and careful. Florence and Frances had mostly been held captive by their own thoughts.

Florence was on pins and needles to find out who the killer might have been. She still thought Jack might have killed his wife, but Frances had made a very convincing case that it was Meredith. Tomorrow would reveal all.

Frances still had a few unanswered questions that were bothering her. She really wanted to speak with Gerald and she also wanted to speak with Dr. Garnet. Those were the two men she hadn't had the chance to pepper with questions yet, and she wanted to know if they were involved. And if they were, then how?

She hadn't seen Gerald since that first night for dinner, but she had the impression that he was staying at the Forsyth residence for a few days. Lady Marmalade had the impression that he lived in Manchester close to the Forsyth Motor Manufacturing plant. That wasn't a long drive from Puddle's End, so he might have already left back for Manchester, though Frances hoped not.

She wanted to ask him about the insurance policy. That didn't seem like such a good idea, now that he had been identified as being at the docks. He didn't need the company anymore now that he had a hundred thousand pounds coming due.

That was a small fortune, at least for the Forsyths, or so Lady Marmalade would guess. It might not be enough for Gerald to retire on, but it would be more than enough for him to start over with. He'd have no money concerns again if he was careful with it.

And what about the study? Why did Jack utter those two last words? Could it have been a red herring to put his son off the trail of the gold, or could there actually be something to it? Lady Marmalade needed to find out what the study might hold exactly.

She was certain who had killed Ginnie and she was now quite certain who had killed Jack, though she wanted to button it down completely before she got them all together tomorrow afternoon with Inspector Gibbard's help.

"You want to go back to the Forsyth estate?" asked Florence, not taking her eyes off the road, her gloved hands both gripping the steering wheel firmly.

"I do, Flo. I want to take a look at the study. I want to know why 'the study' were Jack's last words."

Florence nodded. The roof of the car had been pulled over and buttoned down to the red frame. The clouds were ganging up on the sun and it couldn't blink out a moment's warmth before being tucked back in behind gray fluffy clouds. Because of that it was cooler and so the top had been pulled over and that made it quieter too.

"You know," said Florence, "I was wondering about that too. Do you think the gold might be in the study someplace secret?"

"I don't think so, Flo. It might be and perhaps we'll find out, but I think it has already been taken."

"Really? By whom?"

"I can't say for certain yet, but I plan to find out by tomorrow. Later, I need to make a call to Eric. I have a few questions to ask him. He's a whizz with financial matters and gold especially. I think he took a liking to it during the Second Boer War."

Frances smiled. She was glad he had made it home safe from that war. A war the British should never have fought in the first place. At least that was her opinion, as unpopular as it might be. Though not without merit. It was an ugly war, and the concentration camps and deaths of the many children seemed very un-British to her.

"I don't think you ever told me that Eric served in the Boer Wars."

"Yes, the second one. He was there in '02 for the last of it. He doesn't like to speak about it. I think it had a lasting impression on him and that was one of the reasons he used to not get involved in the Great War."

Florence nodded. Puddle's end was up ahead as the came round the last bend and the railway station was in sight.

"I wondered why Eric was always around during the war years. You're lucky you had him with you. The toll was so great on so many others."

"I know. War, it seems to me mostly about state sanctioned murder. Yet if it helped to end all wars then I suppose the sacrifice might be considered worth it. Though with the current state of affairs I fear, my dear Flo, that we might yet be due a second one."

"I hope not."

That's all Florence had to say about it. She disliked war, and she disliked talking about it more so. And Frances was right, the world stage looked ready to teeter into the cauldron of more fighting and division. And this time the guns were bigger as were the bombs and the planes were faster. It was a ghastly thought to think about. So she turned her thoughts to other matters.

"So you just want to have a look at the study, do you?" she asked.

"That's one of the things I'm hoping to do. I'm also hoping that Gerald might be around. He lives in Manchester, correct?"

Florence nodded.

"But I thought I overheard him mentioning that he was staying at Jack's estate for the week."

"Yes, that's right. Though I suppose with everything that's been going on there lately, that might have changed."

"That's what I'm worried about. I'd rather not have to drive all the way into Manchester to speak with him. I also want to try and find out if and how Dr. Garnet might be related to all of this. And then there's Enoch, I think he might have a few things to say that could enlighten us even further."

Florence looked over at Frances briefly.

"How so? I didn't find our last visit with him to be exceptionally enlightening."

"Yes I agree, however, this time I think he has a better stake in the outcome. I think it all revolves around the gold, Flo. I think that might be the key to Jack's murder and in a roundabout way, Ginnie's too."

"You know, I've been thinking about that too. All this talk of gold and yet nobody has actually seen any. I wonder if it's even true?"

"I think it is. I think if we get a greater idea of what this gold was worth, not just in monetary terms but in other ways too, I think everything will become much clearer. You see Flo, the whole Forsyth clan seems on the edge of, dare I say, destitution."

Frances looked over at her friend and Florence smiled and nodded.

"That might be a fair assessment," she said.

"And what I've learned over the years is that the destitute are often liable to doing all sorts of egregious and illegal things. When you're living a lie, lying becomes almost like truth to you. You start to lie for all sorts of reasons to get what you want and to continue the facade."

"I find the whole thing, Fran, to be quite depressing to be honest."

"I know. The reasons why people do the things that they do to each other are often insignificant and petty."

"That's just it. Ginnie seemed like such a lovely woman. I didn't know her that well, but just was always very decent to me."

"I understand, Flo, I do. It appears as though Jack might not have been the nicest man, but even still, as Lottie said, he didn't deserve to be murdered. There are more civilized ways of handling these things."

"I don't know how you do it," said Florence, glancing at her friend as she drove through Puddle's End towards the Forsyth estate on the outskirts of town.

"I don't go looking for it. I couldn't imagine being a full time detective. No wonder Gibbard seems frustrated and grumpy. Having to deal with that element all the time, it's enough to make you bonkers."

Florence laughed.

"Though truth be told, Flo, what makes it all worthwhile is seeing justice served at the end of the day."

"And thank you for doing that, my dear friend. It is so good of you to help out in this case. I know it isn't the break that either you or I were hoping for when I picked you up at the station on Monday."

"Not at all, Flo, I'm happy to help. And I'll just have to come back up again so we can enjoy a more relaxed time together. No visiting any of your friends though, I'm not taking any chances next time!"

Florence laughed.

"Heavens, no. In spite of what you might think, I do enjoy a quiet life out here in Puddle's End. That's one of the reasons I moved out here."

Florence turned left into the driveway of the Forsyth home and up above at the top of the driveway was a police car and one other that she didn't recognize, though Frances remembered the 1936 Rolls Royce Phantom III from her first visit to the home. It was either Gerald's or Dr. Garnet's car. Frances hoped it was Gerald's.

Florence drove up and parked next to the Rolls Royce. It was immaculate and very well cared for. You could tell that the owner took great pride in maintaining it. And even after almost three years there wasn't a scrape or ding on it that Frances could see.

Florence and Frances got out of Florence's red Alvis and walked up to the main door. James answered it, doing his best to stand tall and smile broadly. Though the weight of the day were pulling down both his shoulders and the corners of his mouth.

"We're getting to the bottom of this James," said Lady Marmalade. "Won't be long now and we'll all be able to rest and get back to normal."

"Thank you, my Lady."

"Who's all here?" asked Florence.

"The inspector with one of his constables. They just brought Garrett home not long ago and he's quite upset about the whole ordeal."

"I can imagine," said Florence.

"Ms. Church is still here and Mr. Gerald Forsyth showed up earlier this afternoon. I think he's packing upstairs and getting ready to head on home."

"Is Enoch around?" asked Frances.

"Yes, my Lady, he should be out in the garden or shed I imagine."

"Listen, James, we just need to do a little snooping around the study, if you don't mind. Perhaps you can let everyone know we'll be with them shortly."

"As you wish."

James closed the door behind them and plodded slowly down the hall towards the living room. Frances and Florence walked a few strides down the same hallway and then took a right down a secondary hallway where they took their first right into the study.

The study was bright and large. To the left was a large wooden table with a bookshelf behind it up against the wall. To the right was a large brown leather couch that was well worn with use but by no means near the end of its usefulness. There was a large low wooden coffee table in front of the couch with assorted magazines on it. These included Lloyd's List as well as The Scots Magazine.

Opposite where Frances and Florence had just entered was a large window that opened up onto the front yard and driveway. Frances walked over to the desk. It was strewn with papers, perhaps from Garrett's attempt at making sense of his father's last words.

Frances took her time combing through all the scraps of paper. Most of them, perhaps eighty percent or more, appeared to be invoices and there were duplicates amongst them too. Some said sixty days overdue, others ninety and a few more were one hundred and eighty days overdue.

There were even a few solicitors' letters demanding payment on behalf of some clients. It was clear to Frances that she was witnessing the beginning of the end of Forsyth Motor Manufacturing.

The only two left to run it appeared to be Garrett and Gerald. Frances didn't hold a lot of hope that Garrett could run this business, and as for Gerald, that remained to be seen.

Under the many papers all over the desk, Frances found a desk calendar with the month of April. There were some meetings later in the month regarding business matters as well as a meeting with his solicitor.

It also appeared that there was some smudged charcoal across much of March. It was hard to make out what it was, but it seemed to have been from a letter written in duplicate with carbon copy. What Lady Marmalade could read of it was, 'equal share of proceeds...business matter will be finished...our cost ten pounds each...Gerald'. It was a strange and cryptic scribbling that didn't make much sense.

But what Frances found interesting was a cryptic note on the 7th of April. All it said was "AE to FC, 12".

"Take a look at this, Flo," said Frances to Florence who was on the opposite side of the desk. Florence walked around to take a closer look.

"Interesting," she said, "and what about this one?"

She pointed to another cryptic hastily written scrawl that said "AD, 02, Liverpool". which was written on the desk calendar square for the 6th of April.

"Very interesting indeed, Flo, I think this is part of the key. But I don't think it's what we were meant to find in the study. If we're meant to find anything at all."

Frances lifted up the desk calendar but there was nothing underneath it. She pulled out the sheets from the bottom right and top right envelope corners, but there was nothing in between any of the sheets.

"Why don't you take a look at the bookshelf and see if you find anything interesting or related to what Jack's last words supposedly were."

Frances stayed focused on the desk. There were three trays to handle mail and none of them contained anything of note. A letter from the bank that warned of Jack's account closure if he didn't repay his loan. A letter from another solicitor that was unopened and the last income statement from Forsyth Motor Manufacturing which didn't require you to be an accountant to realize that the company was taking it's last dying breath.

Frances next looked in the small cigar box that was on the desk, but it just held cigars as would be expected. The holder of pens and pencils was empty except for two pencils and one Swan fountain pen.

Next she took to looking into the main drawer. It seemed that whatever it held was probably stolen or now lying strewn across the face of the desk. There was a pad of paper and a brass key. What the key was for she had no idea.

She was just about to start opening the side drawers when Florence spoke.

"I don't know if this is anything, but it's interesting nonetheless."

Frances stood straight and turned to face the bookshelf that was behind her. Florence was pointing at a book's spine.

"Odd. This book is called 'The Study of Deceit'. It's the only book I've seen on here so far that has the word 'study' in its title."

"Well, let's take it out and have a closer look," said Frances.

Florence pulled it out and handed it to Frances. Frances looked at it. It was burgundy in color, written by a Dr. Reginald Masterson, an author she had never heard of. It didn't have a dust jacket and was of average size in all three dimensions.

"Strange," said Frances, "I wonder what it might be about?"

She opened the front cover and went to flip through to the index, but the book opened rather unexpectedly by itself about one third of the way in. There was a small piece of paper folded in half, stuck between pages forty seven and forty eight.

"We might have something here, Flo," said Frances grinning.

Florence smiled widely.

"Oh, do tell!"

Frances took the paper out and opened it up. It was about half the size of a regular sheet of paper and this was written on it:

Jack,

I've had it. I want what's mine and I'm going to come and collect it.

If you don't have it by Tuesday I'll take it from the gold. Yes, I know about that and I know about Albert Dock on Wednesday night.

I swear I'll kill you if I don't get it, for all the trouble you've caused.

DG

"Oh my," said Florence. "That is quite something isn't it. But who on earth is DG? Do you think he could have killed Jack?"

"That is a puzzle, my dear Flo, and who's to say DG is a man. Could it not have been a woman just as likely?"

"Well, I suppose so, but didn't Lottie tell us she saw a man shoot Jack?"

"Not exactly, Flo. She saw a man holding a gun run away from the scene and he was in the vicinity of where the shot might have come from. But she didn't actually see him pull the trigger, did she?"

Florence put her finger to her mouth and furrowed her brow.

"I suppose not. I give up, Fran, I have no idea who did it and I'm not going to try anymore. I'll wait for you to spill the beans."

"And the beans I shall happily spill. I believe this is exactly what Garrett was supposed to find. I think it helps point to Jack's killer."

Before Florence could speak, they heard brisk footsteps coming down the hall towards them. They turned to look at the study door just before he entered.

Twenty Three

Inspector Gibbard walked his thick frame through the door. He raised an eyebrow when he saw it was Frances and Florence.

"Oh," he said, "it's you two.'

Frances looked at him and smiled. His gruff and grumpy facade was not worth the bother in getting upset over.

"I'm so glad you're here Inspector," she said. "Did you bring Garrett back?"

"Yes, well we had to, on closer inspection of the revolver. Apparently his revolver didn't have any bullets in it so he couldn't have shot his father could he?"

It was a rhetorical question, but Lady Marmalade decided to answer it anyway.

"Quite. We heard the same from Ms. Lottie Daubney. I don't suppose you've had a chance to speak with her yet have you?"

Lady Marmalade was poking the bear. She couldn't help herself, and besides the stick she was poking with was long and thin, meant more in jest and fun than seriousness.

"No."

"We have something here, Inspector, that you might like to take a look at. We could use your expertise in helping uncover its meaning."

Frances held the letter out for Gibbard. He came round to their side of the desk. There was a lot of space behind the desk for the three of them. He took the letter from her and read it silently. Frances watched him read it, standing to his left and to her left was Florence, also intently staring at the inspector.

"Interesting," he said, still looking at the paper in his hands.

"Florence found it in this book," said Lady Marmalade pointing to "The Study of Deceit" which was now closed, spine facing them, on the desk. Gibbard looked at it but didn't pick it up. He glanced back at the paper still in his left hand. Then he looked over at Lady Marmalade. They were standing closely together, the three of them, all crowding around the page in Gibbard's hand as if he were holding a newborn baby.

"I was going to ask the two of you what you were doing in here."

"It was something Jack said with his dying breath," said Florence.

"I see."

"We've just come back from seeing Lottie and she told us that Jack said 'the study' as his last words."

"Go on."

"Well, we wanted to know why they were at the docks to confront Jack and one of the things she said was that Garrett had wanted to know where this gold supposedly was."

"Ah, the gold that everyone speaks about and yet nobody has seen," said Gibbard.

"Anyway, we thought that perhaps the gold was here in the study or something might be here in the study that would lead us to the gold." Florence looked at Frances. "Does that sound about right?"

Frances nodded.

"Let me guess. I suppose the two of you also haven't found this disappearing gold?"

"No, we haven't," said Frances, "but I think that was the point. I don't think Jack was trying to tell Garrett where the gold was, but rather to lead him to his killer."

"How so?"

"I think that Jack saw the man who killed him and gave Garrett this cryptic message of 'the study' to lead him here. However, I saw Garrett rummaging in here earlier this morning when we just arrived, but I think he was looking for the gold."

"So perhaps Garrett has found the gold and stashed it away somewhere?"

Gibbard was smiling. Why all the concern over this alleged gold that nobody had seen was beyond him. Frances shook her head.

"No, I don't think he found the gold here. I don't think the gold was ever here."

"Then why lead his son to his study?"

Frances was almost getting impatient with the inspector. But she bit her tongue and tried to explain it more clearly.

"The answer, Inspector, is in your hand." Frances took the paper from Gibbard. "This note, I believe is from the killer and Jack wanted us, or more likely his son, to find it."

Gibbard looked at the note again.

"Yes, I can see that," he said, "but it was stuffed in a book on this bookshelf I presume," he turned around and waved his hands across the bookshelf. "That's not how you leave something you want found."

"True, Inspector, but we are standing in his study and the book has 'the study' in its title, I think that was about as obvious as Jack thought he could make it while still keeping it safe. I think whoever gave this to him was someone close to him who might easily have access to his house and study and therefore perhaps come back to find it once they realized how damning this letter is."

"I agree," said Gibbard, "that this certainly looks damning, but who on earth is DG. I haven't met anyone yet with those initials related to either Ginnie's or Jack's murder."

"Yes, I know, that's one piece of the puzzle that needs to be sorted out. And I suspect that if we determine who DG is, we might find our gold too."

Inspector Gibbard smiled.

"This gold that everyone talks about but nobody has seen."

"I think there are some who have seen it."

"Really, and who might that be?"

"I believe Ginnie knew of this gold and where it was. Obviously, if this gold was real, which I believe it was, then Jack must have known where he kept it. And I believe the Enoch has probably seen some of it. And lastly, as I mentioned, the person who stole it knows where it is and that person might be the same one who killed Jack."

"And what about who killed Ginnie then. Is this person one and the same?"

"No," said Frances.

"Meredith killed Ginnie," said Florence unable to stop herself before she thought better of it. Frances winces ever so slightly. Gibbard raised an eyebrow and looked askew at Florence.

"Is that so? And you know this how?"

Florence didn't say anything, she was a little embarrassed.

"This was the other thing I was hoping you could help us with, Inspector," said Frances. "I'd like you to join us here tomorrow at noon, where I'll enlighten you as to who the killers are. For as Florence said, Jack and Ginnie were killed by two separate people."

"I see, so you'll come in here and announce the guilty and then let me cart them off?"

"If you want to put it this way, Inspector. Though I'm certain you'll be quite aware of the murderers yourself as we discuss the evidence tomorrow, together. Of course I will bow to your authority and expertise."

Frances smiled at him and he seemed to thaw from her warm smile and kind words.

"Very well."

"But if I might, Inspector, ask a small favor. It would be most helpful if you could insure that everyone is present. Garrett, Meredith, Luther Garnet and Gerald Forsyth. I've already informed Lottie that we need her here and Florence has agree to pick her up from the station at noon and bring her back here."

"I'll give you leeway this one time, Lady Marmalade as I've spoken with Scotland Yard and they speak very highly of you. But don't let me down. You're in Blackpool's yard now and we don't take well to meddling amateurs however well respected they might be elsewhere."

Inspector Gibbard was trying to save face more than anything else. Frances nodded politely and smiled sweetly at him.

"I wouldn't have it any other way, Inspector. You've been most gracious to me and I'll never forget that. I will just offer my opinions tomorrow as we have an open conversation with everyone here. You'll very much be making the final decision as to who or if anyone should be charged, but I think you'll find the evidence quite compelling."

Inspector Gibbard nodded.

"I was also wondering if you've had the chance to find out if Gerald and Luther own any guns?" asked Frances.

"I did," said Gibbard. "Gerald owns a hunting rifle and that's all. Luther owns an assortment of revolvers and hunting rifles. One of which happens to be a Webley."

"Like the kind that shot Jack?"

"Yes. But don't be getting all excited, it's a common revolver in these parts and it doesn't mean anything."

"Of course not, Inspector, but I imagine that in the interest of thoroughness, you'll be inspecting it as well?"

"We will get around to it."

Frances brushed away some of the papers that had moved back over the desk calendar. She picked up the book and put it back in the bookshelf where it had come from.

"I wanted to show you these two items as well, Inspector," she said, pointing to the squares on the calendar for the days of the 6th and 7th of April.

"See here on the 6th, it says 'AD, 02, Liverpool' and on the 7th it says 'AE to FC, 12'."

Frances' fingers underlined each of the short sentences written in Jack's quick and ugly scrawl. Gibbard nodded his big head and Frances noticed his ear like a pinched cabbage leaf on the side of his head.

"What do you make of it?"

"Well, I think the first one is quite apparent is it not, Inspector?"

Frances wanted to give him a chance to figure it out for himself. He squinted his eye and furrowed his brow, his bushy eyebrows coming together like two worms about to kiss or fight, not certain of which.

"Hmm, yes, I suppose so. Albert Docks I imagine."

"That's right, I think he was meeting whoever it was he was supposed to meet for two a.m. at Albert Docks. Remember that Meredith said he was picking up a couple of young women and some gold."

Inspector Gibbard rummaged his hand through his short hair. He vaguely remembered something like that. He much preferred cases that were simpler and more straightforward. Perhaps all these new ideas that Scotland Yard had of keeping notes about their different cases wasn't such a bad idea. He thought now how he might like to have had a notebook to refer back to.

"So what do you make of the 7th then?" asked Gibbard.

"I think that's referring to the gold, and perhaps the women, though I'm not sure about that part of it. AE I believe refers to American Eagles. I think this gold was American gold coins. I'm going to have to speak to my husband Eric about that and see what he has to say. He's very knowledgeable about those sorts of things. The FC I believe refers to The Flying Chan, which is Lee Chan's restaurant that we spoke about earlier today too. I'm almost certain that Jack was supposed to deliver this gold and perhaps the women too, to Mr. Chan on Good Friday. In other words, today."

"If what you're saying is true, then this Mr. Chan is a bigger problem than we've realized and frankly, my Lady, we've never even heard of him."

"He could be one of the biggest smugglers of opium, women and apparently gold that England has remained ignorant of."

"And if he's conducting business right under our noses then I'm going to make sure to put him out of business," said Gibbard.

"I know you will, Inspector, and the sooner the better. Indirectly, I'd argue that Mr. Chan is perhaps responsible for both of these murders. It is because of Jack's weaknesses for Mr. Chan's wicked ways that both Ginnie and he ended up murdered."

"I had another question for you, Inspector," said Frances.

Gibbard looked at her and nodded.

"Did you get the letters that Garrett had in his pockets?"

"We got the one from his pocket and the other from Ms. Church."

"Good, the one that was in his pocket, it no doubts refers to the same event that I think Jack wrote about here. Don't you agree?"

Frances pointed at the desk calendar under the writing written in the square for the 6th of April.

Gibbard nodded.

"Have you had a chance to determine who this woman, Rachel Badcocke is?"

"That letter was mailed from Manchester and I have a man looking into it as we speak. Why do you ask?"

"Well, I want to rule her out from this mess. I don't think she's played any role but I'd like to find out more about her when your constable has interviewed her."

"And why don't you think she's involved?"

"Well, quite simply, her name hasn't come up with anyone else in conversation and someone who's planning something foul and writing a legitimate threat is unlikely to sign a letter off with their full name I shouldn't think."

"Good point."

"So perhaps we could meet here earlier than noon tomorrow just to clear up a few small items on Ms. Badcocke?"

"Very well."

"Thank you, inspector, you've been most kind. I do appreciate all your help. If you don't need us, Florence and I have some more questions for some of them members attached to this home."

"As you wish," said Gibbard.

Frances and Florence left the Inspector in the study, after Frances had handed the letter written by DG back to him. Gibbard stood, behind Jack's desk in Jack's study staring at the paper in his hand trying to make sense of the whole sordid affair.

Twenty Four

Frances and Florence were walking into the living room when they bumped into Gerald Forsyth coming down the stairs from his bedroom. He was carrying a large suitcase that didn't seem exceptionally heavy.

"Good day, ladies," he said, tipping his hat that he was wearing. Likely the same one that he was wearing when Lottie saw him at the docks last night.

Frances and Florence stopped to talk to him for a moment.

"You aren't leaving already, are you?" asked Frances.

"Yes, I'm afraid I am. I can't say I feel at peace in here much since the awful events of this past week."

"Yes, it has been quite the ordeal. Though surely Garrett needs you more than ever at a time like this," said Frances.

Gerald put his suitcase down realizing that this wasn't going to be a quick and easy goodbye.

"Garrett is a grown man Lady Marmalade. He knows where I am if he needs to get hold of me. I'm not far away in Manchester."

Frances nodded.

"Yes, I know. Still, he'll need help in getting his father's affairs in order, and surely you and he need to work on the business together and see if it can even be salvaged."

"That might be possible. I dare say that might be the only good thing to have come out of this mess."

"What is?"

"Well, the fact that Jack is dead now. It might mean he might not have been able to bleed every last penny from Forsyth Motor Manufacturing and Garrett and I might actually have a chance of turning the company around and if not bringing it back to its former glory, we might be able to limp it along until we can sell it."

"That would be your plan then?" asked Florence.

Gerald looked over to Florence. His arms were crossed across his chest.

"Can't say for certain. I'll need to take a look at the books. But I wouldn't be surprised if that is our best opportunity at getting something out of the business that my father started at the beginning of this millennium."

Gerald leaned down to pick up his suitcase.

"If you ladies don't mind, I do need to be off. I have affairs in Manchester that need attending."

He stood up and waited for Frances and Florence to allow him past. They didn't move.

"I'm terribly sorry," said Frances, "but we can't let anyone go until tomorrow evening. You see, the inspector and I haven't quite had the chance to arrest the murderer or murderers of Jack and Ginnie. And until we do, all of you are still suspects."

"This is utterly absurd," he said. "Not to be rude, Lady Marmalade, but you aren't the police and I'll be going if I wish. Good day!"

He tipped his hat to her and maneuvered around her to get going.

"Not so fast, Mr. Forsyth," said Inspector Gibbard stepping into the main hallway, having just come out of the office. He was folding a sheet of paper and putting it in his pocket. "Lady Marmalade might not be the police, but I am. And nobody is allowed to leave until this ugly mess has been wrapped up. If you're innocent, Mr. Forsyth, and I say it with a big 'if', you'll be free to head back to Manchester tomorrow evening."

"I say, this is totally preposterous. Never in all my days have I seen such incompetence and heavy handedness by the police. This isn't a Bolshevik revolution you're dealing with here, Inspector. This is civilized bloody England."

"It might not be a revolution as you say, Mr. Forsyth, though your tone and demeanor suggest otherwise. Nevertheless, this estate has seen two tragedies, two murders in one week and I'll get to the bottom of it one way or another. You will be inconvenienced for one day more. That's all."

Gerald was still holding onto his suitcase. Lady Marmalade touched him on the elbow to try and calm him down.

"Tomorrow is also Good Friday, Gerald, businesses are closed. Surely you won't be missing anything that can't wait until next week."

Gerald sighed heavily for emphasis. His thin lips shaking like the fragile leaves of autumn. He put down the suitcase again.

"Very well, but I'll be off tomorrow night at the first opportunity."

"You're terribly kind, Gerald. And I'm sure Garrett will appreciate having his uncle around for another day. Perhaps you could spend this evening productively trying to assess the company's records?"

Frances turned and continued down the hallway. She was followed by Florence and they stepped into the living room. Garrett was sitting down in one of the chairs with another Scotch in his hand. Meredith was still sitting in the same couch that she had moved to when they had been served tea. It looked as if she hadn't stopped drinking Tom Collins' all day. Another one seemed freshly poured into the glass she held in her hand.

Garrett stood up as soon as he saw Frances and Florence enter the living room. He intercepted them as they made their way towards the French doors. He put his hand out to stop her and held her forearm with his free hand.

"Thanks for coming back," he said.

Frances smiled at him.

"Did you see Lottie? Did she tell you what happened? Do you know you killed my father?"

"I did see Lottie and she was most helpful. She'll be joining us all tomorrow when I identify those responsible for your mother's and your father's murders."

"Thank God. The police released me not long ago after they realized my gun hadn't even been shot. It didn't even have any bullets."

Garrett smiled wearily.

"I'm glad," said Frances. "But you still made some unwise choices."

He nodded and looked down.

"Yes, I suppose I did. You have no idea how difficult it's been living here these last few years as Jack ruined everything."

Frances looked at him for a while.

"Have you seen Enoch?" she asked.

Garrett looked back up at her.

"Not since I've been back, but he should be out back somewhere I imagine, unless he's skipped out."

Frances turned and let herself out of the living room and into the garden outside followed by Florence. She stopped just outside the French doors and took a look around. She couldn't see Enoch anywhere, so she went to the greenhouse and took at look inside. He wasn't there.

"Must be in the shed I imagine," said Florence. Frances nodded.

They walked to the opposite end of the garden to the shed and Frances stopped by the doorframe. She peeked in but it was dark inside and her eyes hadn't adjusted. She knocked on the open door.

"Hello," she said, "Mr. Habbit?"

"In 'ere at the back," he said.

Frances walked in and blinked a few times trying to adjust to the low light. It was tidy inside the shed. A workbench was clear on its top and held a vice at the near end to the door. The tools were clean and all placed neatly hanging up on the sides of the shed. Towards the back she saw Enoch sitting on a chair with a pair of hedge clippers in his hands.

Frances walked up to him, scooting around a wheelbarrow that was tipped up against the far wall. When he saw it was her he stood up.

"My Lady, good to see you a'gin."

"Thank you, Enoch, I wasn't sure you'd be here still, in light of the recent events with Jack."

"I heard he was murder'd. Terrible bus'ness this house 'as seen."

Enoch sat back down and continued to oil the hinge of the hedge clippers and snap them back and forth, the blades chomping against each other and making a soft whistling sound.

"I thought with all the police coming and going from here, a man such as yourself might not want to be around."

"That's a fact. But they already lock'd me up one time and I got nothin' to do with Jack's murder. 'Sides, I got to fig're out where them gold's at."

"That's what I wanted to ask you about, Enoch. You were overheard passing a letter onto Jack a little while ago about this gold. Can you tell me about that."

Enoch didn't look up at Lady Marmalade. He sat on his old chair, his knees wide apart and his elbows resting on each knee. His big hands covered with black stains of dirt and oil. He took a rag that was draped over his knee and he started to polish the blades of the clipper. Cleaning them and wiping the excess oil off.

He was methodical and thorough and slow with it. You got the impression he was careful in taking good care of his tools. Especially the sharp ones.

"I had a message fir Jack from my employ'r. T'morrow he was s'posed to bring the gold to Mr. Chan. Now 'es dead I've gotta get there inst'd."

"What kind of gold was it, Enoch?"

"They were big coins. Had 'n eagle on one side an' a lady on th'other. Bigger 'n a shilling and shiny gold."

"So you've seen one?"

"I did see one. Jus' the one. Mr. Chan wanted t' make sure that Jack brought the right ones with 'im t'morrow."

"How many was he supposed to have?"

"Thirty-six. Las' night he was s'posd t' pick up fifteen."

"So he already had twenty-one of them on him?"

"That's 'bout right. But I nev'r knew where 'e kept 'em. I been tryin' to figure it out but I can't find 'em."

"You won't find them, Enoch," said Lady Marmalade, "because they're not here. And when they do show up, the police will take them as evidence and neither you nor Mr. Chan will get them. Because I imagine they're not legally Mr. Chan's."

Enoch looked up then and stopped his wiping.

"That's not gonna be good f'r me."

Then he went back to wiping the hedge clippers and after a few more strokes he got up and put them back in their place on the wall.

"I imagine Mr. Chan won't be happy with that."

"No ma'am they're worth a fortune 'e said."

"If I can offer some advice, Enoch. You might do well to move on somewhere else. Things aren't likely to go well for Mr. Chan moving forward."

Enoch turned and looked at Frances and Florence. He was a big gnarled tree of a man. Looked like he'd been hewn roughly from wood. His hands hung by his sides like hammers. His eyes looked sad and his mouth hung down more in a frown than a grimace.

"You can choose a better way for yourself, Enoch. Take this moment to make a fresh start."

Frances was looking at him and the big man stood still and thoughtful as a large oak. No inkling about what he was thinking.

"I reck'n you been kind to me, ma'am. I hear a war migh't be startin'. Maybe'n war I'll find my way back 'ome."

Frances turned to leave and Florence followed her out. As they walked back towards the house, leaving Enoch in the shed, Frances turned to Florence.

"He's a big scary man that Enoch. But I think there's a corner somewhere inside him where the light still shines. Hopefully he'll find it."

Florence didn't say anything as they walked the rest of the way back up the way they'd come. She looked towards the house and she saw Garrett staring out the window after them. He had a puzzled look on his face.

Twenty Five

Garrett opened the door for them as they got back up to the house.

"Did you find him?" he asked.

"We did," said Frances, walking past him and into the middle of the living room. Agnus was bringing in a tray of tea and assorted small cakes, including whipped cream, jam, scones and crumpets. She put the tray in the middle of the table which was centered in the living room and around which the two couches and a couple of chairs huddled themselves.

"That's a treat," said Florence, "I was just about to die of thirst.

Florence and Frances took the two available chairs opposite from where Meredith sat. She looked at them carefully, sipping her Tom Collins and not saying much at all. Gerald was in the living room now and he came over and sat next to Meredith. Garrett came over holding a finger's worth of Scotch in his tumbler. He swallowed it down in one go and sat down in the second couch which he now had all to himself.

He placed the tumbler on the edge of the table closest to him and reached across for a plate which was lined with colorful colored flowers. You could tell it came from the same set as the teacups, saucers, milk jug, sugar bowl and teapot. He placed a scone which was warm from the oven onto the plate and broke it open in half. He put a dollop of cream on each half followed by a spoon of jam. He sat back and started to eat.

"Who'd like some tea?" asked Gerald, looking first at Lady Marmalade and then Florence, Meredith and Garrett. Frances, Florence and Garrett all asked for tea. He served them up in the order he had looked at them.

Frances put cream and sugar in hers, as did Florence and Garrett and finally Gerald after he poured himself last. Frances took a scone and added whipped cream and jam to both sides. Florence took a crumpet which was already glossy with butter and she added a spoonful of jam to it.

Meredith watched, almost with contempt, as the four of them took crumpets and scones. Gerald taking his time to decide upon a crumpet and a scone. Finally, perhaps with the temptation being too much, Meredith reached out and took the one and only Shrewsbury cake which she placed on a plate and rested on her lap.

"This is exactly what I needed," said Florence. "What a trying day it's been."

"I'd say. I've been arrested, taken to jail and released, all in the space of few hours," said Garrett.

The grandfather clock chimed four times as the five of them sat in silence listening to the old clock.

"I imagine you'll miss Agnus, and James too," said Frances.

Garrett looked at her for a moment and chewed on a bit of his scone.

"I shouldn't think so, she's not going anywhere that I'm aware of."

"But my dear Garrett, they're both quite behind in having received their pay. They're still owed half of it for the past year."

Garrett, frowned and looked at Frances.

"Well, I didn't know that. I'll make sure they get paid up after the estate's all taken care of."

"I've already promised them I'll see to it. But you don't even know the state of Forsyth Motor Manufacturing. It might be unsalvageable."

"Or it might not," interjected Gerald.

"That's what I'm planning on finding out," said Garrett.

"Perhaps you'll be putting up some of your new found winnings to keep the business going?" said Frances, looking at Gerald.

Gerald looked back at her with a sour look on his face as if he'd just bitten into a lemon rather than the creamy scone that marked the corner of his mouth with cream. He didn't say anything right away but chewed and swallowed his food.

"I'll say. You've got quite the nerve coming here and talking like that. I'd hardly call it winnings under these circumstances."

"What would you call it, Gerald?" asked Lady Marmalade.

"What it bloody well is, which is an insurance policy."

Meredith looked at him sideways.

"And a large one at that. Which unfortunately, Gerald, makes you a suspect."

"Unfortunate indeed, for you. I didn't kill my brother!"

"That's what everyone says," said Frances, "even the guilty as sin."

"Do you have any guns, Gerald?" asked Garrett.

"No I don't."

Gerald looked at Garrett with fire in his eyes.

"Inspector Gibbard suggests otherwise. He seems to think you have a hunting rifle," said Frances.

"Because I do. A hunting rifle is not a bloody gun. Not the kind that shot Jack."

"How do you know what was used to shoot Jack?"

"Because I was there."

Gerald looked at Meredith and Garrett. They were both looking at him with thinly veiled hostility.

"You two bloody well know I was there. We all saw each other and we all saw what happened. Though none of us seem to know who did it. Do we?"

Meredith broke eye contact with him and looked longingly into her quickly disappearing drink.

"I told you I was going to speak to him," said Garrett.

"Yes, well I didn't quite trust you and from what I overheard you weren't speaking to him about the business were you?"

"I was going to get to it," said Garrett.

"But instead he got shot and now we're left with his mess to clean up."

"It was, at the very least, Gerald, poor decision making to head out to the docks. Wasn't it?" asked Frances.

"Very easy to find fault in hindsight," said Gerald, "but I wasn't expecting him to get shot. I didn't go out there to get him shot either."

"Well, that remains to be seen. You might have been working in conjunction with the murderer."

"You won't find anything to implicate me, because there's nothing there."

"Perhaps so, Gerald, but why did you decide to take out a one hundred thousand pound insurance policy on your brother with you as the only beneficiary?" asked Frances.

Gerald finished up his scone and started on his crumpet. Florence had finished hers and placed her plate back down on the table. Frances was only half finished and took the time to sip her tea.

"My brother Jack, as it is well known now, was careless, a cad and in trouble with bad people. I wasn't going to let him ruin me along with himself. I thought that at the very least, if he ruins the company and his life, at least I'll have something to start over with. As it turns out, it was a good decision."

"And what about this gold that we all keep hearing about. Were you not out to get it?"

"No, I wasn't, not like Garrett. I knew the danger that Jack was involved with. These people aren't nice people. The last thing I wanted to get involved with were the same nasty people that Jack was involved with. And the surest way to get started down that dead end was to steal from them, or take their gold."

Gerald looked over at Garrett.

"And I told you the same, didn't I? You should have listened."

"Well, it makes no difference now," said Garrett, taking the last bite of his scone and then putting his plate down on the table next to his empty tumbler, "because I never got the gold nor did I see any of it."

Gerald turned back to look at Lady Marmalade.

"And I plan to make a fresh start with this money I'm due, which will likely take months to collect. In the meantime, Garrett and I will try and salvage what we can from the business before the vultures pick it bare."

"I'm sure the company is quite sound," said Meredith, finally speaking up.

They all looked at her with confused faces.

"You've got to be joking, and have you not been paying attention to anything we've said this whole time?" asked Garrett.

Meredith looked at Garrett harshly and pursed her lips.

"Jack assured me that everything was fine, that he just needed to pay off his last few debts and that he was going to get back on track with the business so we could be together happily."

Garrett shook his head and laughed.

"Meredith, are you that blind to what kind of a man Jack was?" asked Gerald. "He was a thief, a liar and a cheat."

"Not with me he wasn't."

Meredith was getting her hackles up. She didn't like getting attacked, especially regarding her feelings for Jack. None of them knew him like she did. And he was honest and kind and loving with her.

"After everything you've seen and heard. After I showed you that bloody letter from that other woman...Rachel I think it was, you still believe my father was your knight in shining armor?" asked Garrett.

Frances was watching the back and forth as if she was watching a tennis match. Only now the volleys were getting harder and more pointed.

"Jack promised me that there was no one else. I don't care what that stupid letter said, I believe Jack. He was a handsome man and women liked him. That couldn't be helped, she was obviously very misled by any simple kindness he might have offered her at one point."

Frances couldn't help but shake her head. She couldn't have found Jack to be handsome in a thousand tries and his kindness, well, he was more like a snake in the grass or a wolf in sheep's clothing. But love is blind and it'll have you do all sorts of silly, and even dangerous, regrettable things. Meredith looked up at Frances and saw her shaking her head.

"What?" said Meredith with spite thick as treacle in her voice.

"Nothing, my dear, I just think you and I have very different tastes when it comes to the attractiveness of men."

"Quite," said Florence, "Jack was not an attractive man by my standards."

"Each to his own," said Meredith getting up and walking over to the bar where she mixed herself another drink. She wobbled a bit getting there. Probably had enjoyed way more Tom Collins' than she needed.

"What I'm curious about," said Frances, looking from Gerald to Garrett and across to the bar at Meredith, "is that the three of you are now partners in Forsyth Motor Manufacturing and yet only one of you seems likely to come out ahead financially from Jack's death."

"That's purely coincidental and quite by accident," said Gerald.

"Yes, but you set up the insurance policy just in case."

"Well, as it turns out my instinct was right then, wasn't it? In any event, one could argue that we all, sadly, in a way, benefit from Jack's untimely departure because the company might now be salvageable."

"You might be right, and I'm not intimate with business and financial matters as you likely are, but I fear that the company might not be as salvageable as you all think. And from what I gather, none of you seemed to have taken any interest in the company until very recently and, correct me if I'm wrong but none of you have actually looked at the books, have you?"

Frances looked around the room. Meredith had decided to stand up by the bar and lean against it for support, moral and otherwise it seemed. Gerald finished up what was on his plate and as Lady Marmalade waited for them to answer she finished her scone and put her plate down on the table. None of them would say anything.

"I didn't think so," she said. "And this brings me to the crux of the matter. All three of you were there at the docks when Jack was killed. All three of you could have been working with the fourth. The murderer, and I imagine if I look closely that the thread that weaves all of this together, including to a degree, Ginnie's murder, is Forsyth Motor Manufacturing."

"That is outrageous and preposterous," said Gerald.

"Listen, Lady Marmalade," said Garrett, "you spoke with Lottie, I was there, but I didn't have anything to do with my father's death. Hell, my revolver didn't even have any bullets in it."

"Quite right, doesn't mean that you all couldn't have been playing a role in some big conspiracy to kill Jack."

"Ridiculous," said Gerald.

Meredith leaned up against the bar her eyelids heavy, her lips resting on the rim of her glass, saying nothing. Garrett just looked and blinked and stared blankly at Frances without saying anything.

"If it is some great big conspiracy then what have I gained from it all, if as you say, the company is bankrupt?" asked Garrett at last.

"That's what we shall find out. Because you are correct, you haven't gained anything from this directly have you. Nobody here has seen the gold, have they?"

Frances looked around again at each of them in turn. Garrett shook his head, as did Gerald. Frances stared at Meredith until finally she shook her head.

"I told you already that I haven't seen any of the gold."

"That's right. So then, where is it?"

"Maybe there wasn't any," offered Meredith.

"Exactly," said Gerald.

Frances stood up. It was almost four thirty now and she needed the afternoon and evening to piece this mess back together. She also wanted to speak with Eric about gold and eagles and things of that matter. She looked at Florence.

"If you'll excuse us," said Frances, "we must be off. There is no need to trouble the three of you anymore until tomorrow. If you don't know, Inspector Gibbard and I will be here tomorrow at noon to arrest the guilty. Good day."

Florence walked with Frances out the living room and down the hall until they were out of the house. Nobody had risen as they had left and nobody had said farewell. Florence thought it quite rude of them, but then again, it seemed like Frances made quite the abrupt departure.

"That was awful quick," said Florence as they climbed into her car.

"Yes, it was."

"Do you really think that this might be some big conspiracy?"

"I don't know, Flo, that's why I need to take my time this evening and review all the evidence. I was hoping to unnerve them all and keep them on their toes until tomorrow. I also want to ask Eric about a few matters related to gold. And at the end of the day, I was tired and I didn't have any other questions to ask them."

"Well," said Florence as she drove them out of the driveway and towards her home, "you've kept me thoroughly in the dark, Fran. I can't wait to learn who did it."

"Me too," said Frances, laughing.

"You can't be serious," said Florence, looking at Frances quickly.

"No, of course not," she said and they both laughed together.

Twenty Six

It was a sunny day, and it was Good Friday. It was also a good day to bring justice to bear for Ginnie and for Jack. Frances watched as Florence drove away from the Forsyth estate. It was quarter to twelve and the sun was burning an arc across its zenith. Eric had been most helpful after he had gotten over the shock of the week's events.

As Frances stood out there waving at her friend who would be back soon with Lottie, she couldn't help but to think that the bright, clear day was a metaphor for the clarity she had regarding the murders. And if she lay out the breadcrumbs carefully for Inspector Gibbard she was certain he'd be amiable to seeing the truth.

Frances turned away as Florence exited the driveway and headed out onto the road. She walked up to the main door and knocked on it. It wasn't long before it was opened by James. He looked well rested though somewhat worried.

"Good morning, James," she said as she entered.

"Good morning, my Lady. Do you think justice will be served today?"

"I believe it will, James, I believe it will."

"I'm very pleased to hear that, my Lady, it has given me no end to worry. Same for poor old Agnus."

"I can imagine."

Lady Marmalade wasn't wearing a coat and her handbag was small and light. She was dressed in gray slacks with a pale salmon blouse with a tightly knitted shawl over her shoulders. She took off the gray chiffon scarf around her head and tied it around her neck loosely.

"Where is Inspector Gibbard?" she asked James.

"I believe he is in the study with the others," he said.

"Thank you, James."

Lady Marmalade walked down the hall and turned into the living room where everyone was gathered so far. Everyone except for Lottie and Florence. Inspector Gibbard was standing to one side of the living room with two of his constables. Frances walked over to him.

"Good morning, Inspector," she said.

"Good morning," he said.

Frances looked around and saw Dr. Luther Garnet sitting down in the one couch, next to Meredith. Garrett and Gerald were seated in the other. On the table by the couches was a tray with a teapot and used teacups and the crumbs of what might have been cakes or toast or crumpets.

"I see you managed to find Luther. Thank you for bringing him."

Gibbard nodded.

"Did you happen to have one of your men visit Rachel Badcocke?"

"We did."

"And?"

"Well, there's nothing really to say about her. She's young, in her late twenties and she's a charwoman. She thinks she's in love with the late Jack Forsyth. As we're getting to know him, it seems that he strung her along for quite some time. Rachel says she's been with him for almost a year now."

"Did you tell her he'd been murdered?"

"Yes and she was very genuinely upset about it. She didn't know and she was at home all of Wednesday evening. She rents a room in a boarding house and the other renters remember her coming home just after six and not leaving again until six the next morning."

"She might have snuck out."

"Not likely, this particular boarding house has a curfew. They lock the doors at eleven during the week. Besides, she has no car and had no idea where Jack was. She assumed he must have been murdered here at home. She's an attractive woman, but by no means would I say she was the brightest. And certainly naïve."

"As I suspected, Inspector, thank you for your trouble."

He nodded at her, standing erect and tall with his hands clasped behind his back, watching over everyone like an owl surveying a field full of tasty morsels. Frances looked around the room. Everybody was particular somber and sober. Nobody was drinking alcohol, the only drinks out at this time were the mostly empty teacups. Luther was sitting upright in in the couch wearing a black suit and white shirt, his doctor's bag snugly between his legs.

Garrett was dressed in gray slacks and a white shirt with red suspenders. Meredith was wearing a black polka dot dress which fell below her knees, with long sleeves, and Gerald was wearing a light brown suit.

"Did you happen to find Dr. Garnet's revolver, inspector?"

He shook his head.

"Not yet, he said he'd lost it a few weeks ago so we're looking into that and we're also searching his home. I have one of my men still there."

"Good, I hope it turns up."

Gibbard turned to look at her and leaned in towards her.

"Are you sure about this, Lady Marmalade?" he asked in a hushed voice.

"Quite sure, Inspector and I believe you will be too when we're all done."

He leaned away from her and looked into her eyes, he was searching for a crack but he found none, so he nodded instead.

"Very well."

The clock standing still in the corner like the never blinking centurion struck noon. Lady Marmalade waited until it went silent. Then she went and stood in front of all the guests who were seated in the living room. She looked at each of them in turn.

"On Monday evening I was invited by my friend Florence Hudnall, whom all of you know, to dinner here at the Forsyth home. Ginnie Forsyth had graciously extended an invitation to me, a stranger, to dine with her and her guests."

Frances stopped for a moment as she heard the front door being answered by James. Then there were footsteps and Florence entered into the living room followed by Lottie. Frances turned to them and smiled. She extended her arm pointing towards the clutch of chairs and couches.

Florence came and sat down in an armchair that was to the side of the couch where Meredith and Garnet sat. Florence was closer to Meredith than Luther. Garrett was patting the couch next to him. He had moved up closer to Gerald, though he wasn't that close as the couch he was sitting on was larger than the one that held Luther and Meredith.

Lottie smiled and came over to sit by him. Lottie looked over at Meredith and Luther nervously as she came up to where

Garrett sat. Garrett patted her knee when she was seated and smiled warmly at her.

"The woman sitting next to Garrett who some of you have not met is Ms. Lottie Daubney. She was the woman with Garrett when Jack was shot. She also happens to be Jack's daughter through Ms. Maude Daubney."

Frances paused to let that sink in. She watched Meredith who looked over at Lottie with some disdain as if she might have been naked.

"I don't believe it," said Meredith.

"There is a lot that you don't believe, my dear," said Frances. "Nevertheless, she is Jack's daughter and she has the paperwork to prove it. I've seen the letters that Jack wrote to her mother when Maude shared the good news with him that she was pregnant with Lottie."

Frances looked at their faces. Only Meredith wasn't looking back at her, she was still looking Lottie up and down. Lottie who sat quietly and stiffly on the edge of the couch next to Garrett. Her hands clasped together in her lap and her eyes cast down. She was clearly nervous.

"One could almost say that Lottie is the reason why Ginnie was murdered. That and the gold of course. Everything comes back to the gold, which only one of you in here has actually seen."

They all looked around at each other wondering who that might be.

"But first, I want to talk about Ginnie's death. Her unnecessary and callous murder, committed by one of you here."

Again they all looked around at each other trying to determine who that might be.

"You see," continued Frances, "Ginnie was murdered in the greenhouse which seems a terribly odd place to murder someone. What, after all, do tomatoes and flowers have to do with murder?"

It was a rhetorical question, not one that Frances was looking for an answer. But she gave her audience time to let it sink in.

"The answer of course, is that tomatoes have nothing to do with murder, but gold and dark secrets do. You see, Ginnie had had enough of Jack's philandering ways and she'd found her way out of her failing and miserable marriage."

"How is that?" asked Gerald.

"She had found the gold. The gold that everyone here has been chasing."

"I wasn't chasing any gold," said Meredith.

"Not directly no, but you were hoping to keep the gold with Jack and therefore solidify your future with him."

"You see, the greenhouse held the secrets to Jack's undoing. Ginnie had stumbled upon two letters that Jack had hidden in the greenhouse. These two letters were hidden by Jack in the greenhouse because that was the only area where he thought they would remain safe. But Ginnie had uncovered them."

"And what was so secretive about these letters?" asked Luther.

Frances looked at him and smiled.

"You know," she said. "All of you know of at least the content of one of the letters, and some of you know about the content of both letters."

Frances looked at Gerald and then at Garrett and Luther.

"I haven't seen any of these letters," protested Meredith.

"You have, Meredith, you have."

"I meant," said Meredith rolling her eyes, "that I only saw the one after Garrett threw it at me so rudely."

"I'd like to know what these letters mentioned," said Lottie, looking up at Frances.

"The one letter was yours, Lottie," said Frances. "Lottie had written to Jack demanding that he meet with her or she'd tell everyone about the truth of his affair with her mother. You all know about this letter because Ginnie mentioned it to you. Garrett overheard her having an argument with Jack and he mentioned it to you Gerald."

"So what, came as no surprise to me," said Gerald.

"And Ginnie told you about it too, didn't she Dr. Garnet?"

Garnet nodded and leaned down and fiddled with the buckle on his bag.

"She told me about it, she told me about the gold. I told her she should take it and make a fresh start of it. We all know Jack was no good."

"That's right, he was no good, to her at least. And that is exactly what I believe Ginnie was planning on doing with her life. She knew where the gold was and that it was worth a substantial amount, even as a reward for turning it in. It would earn her a fresh start. But it wasn't just Lottie's letter. Lottie was born of one of Jack's earlier affairs. That happened a long time ago and Ginnie might have forgiven him those early indiscretions. But he hadn't stopped being indiscreet."

Frances turned to look at Meredith sitting smugly in the corner of her couch by Florence.

"For you, Ms. Church," said Frances, "wanted to ruin his marriage and so you planned it that she would find you and Jack in bed together."

Meredith shrugged her shoulders.

"He was supposed to have left her a long time ago. He promised me that and I was just trying to help him keep his word."

"Except he wasn't only with you, Meredith, he was with others. And one of the others had written to him from Manchester demanding that he keep his promise to leave Ginnie and move to Argentina with her."

Frances kept her gaze sharply on Meredith. Meredith lowered her eyes for a moment and her face flushed.

"And you knew about this too, didn't you?" asked Frances.

Meredith said nothing.

"Because Ginnie told you, but you wouldn't believe her. She said she had proof, it was all in the greenhouse if you'd just follow her there. And you did. But before she could show you the letter you beat her over the head and strangled her to death, rather than face the truth that Jack was not the kind of man you thought he was. His promises were empty, very much like his bank accounts."

"You have no proof of that," said Meredith, coolly.

"Oh, but I do. When we arrived that afternoon, after Ginnie had been murdered by you, I noticed a few things that you had forgotten to cover up. Your shoes were scuffed from the same dirt that I noticed in the greenhouse and your nails were not painted any longer. In fact your nail polish which just the night before had been perfect had been stripped off. Why? Because you had strangled her and scuffed your nails against the dirt floor of the greenhouse."

Meredith looked at Lady Marmalade with a hateful spite in her eyes.

"You don't know what it's like to lose a husband. And the only man who can bring you any comfort was his brother, Jack. Ginnie was trying to ruin that. She wanted to ruin my second chance at love."

"I think she was just trying to protect you. She was leaving him, I'm sure of that. She was going to take his gold and leave him."

"She was a vindictive cow. She was upset because she couldn't give Jack what I could. So I did it. She said she had a letter to show me that would show me exactly how Jack was playing us both. She told me I was such a naïve simpleton to think that Jack would ever leave her for me. She laughed it off as if it were the funniest thing she had ever heard of. So I did it. I showed her and I don't care anymore, Jack's dead and with him has gone my hope at a second chance of love."

Frances looked at Meredith as she had her tirade. How blind love could be. There was no explaining it. The desperate will do anything for a chance, for the hope of keeping their dream alive, even if it is just a mirage.

Inspector Gibbard stood silently watching the whole event unfold. He smiled a little when Meredith came out and confessed. His constables looked at him but he didn't give them the nod to arrest her. There was more to come. Lady Marmalade was just getting started.

"Meredith said she wasn't after the gold. So how is the gold involved in my mother's murder?" asked Garrett.

"Indirectly. Your mother was going to take the gold and leave. You see, the gold was kept in a small box where the letters were kept in a small recess in the floor of the greenhouse. But when I went to look, the only things remaining were the letters. The gold was gone. At first I assumed it was taken by Ginnie, but she hadn't the time to access the box to show Meredith the letters, let alone take the gold. No, the gold was taken by someone the day of Jack's murder."

"And who was that?" asked Meredith, glad to have the attention off her for now.

"We'll be getting to that. I believe that at first the idea was not to murder Jack, but rather find where the rest of the gold was and then steal it and leave him holding the bag and having to deal with the consequences."

Frances looked around again at the blank faces. She might as well have been giving a speech, as no one seemed interested in contributing to the conversation.

"You see, this gold that everyone has been after is incredibly valuable. I've learned from my husband, Eric, that several years ago, the United States government minted double eagle gold coins. The 1933 minting being the last. These coins were never released to the public, but some of them went missing and the American government has promised a reward of ten thousand dollars for each one safely returned. Obviously, you can get more a private sale."

"If it was all about the gold, then why kill Jack in the first place?" asked Meredith, starting to become interested in why Jack had been killed.

"I believe that was out of revenge for Ginnie's murder," said Frances. "Though it made finding the gold all that more difficult."

Florence looked at Frances but couldn't quite figure out where all of this was going.

"Why did it make finding the gold all that more difficult?" she asked.

"Because the only person who knew where the gold was, other than Jack, was Ginnie, and she was now dead. However, I believe she gave some idea of where the gold was to the person who killed Jack."

They all looked around at each other.

"Who killed Jack?" asked Meredith.

"One of you killed Jack, but it was a conspiracy of a few of you."

Frances took her time looking around at everyone present. Meredith looked at Luther sitting next to her, then over to Gerald and Garrett.

"And Lottie knows who it is. Don't you, Lottie?"

Lottie looked up at Frances nervously and nodded quickly.

"The person who killed Jack is Dr. Luther Garnet," said Frances.

She waited and watched as everyone turned to look at Luther. He didn't say anything.

"Says you," he said.

Frances looked at Lottie.

"Am I correct, Lottie? Is Dr. Garnet the man you saw running away from the docks with the gun in his hand?" asked Frances.

Lottie nodded quickly, glancing over at Dr. Garnet and then at Frances.

"My God, I suppose it had to be," said Garrett. "Why?"

"Don't start with me, you bloody well know why. Your father killed my sister, that's why?"

"No he didn't," said Garrett, "you just heard Meredith confess."

"If he hadn't been playing around with that whore, none of this would have happened."

Meredith looked at Luther with her mouth opened, stunned for a moment. Then she slapped him across his left cheek. It stung, you could see him wince.

"Bastard!" she said.

"That's enough!" said Frances. "Dr. Garnet might have pulled the trigger, but he wasn't acting alone."

She looked over at Garrett and at Gerald.

"The two of you were cooperating with him."

"Certainly not!" exclaimed Garrett.

"Ludicrous," said Gerald.

"I don't believe you knew that Dr. Garnet was going to kill Jack, but you all were planning on robbing him of his gold and splitting the proceeds."

"You have no idea what you're talking about," said Gerald.

"Agnus overheard you and Dr. Garnet talking about it on the side of the house when she was in the kitchen cleaning up after lunch. She overheard the two of you. You said, Dr. Garnet, that you knew about the docks. That it was your chance to get all of the gold, that Jack would be the one left holding the bag."

Gerald shook his head in disbelief, trying his best to throw off these accusations from around his neck.

"And you, Garrett, you were overheard arguing with your father in his study, when he caught you looking at his desk calendar. James overheard you telling your father you were just in there looking for a book. But in actuality you were confirming the information that Gerald shared with you about your father visiting the docks for his last collection."

Florence saw it plain as day now. A conspiracy to rob Jack of the gold that wasn't his so that they might not be all left destitute by Jack's wicked ways.

"If I'm correct, Inspector," said Lady Marmalade, "you'll find that somewhere with Dr. Garnet or at his residence will be three portions of gold, each made up of seven 1933 American Double Eagle gold coins. One for Dr. Garnet, a second for Gerald and a third for Garrett. You should also find, on each of these three a letter signed by Mr. Gerald Forsyth promising to split the insurance with all of them equally."

"How do you know that?" asked Gibbard.

"I uncovered evidence of it on the calendar upon which he had written the letter in triplicate."

"Constable," said Inspector Gibbard.

One of the constables moved forward to arrest Dr. Garnet. He leapt up from the couch and grabbed his doctor's bag and as he did so, three red velvet bags fell out, clanging softly with the sound of heavy coins. He reached into it with his right hand and pulled out a Webley revolver. He stepped past Frances and pointed his gun at all of them, waving it around.

"I know how to use this. I've done it once. I can do it again. Ms. Church, if you don't mind, please bring me those bags."

He pointed the revolver menacingly at her. She got up from the couch and picked up the bags. She opened one up and pulled out a coin and looked at it. She started to cry.

"Judas," she said, as she came up to him.

He held out his open doctor's bag.

"Put them in there."

The revolver in his right hand was tilting lower.

"You killed him for twenty pieces of gold, you Judas!"

She looked at the three bags in her hand and without thinking she struck him across the cheek. This was the second time. The moment she did that a loud crack could be heard as if lightning had just erupted in the living room.

Nobody knew what had just happened, until they saw Meredith fall to the floor and blood seep from a wound just below her heart. Quickly her white and black dress started to become stained with red.

A constable took this opportunity to tackle Dr. Garnet, wrestling the revolver out of his hand. The other constable helped him subdue Dr. Garnet. They both picked him up from the floor and the first one put handcuffs around his hands. The second one passed Dr. Garnet's bag and revolver to the inspector.

Gibbard looked inside and pulled out a tri-folded piece of paper. He read it silently and then looked at Frances.

"This would be your letter that explains how Gerald was going to share the proceeds from the insurance policy between the three of them."

"Constables," said Gibbard. "Take these three men away."

He came over to Meredith who was lying on the floor. He put his head down to her face and listened for a moment. James came rushing into the living room.

"Oh my," he kept saying.

Frances looked down at Inspector Gibbard.

"Will she make it?"

He got up slowly and looked up at Lady Marmalade, still bent over her. He shook his head.

"I'm afraid not. She's dead."

Frances looked over at James and got his attention.

"Call the coroner please, James, and get a blanket too if you don't mind."

He glanced back down at Meredith's still body on the floor, the blood had now trickled onto and stained the carpet.

"Yes," he said, stammering, "yes, my Lady."

And he turned around and was gone as if he'd just been a momentary apparition. The constables were pushing Gerald and Garret and Luther from the living room. Garrett looked back at them.

"It was never supposed to be like this. What was I supposed to do, I've never worked a day in my life. I was just supposed to get a second chance."

It seemed to Lady Marmalade as she stood there, still in shock, that second chances had long run out in the Forsyth household. She looked over at Florence who had her hand over her mouth, and who was now standing bolt upright, quite still, her eyes looking down at Meredith.

"Good heavens," she said. "This can't be."

Frances walked up to her and placed her hand on her friend's shoulder.

"Those beggars be buggered," said Florence. "I hope there's no pardons for any of them."

Lady Marmalade didn't know what to say. She'd helped to find justice for Ginnie, but the price had been heavy and paid ten times over. She turned and looked at Gibbard. He was standing over Meredith, looking down at her, his face grim and stoic but his eyes hollow. Perhaps he'd seen too many dead bodies in his day. Perhaps she had too.

"I'm sorry I got you involved in this, my dear Flo."

That was all she could say, and it sounded hollow. No words help after the dead have gone silent. The pause is the end and the end is final.